Will Buckley

The Man Who Hated Football

HARPER PERENNIAL
London, New York, Toronto and Sydney

Harper Perennial
An imprint of HarperCollins*Publishers*
77–85 Fulham Palace Road
Hammersmith
London W6 8JB

www.harperperennial.co.uk

This edition published by Harper Perennial 2005
1

First published in Great Britain by Fourth Estate 2004

The author would like to acknowledge the quote on p.252 from an
article by Peter Cook published in *Vox* magazine in 1994 and further
quoted in *Tragically I Was an Only Twin: The Complete Peter Cook*
edited by William Cook and published by Century in 2002

A catalogue record for this book
is available from the British Library

ISBN 0 00 717555 8

Typeset by Palimpsest Book Production Limited,
Polmont, Stirlingshire

Printed and bound in Great Britain by
Clays Ltd, St Ives plc

WILL BUCKLEY is a sports journalist for the *Observer*. He lives in Norfolk with his wife and three children. This is his first book.

For automatic updates on WILL BUCKLEY visit harperperennial.co.uk and register for AuthorTracker.

'It's the attack on the fools at the heart of the beautiful game that gives it its potency'
Jack

'The author draws knowingly on the relationship between sport and media. In Jimmy Stirling, we have a comic anti-hero, a periodically competent hack jaded by the goldfish bowl he inhabits'
Irish Independent

'Quotes from Stirling like "Fuck you and your fucking awful newspaper" might not go down too well with *Observer* top brass. But for readers it adds a sense of naughtiness to an already hilarious exposé'
Arena

'Jimmy Stirling is so wickedly, relentlessly funny, so preposterously brave in sharing the conscious nightmare that football journalism can be if you are not – how can I put this – up for it, that he cannot be me'
Patrick Barclay

'Deliciously funny reading. Cutting a comically unfortunate figure as he stumbles from one absurd situation to the next, Stirling manages to remain, incredibly, likeable, not least because he often says the things we wish we had the balls to. A brilliant first novel'
Jockey Slut

To my family

1

'But I thought you liked Sugar Puffs?' Jimmy Stirling said to his children.

Charlie sat, arms crossed, upper lip quivering, and gave him that crestfallen look usually reserved for being told that a favoured pet had moved to Lowestoft.

Nancy concentrated very hard on the back of the cereal packet.

It was a Nabisco stand-off.

Stirling couldn't be doing with breakfast. He lit a cigarette and stared out of the window. His position at the head of the table afforded a grim view of his land. In the far distance a paddock, in need of a horse or goat or llama or whatever crackpot animal was the kids' current favourite, abutted a distressed stable. In the mid-distance assorted crumbling outbuildings, a leaky woodshed and a pile of cut-price manure. In the foreground an unmown lawn surrounded by gone-to-weed borders. Running crash-bang through the middle, a barely gravelled drive under which a flood was already beginning to bubble. It was called The Priory. It was too much and it was home.

He was still alternately baffled and furious to be living in South Norfolk. The move from Soho to So-No had taken him by surprise. One minute the family – B, he and the twins – had

1

been crammed into a bijou flat off Berwick Street and at the centre of all the action generated by scripts in development and soft-pencilled auditions, the next he was staring at sheep. As ever, fear, greed and negligence had been the root causes of his downfall. The fear that the increasingly delicate twins wouldn't stack up at the solitary non-paying primary school – a disused police station with a heavily fenced-in lump of tarmac to the rear just behind Cambridge Circus operating under the name Our Lady Of Victories. The greed that strikes one when people mistake development for completion and soft-pencil for signed contract and offer you blue-sky prices for your one-and-a-half-bedroom flat. The negligence that afflicted Stirling when, waiting for day after day in a Novotel near Bari to interview a moderate central defender supposedly on a pre-season tour with Everton, he failed, on the daily check-call home, to pick up on the significance of the word 'prospectus'. By the time he returned to Soho with a notebook packed with 'a game at a times', 'all credits to the gaffer' and 'at the end of the days' an offer had been made and, it being received in South Norfolk, quickly accepted.

Stirling waited for the gazumpers and gazunderers, but everyone behaved honourably and the family was on the move. Over a February weekend they transferred the contents of their flat and reassembled them sparsely in four of the thirteen rooms that they now owned. In an attempt at good parenting and a bid to sunder the twins' increasingly spooky interdependence, Jimmy and B had allocated them a room apiece complete with en suite bathroom and optional study. Charlie and Nancy had giggled to each other at such munificence. After a week of frenetic furniture activity, quite impressive in five-year-olds, Nancy was reunited with Charlie. Although, on the plus side and as they might one day have to explain to the Social Services, they had to be congratulated on being brave enough to sleep in separate beds, albeit ones without a cigarette paper between them.

So it was that the Stirlings had passed a cold grey spring enlivened only by regular flash-flooding, holed up in the east wing of their property. The family moving cautiously from kitchen to TV room and then upstairs to their respective bedrooms. There was no financial possibility of living anywhere else for the next couple of decades. The rest of the house could wait.

The phone rang. That wasn't meant to happen. He picked up the hand-set with caution.

'Hello,' he said quietly.

'Sorry to call so early, Jimmy, it's Derrek here.' (Derrek Senior, his boss.) 'I was just having a word with the lad' (Derrek Junior, his nemesis) 'over the Shredded Wheat' (they were both fat) 'and we thought it might be clever to redirect you tomorrow to Halifax.'

'But what about Ipswich?' asked Stirling.

'Didn't you do them last week?'

'No, that was Norwich.'

'Same difference.'

'Not entirely, one's in Norfolk and the other's . . .'

'Whatever. The thing that grabs my goat is that Halifax are playing Lincoln.'

'Wow.'

'Don't be a cunt, Jimmy. As you well know Lincoln finished second from bottom of the Third Division and Halifax finished bottom and were only saved from relegation to the Vauxhall

Conference by Kidderminster having problems with the local council over ground redevelopment, so what we have tomorrow at The Shay is two teams who, even this early in the season, could be on the brink of sliding into utter oblivion.'

'And . . .'

'If that's not a story that cries out for the Stirling touch I don't know what is.'

'Whatever.'

'You don't have to worry too much about the details. Just make it sing.'

'It don't mean a thing . . .'

'Good man. It could be an award winner. Ciao.'

'Ciao yourself,' said Stirling an irritating second after the line went dead. 'Bollocks.'

'Dadda . . .' said Nancy.

'. . . That's a bad word,' continued Charlie.

'Sorry. Sorry. Sorry.' He lit another cigarette. 'So what are we going to do about this Sugar Puffs situation?'

Stirling had become a football writer for want of something to do. Having made a modest living for one during the fag end of the Eighties writing 'Are You Mad?' quizzes for the lads' magazines he had struck lucky when a newspaper sent him to report on Southampton v Coventry. For once, he was in the right place at the right time. Doors opened. A longish stint doing football, a summer of tennis, a year on a tabloid, a good Olympics, and now he was Chief Football Writer on a Sunday paper with a long past and short future. His unopinionated column was published every week, his interviews whenever he got round to transcribing them, his think-pieces when the mood took him. And every Saturday, because it was expected that you not only work but be seen to be working one day a week, he would make the effort to watch some live sport. It was a terrible living and it was his only living.

'Has everyone finished their breakfast?' said B, waltzing into the kitchen in a kimono, thong and green wellies.

'Getting there,' said Stirling.

'Toast, yoghurt, fruit, vitamin pill . . .'

'Not yet. Bit of an impasse on the Sugar Puffs.'

'Come on darlings. Finish your cereal and you might find Mummy has a surprise for you.'

The twins started shovelling the honeycombed nuggets into their tiny mouths. Astonishingly easy.

'Who was on the phone?' asked B.

'Big Derrek,' said Stirling.

'And . . .'

'He's sending me to Halifax tomorrow.'

'You told him where to stick it.'

'Not exactly.'

'Jimmy, you're meant to be Chief Football Writer. Chief football writers don't get sent to Halifax.'

'Yes but . . .'

'No yes buts. If you want to go, go. Just don't moan to me about it.'

And she sashayed off to slice up a couple of Kiwi fruit, arrange the slices over two dollops of natural yoghurt and, with a vitamin pill as the centrepiece, serve up the concoction as 'Wizard Pudding' for the twins. They gobbled it up.

B was right, of course. She was always right. In dozens of years of being together Stirling had never won a single argument against her. Even when they had had an argument about her winning every argument she had won the argument on the grounds that as Stirling always did exactly what he wanted to do they only ever argued about things when she was in the right. He loved her logic. He loved her feistiness.

And this time she really was right. It was ridiculous that a sports writer of his standing was being dispatched to Halifax. If he had any pride he would have told the fat man to swivel. If he had any sense he'd walk away from a job that caused him such dismay. Aside from anything else he took exception to being called a cunt before nine in the morning.

But Stirling hadn't opened an envelope since the family had moved to Norfolk six months ago. He had been able to pull off such a cavalier approach to personal finance thanks to one of those fancy new banks offering consumer-friendly new all-in-one accounts that seemed to spend all his money on advertising their cleverness and in return allowed him to spend as much as he liked until he spent that little bit too much and they repossessed his home. He lived in terror of accidentally pressing the balance enquiry button at the cash-point machine. For even though he had no idea how great was their debt he was as certain as could be they were spending at least twice as much as he earned. And if he flounced out there would be no redundancy, no pay-off, no anything. The factor by which they were spending more than he was earning would become infinite. Bankruptcy would loom. Far from being in a position to tell anyone to stick it, he was utterly stuck.

The twins appeared in the kitchen. Dressed, teeth cleaned, hair brushed, all without a Stirling finger lifted.

'Will you come swimming with us, Dadda?' asked Nancy.

'I'd love to,' said Stirling. A lie.

'But . . .' said Charlie.

'But I've got a driving lesson.' A truth.

'Daddy . . .' said Nancy.

'. . . you never come swimming,' said Charlie. As near to true as made no difference. Stirling didn't enjoy taking his children swimming. He couldn't swim and nor could they. Standing would be a more appropriate verb for such activity as went on at the Bungay Sports & Leisure Centre. What's more, due to a late puberty, a small bone structure and delicate features, he had always found public changing rooms harrowing. He was as competitive as the next man, but not when it came to communal showers. His lack of confidence in this field was a publicly unexpressed factor behind his surprise decision to give up team sports at the age of twenty-seven. And, finally and clinchingly, the fact that (unlike in Soho) none of the Yummy Mummys could be arsed to wear bikinis and had tattoos creeping out from unalluring one-pieces did little to boost Stirling's detumescent libido.

The twins looked disappointed. 'Listen, darlings,' he said, 'when, and it will be "when", honestly, I get this driving cracked I'll be able to take you anywhere. We could go swimming . . . we could go to the Steam Museum . . . the Dinosaur Park.' He faltered. There wasn't an abundance of 'things to do' in Norfolk.

'Promise,' said Nancy.

'Promise,' said Stirling.

'Really promise,' said Charlie.

'Really promise,' said Stirling.

Thinking it was the least he could do, he helped B bundle the kids into the car and gave them a positive send-off. On his return, there was an answerphone message. Could this be Big Derrek's first recorded apology? He hit play.

'Sorry, Jimmy, George here. I can't make today. Everything a bit in the air and my therapist has advised me not to give any driving lessons for the time being. I'll be in touch when I know a bit more what I'm doing.'

George had always seemed relatively sane to Stirling. Very calm, really, when you considered the circumstances under which they met. Oh well, that was the day's social life jiggered.

2

'You're cracking up,' said B.

Before Stirling could reply the train went into a tunnel, and by the time it emerged into yet another dreich East Anglian morning the battery on his mobile was dead.

According to football writers, it was a golden age for football writers. Never had they been given so much space to write about their only subject. Previews, exclusive interviews, predictions, match reports, chalkboards, analysis, comment, quotes, marks out of ten, more exclusive interviews, sport think-pieces, yet more analysis – all this for Bolton v Middlesbrough. And if Man United or Liverpool or Arsenal or Leeds or Chelsea or Newcastle were playing then yet more angles would be exhausted in order to fill the thirty-two-page supplements. World News, meanwhile, had been pushed off the map. The 'top people's papers' could tell you more about the state of Steven Gerrard's groin than what might or might not be happening in the entire continent of Africa. The PR people conned the marketing executives who conned the newspaper editors that all this senseless coverage was 'adding value', if not sales. And because newspaper editors were never more uncomfortable than when not doing something someone else was doing they all fell into line. There was no escape.

The main beneficiaries of this craven monopoly were the football writers. Previously considered too drunk or infantile to work for anything other than the 'toy department' (an insult they took as a compliment), they were now accorded a prominence that was once given to erudite book reviewers or distinguished war correspondents. Their salaries and picture bylines bloated. Editors not only noticed them but sought their opinion on the issue of the day – usually something as riveting as the English left-back crisis.

If they had been restricted to newspapers they could be easily avoided, thought Stirling, as he tossed the Saturday sports supplements on to the far seat. Recently, though, the football writers had begun to proliferate in other media. They'd been gifted their own TV shows, radio stations had been given over to their mangled abuse of the language, and, worryingly, they had started popping up on *Newsnight*. Out went the Asics jackets and other freebies from sports manufacturers and in came dark suits, ironed shirts, big ties and shades, a transformation consolidated after an incident in a Luxembourg lap-dancing bar when six 'Chiefs' had been arrested and while spending the night in jail had passed the time re-enacting favourite scenes from *Reservoir Dogs*. So tickled had they been that they had decided, on a whim, in the Principality's only prison cell, to dispense with their old nicknames – Bandit, Kipper, Doggo, etc. – and start to refer to each other as Mr White, Mr Green, Mr Brown. The Tarantubbies had been born – Football's finest. On being deported each and every one of them had condemned in print the 'drunken hooligan minority' who had taken the shine off England's gutsy 2–0 win against the part-timers. It would have been laughable had they not been paid so much more than Stirling.

Grantham, Leeds, Bradford Interchange, New Pudsey, Bradford Interchange again, Halifax. He was there. An attenuated streak of piss looking like the advance man for a famine, he walked, as briskly as he could while smoking, towards the floodlights. It was August but it was dark enough for them to be operating at their maximum capacity of 20 per cent. As ever, given the choice between left and right, Stirling chose wrong. Having circumnavigated four-fifths of the crumbling Shay Stadium he found an entrance, asked three people where the press box was, and finally happened upon it just as the players were coming off the field for half-time. The only task his job required was to turn up on time – and it was beyond him.

A row of sullen men sat whispering into phones and tapping away into laptops.

'Jimmy Stirling?' he said.

No response.

'Hi, I'm Jimmy Stirling. A seat should have been booked in my name.'

'Need to get here early if you want a seat,' said a man with a face which if Stirling had any condition on him at all he would have punched on sight.

'Look, I'm sorry but I've come from Norfolk. The taxi-driver overslept so I missed the 6.17 and went for a coffee and waited an age for my change and just missed the 7.17 and the 8.17 was cancelled and after all that there were ongoing problems at Peterborough . . . I won't bore you with the details. I think there should be a seat reserved for me.'

Ugly and his Fat Cousin were occupying four seats. Now

the Cousin was arguably a two-seat man but Ugly was really quite slim for a football writer.

'Any chance of you two moving up?'

No response.

'I just wondered if you could move along a bit,' he said with more conviction.

'We need our elbow room,' said Fat Cousin.

Stirling paused. No one said anything.

'So where can I sit?'

'Plenty of room in the stands,' said Ugly, gesturing with his thumb towards an admittedly sparsely occupied seating area.

'Thanks,' said Stirling. 'I don't suppose there's a spare team-sheet?'

He made his way up to the stand. The office would need 850 words on the whistle. This was not a problem but some information about the first half would be handy. The score, for instance. He looked around for a reliable witness and, failing to find one, settled for a man eating a pie.

'OK if I sit here?'

'Unnugggh.'

He sat down and took his laptop out. Turned it on. A procedure which always made him feel a little bit more professional.

'Got enough room for your pretty little elbows?' he shouted down at the press box before turning to his neighbour.

'Good game?'

'Not bad.'

'Any goals?'

'Yeah.'

'Who scored?'

'Halifax.'

'Good goal?'

'Missed it.' And then his primary source of information went off for another pie.

Stirling typed in 'Halifax are so unaccustomed to going into the lead at half-time that the manager probably had the bunting out rather than crockery . . .' Total bollocks, but it would do. 'But, just like a Championship Golf tournament only properly begins on the final nine of the fourth day, a Third Division football match between two teams anxious to retain their league status' – the players were now coming back on to the pitch – 'doesn't really kick off until the last forty-five minutes.' Truly crap analogy. 'And after a first half that was only remarkable for the fact that Halifax had finally scored a goal' – the ball was kicked off – 'their players looked nervous on the restart. When you're accustomed to losing it's a difficult habit to break.'

He hit word-count. Eighty-seven. A start. Time to watch some football.

A new problem immediately became apparent. Which side was Halifax? Normally he could overcome his lack of preparation by looking at the home fans' scarves and extrapolating from there. But the supporters' scarves were blue and yellow and, bound to happen eventually, one team was wearing blue shirts and yellow shorts and the other yellow shirts and blue shorts. Either team could be Halifax. Equally, either could be Lincoln. And although you could bluff your way out of most things in the job this was the kind of information you were obligated to know. 'Halifax/Lincoln (subs to delete one) had the better of the early exchanges with the Halifax/Lincoln defence (subs to delete the other) looking as rocky as a marriage in nearby Emmerdale. . .' No, he couldn't file that. Not even as a parody.

But nor, on professional and macho grounds, could he lean forward and tap the bloke in front on the shoulder to ask, 'Who's in the blue shirts?' Aside from anything else the Yorkshireman would probably only fucking lie to him. He certainly would if he were a Halifax season ticket holder and some nancy-boy London hack with a fancy Apple Mac laptop showed up at half-time not even knowing that the mighty Shaymen played in blue and yellow. Or yellow and blue.

The quandary resolved itself around about the sixtieth minute – Stirling didn't wear a watch and relied on his battery-exhausted mobile for the time – when the ball became lodged in the mud in the yellow shirts' penalty area, and after much kicking and missing and huffing and puffing ended up, and Stirling knew not how, in the net. The home fans stirred themselves. The PA went mental: 'Gaaaarrry Jooooooones. The second of the match for the Halifax ever-present.'

'And two more than he scored in the whole of last season. Big jessie,' said the bloke in front.

Stirling got to work.

If at first you don't succeed, try on the forty-seventh attempt to get someone else to do the job for you. Yesterday, on an August Bank Holiday Yorkshire Saturday afternoon as bluff as it was cold, Garry Jones spent much of the afternoon trying to cajole the Lincoln defence into scoring an own goal. He failed. But confronted by yet more evidence of his lack of talent The Big Jessie, as he is semi-affectionately known by the Halifax faithful, surprised everyone at the Shay, not least himself, by achieving something he hasn't managed since the last century – a goal. It wasn't a classic. It didn't need to be. And having scored once, he scored again. The

Jones Boy was on a streak. This might just turn out to be a good millennium for the Halifax Number Nine. An outcome that had previously looked as likely as the so-called A train arriving on time in these dark days for public transport.

The second goal bore all the hallmarks of a poacher with an empty bag. A stray ball, a scrum of bodies, and burrowing away in the middle the rejuvenated Jones to poke it home. Instinctive football. And no more than the mighty Shaymen deserved on an afternoon when . . .

Stirling was into his stride.

Halifax scored again, Jones ('poacher turned goalmaker') setting up a player the PA announced as 'Budgen?', and Stirling reached 850 words at the very instant the referee blew the final whistle and dashed back to the Press Box.

'Any chance of borrowing a phone-line for a minute?'

No response.

'Twenty quid for the first person to lend me a phone-line.'

That got the fuckers moving. He banged off the copy and with a 'see you in the Premiership' to Elbows and Ugly hurried out of the stadium. It was customary for football writers to mill around afterwards to hoover up any free food and booze they could find and lob a few infantile questions at the managers –

Q: Good result, Bobby?
A: Yeah, all credit to the lads, I thought Garry did fantastic what with the drought he's been under and everything but no one at this club will be getting carried away . . .

or

15

Q: You must be disappointed with that, Harry?
A: I don't want to criticise the ref but I thought he was criminal. I don't think I've ever seen a benter ref, but I better not say any more or I'll only get into trouble.'

Stirling, too shy to ask any question he'd like to hear answered, usually gave the pit-a-pat routine a miss. On occasion, if it was a very quiet Saturday night, someone in the office might notice that there were no nannies (nanny goats = quotes, ha ha) from the managers and ask Stirling to refile. This was not a problem. He simply put quote marks at the beginning and end of his first paragraph and added 'said a delighted/devastated so and so after the match'. No one ever noticed. No one in football read his Sunday newspaper for fear of being thought homosexual. If he moved fast he could sneak a quick pint at Leeds station and make his check-call from there.

'Jimmy here, just checking everything's OK with the copy?'

'Who's doing Jimmy?' shouted a work experience. 'Hang on, Jim, Big Derrek wants a word.'

Derrek Senior was a substantial man who had been forced to take a desk job after doctors warned him that the stresses inherent in hauling his big frame in and out of economy class might, at best, bring on a heart attack. As bitter as he was obese, Derrek's sole reason for staying in the job, aside from the endless complimentary buffet lunches organised by Sport England, was advancing the career of his son, Derrek Junior, a piece of nepotism so brazen and obvious that Stirling had picked up on it and gone to some lengths to make a protégé of Junior. He had bought him an overkill of curries, picked at his poppadoms as Junior ploughed his way through the 'all you can eat' option, stood him round after round in The Butt of Lewis. He had, whenever Senior had managed to bludgeon his son's codswallop into the paper, never forgotten to say 'nice piece' to both the 'double "r" in the middle please Derreks'. He'd listened and listened and listened as Junior talked about his beloved Arsenal FC, a team Junior was so besotted with that Stirling had seen him burst into tears while watching Sky Sports Extra when Arsenal had gone a goal down in the seventh minute of the first leg of a Worthington Cup semi-final.

'Sorry, mate, it just gets to me sometimes. How can they be so good and yet so bad?' he had asked, clearing his eyes with a convenient pub towel.

'Beats me,' Stirling had replied, and braced himself for another hour of Arse this and Arsène that, a monologue so limited and unrelenting that it was almost poetic, and one which required nothing from Stirling other than to purchase pints and a couple of packs of KP nuts whenever the protégé paused to stare at the bottom of his glass.

Stuck in his groove, Junior never quite had the time to ask Stirling's opinion on matters Arsenal, which suited Stirling who, by picking the matches he covered carefully and clever use of the remote control, hadn't watched Arsenal playing football since 1997, and wouldn't have had a clue who was in the team if Junior hadn't kept on reminding him.

For a season or two, Father, Son and Jimmy Stirling had coexisted merrily until the Trinity had been busted up over a curry around about Christmas when Junior asked one question too many. With hindsight, Stirling may have been unbalanced by Derek Junior offering to pay for the meal, a unique gesture that prompted Stirling to respond in kind and for the first time in his life order something called a dopiaza. He hated curry almost as much as he hated rice, and hadn't eaten one since finding the courage to admit this to his father a couple of decades previously. Since then, when professionally required to eat in an Indian restaurant – usually only once a month – he had stuck to poppadoms and chutney and made a solid attempt to drink his share of the bill in lager. But if the little twat was offering, he'd go to the top of the menu. Caught unawares, staring at the unholy sludge on his plate, berating himself for his pettiness, Stirling had momentarily forgotten the role he had to play.

'Jimmy, wake up, buddy, I was asking you whether you think The Arse will nick the three points in Lille tonight.'

'I haven't a clue.'

'You're kidding.'

'I didn't even know they were playing.'

'But in your column you wrote that the extra width available to the Londoners should give them the edge against a workmanlike Lille outfit in a country that has traditionally proved to be a happy hunting ground for Wenger's Gunners.'

'I did?'

'Yes, and you—'

'It's OK, Derrek, if that's what I wrote that's what I think.' Stirling had pushed his curry aside and lit a cigarette. 'In truth, Del, not only do I think they'll win tonight 3–0 – Henry two, one in each half; Wiltord one, probably in the eighty-seventh minute – but I think they'll go on to win the whole friggin competition and the Premiership and the FA Cup and the Worthington Cup and, while we're at it, the Football Combination. If it still exists.'

'Don't be silly, buddy. You know I hate counting chickens.'

Derrek finally gave up on chewing an indestructible chunk of curry, removed it from his mouth, and wrapped it in a paper napkin. 'Anyway, whichever way you look at it, you've got to admit it's an important game tonight, Jim. If The Arse can do the business and Dortmund draw in Rosenberg we'll only need three points from our last two games, both at home, to ensure we top the group and avoid some of Europe's biggest guns – your Bayerns, your Lazios, your Real Madrids – in the all-important Stage Two Qualification Round.'

'Wouldn't that be yippee skipee?'

Junior had smiled. A sight more evil than pretty.

'I don't want to go overboard, Derrek, but I honestly think The Arse are so fucking good I'd be amazed if they lost a single game this season. In fact, I'd be faintly surprised if they let in a lousy goal. Ever again.' He paused and added with a contempt so obvious that even Junior couldn't help but notice, 'Listen up, buddy, it's not important. It's only a football match.'

'I can't believe you just said that.'

'It's a game. It's trivial. It's childish. It doesn't matter.'

'Are you fucking mad?'

'Never saner.'

Junior had looked at him, wiped his mouth with a convenient napkin, sadly the one he had already used, leant forward, failed to notice the string of heavily chewed curry gristle that had fallen into his lap, and whispered, 'Everything OK at home?'

Stirling had had the glimmer of an out. He could have claimed that B was suffering from extraordinarily delayed but nonetheless clinical, possibly terminal, post-natal depression, that his children hadn't spoken to him for over a year, that he was facing a sexual harassment charge following an incident involving at least two work experiences. Derrek Junior would have believed him and then, gallingly, tried to empathise. Despite still living at home with his parents, despite, on all available evidence, still being a virgin, his protégé would have felt compelled to dole out marital, parental and sexual advice. It had happened before and it was grisly.

'Never better,' he had replied. 'It's the football that's driving me mad.' And, with that, he walked out. Not quite fast enough to avoid overhearing his protégé angrily asking, 'What do you mean you haven't got any cheese?'

Stirling denied everything, of course, but the untouched curry had left a stain. From that moment he was treated with suspicion. The word 'difficult' kept cropping up. 'Doubts' were expressed about his 'temperament'. Shortly thereafter a 'new approach to management' had kicked in.

'What the fuck d'you think you're playing at, cunt?' shouted Derrek Senior down the phone.

'Sorry,' said Stirling, putting his pint down and lighting a cigarette. There really was no need to swear – it was only a match report on Halifax v Lincoln, for fuck's sake – but sports editors had a nasty habit of morphing into football managers on a Saturday afternoon. They would turn up for work wearing club colours, spend the morning kicking rolled-up balls of paper around, screaming with sub-kindergarten delight on the rare occasions one landed in the bin, and then the whistles would blow up and down the country and they'd go stark staring bonkers.

'There's not a single fucking name in this cunting report.'

'Hang on a minute. Garry Jones should be in there some-where, and Budgen or Budget or whatever, and anyway, as you well know, it was always going to be more a singing mood piece than a traditional match report.'

'I'll give you sodding singing mood pieces. It's the biggest pile of shite I've seen in thirty years in the business. And it's not just me that thinks that. Everyone here thinks you're a total cunt. Complete rewrite by 6.30. Thanking you.'

Stirling bought a local evening paper, another pint, opened his laptop, turned to the match report bylined with a way-out-of-date picture of Elbows and started typing away.

Pettigrew, Barton, Jenkins and Potter, that was the Halifax midfield yesterday afternoon; Flitcroft, Weatherspoon, Philpot and Drago, that was the Lincoln midfield. Mere names to many, but each and every one with the potential to be a hero in the eyes of the 2,043 faithful people who turned up at the Shay Stadium – that's Shay not Shea – yesterday afternoon to witness a match which even this early in the season would go some way to determining which set of unfortunates might retain their league status come the end of it.

In the third minute Pettigrew passed to Barton, who in turn passed to Jones, only for the ball to go out for a goal-kick. Seven minutes later, Lincoln returned the favour, with Philpot finding Weatherspoon who found Drago only for the Maltese schemer to overhit his pass for a throw-in . . .

He worked rapidly but still missed the 19.10 to Grantham which in turn ensured he missed the 21.27 to Peterborough which guaranteed he missed the 23.01 to Cambridge and, with a landslide near Chelmsford somehow complicating matters, it was not until half two in the morning that he arrived in Diss. A long way from Never Pullham.

Miraculously, there was a cabbie on the rank. Usually you had to book them at least two hours in advance, and you could double or triple that figure on a Saturday night. But with his mobile temporarily kaput he had been unable to give any warning of his delayed arrival. Perhaps his luck was on the turn.

'Never Pullham, please,' said Stirling.

'Where?' said the cabbie in that flat, depressed drawl particular to Norfolk.

'It's north of Bungay and Beccles.' Stirling, not being a driver, had very little idea where he lived.

'Unhuh.'

'And west of Great Yarmouth and Lowestoft.'

'Unhuh.'

'If you aim for Lowestoft and then hang a left before we get too close I should be able to find it.'

'It'll cost you.'

'Fine.'

They drove on in silence for miles.

'Been anywhere nice?' asked the cabbie, finally.

'Halifax.'

'Had a good day?'

'No, but there you go. Things can only get better.'

'Wouldn't be too sure about that. If I've learned one thing in life it's that people always let you down eventually . . .'

Jesus Christ, thought Stirling, another depressed East Anglian cabbie. He was fully aware the landscape was bleak, he realised it was unlikely they ever ferried anyone remotely interesting, but couldn't one of the cabbies pull himself together? Recently he'd had the bad luck to be picked up more than a few times by a cabbie called Cedric whose wife – another cabbie – had

22

left him for someone else – yet another cabbie. All three cabbies worked for QuikCabs, the firm that 'owned' the surely unprofitable Diss station cab rank. On every journey the cuck-old cabbie would bring Stirling up to date with his desperate existence – 'Everybody in the firm's taken sides. I'm on my own, now'; 'My new girlfriend's parents won't have me in the house'; 'My new girlfriend's child screams when she sees me'; 'My new girlfriend's left me.' For another cabbie? 'No, for no one in particular.' All delivered in that lifeless Norfolk burr. Last December, Stirling, momentarily concerned that the cuckold might take his own life over the festive period, had uncharacteristically, and significantly, overtipped him, drawing attention to his generosity by muttering, 'Have a drink on me.'

'Who with?' the cuckold had replied before taking an age to fill in the receipt.

Now he was trapped with another one. 'But cars, you can rely on cars, look after them properly and they don't let you down.'

'I'm afraid I know nothing about cars.'

Once more they drove on in silence. Until the car came to a sudden halt.

'I don't think we're there, yet,' said Stirling.

'I know that.'

'Is there a problem?'

'Gone and got a puncture, haven't I?'

'Is there anything I can do?'

'Can you handle a torch?'

Stirling stood on a verge of the A143, within sight of the Brockdish turning, holding a torch for the fiftysomething cabbie with an unmistakable birthmark who in his own sweet time went about changing his tyre. Neither was in the mood for small-talk. Stirling watched. The cabbie toiled. By the time the work was done and they had found his home it was past four o'clock.

'That'll be fifty pound,' said the cabbie.

'What? Oh, fuck it.' He was too tired to haggle. 'Can I have a receipt?'

'Fill it in yourself,' said the cabbie, and sped off.

There was women's tennis on Sky Sports 2 and a repeat of the action from the European Figure Skating Championships in Skopje on British Eurosport. Stirling drank whisky and channel-hopped. He had never really got the hang of figure skating, or whisky for that matter. But then he'd never really fancied barely pubescent girls. Perhaps he wasn't mature enough yet. Perhaps such little delights lay in the future.

Watching Derreks Senior and Junior, on the other hand, watching their own recordings of live figure skating was one of the more repulsive sights in modern sport. 'Here comes the gusset-shot,' one of them would shout to alert the other to press the pause on the remote, and then with the image captured they would trade a high-five and lech at the screen, never forgetting to ask Kath the secretary for her opinion. Why Kath, a seemingly sane woman, continued to work on the desk always surprised Stirling. For five years she had stoically put up with the pair of Derreks' light banter/heavy harassment – an industrial tribunal would, God willing, one day deliver the right decision – and never complained once. On the plus side, he supposed, they always presented her with a bouquet of carnations at the Christmas party. So long as she smiled gracefully whenever a Derrek called her a 'little gem' or 'petal' or 'pet' or 'loveboat' then she was guaranteed a job for life.

There weren't many at the newspaper who could make such a claim, certainly not Stirling, who was always amazed, and disappointed, when another month went by and he found himself still employed as a football writer.

Before he could fall asleep, the twins woke him up.

'Dad, what are you doing?' asked Nancy.

'Just watching some sport.'

'But sport's boring,' said Charlie.

'I know, I know.' He turned it off. 'What do you want to do?'

'Harry Potter,' said Charlie.

'Harry Potter, please,' said Nancy.

If it had simply been a question of watching a video Stirling could have slept his way through it. But, exhaustingly, it would be incumbent upon him to perform.

'I'll be Harry,' said Charlie.

'I'll be Ron,' said Nancy.

'And, Dadda, you can be Hermione,' said Charlie.

3

Stirling could put an exact time on the moment when he had finally, and irrevocably, fallen out of love with football: 2.45 pm, 23 April 2000.

Two days before, Mum had rung to say that Dad had fallen down the stairs and was in hospital. He was in a coma.

Not for the first time. Thirty years before, just as they were taking their first faltering steps to forming an English relationship that would always have sport at its core, his father had fallen down another set of stairs. He had been unconscious for ninety-seven hours. Family legend had it that a card sent by Stirling which depicted him scoring four goals against very modest opposition was the first thing he registered on regaining consciousness. It was unlikely but consoling. Whatever, Stirling had never scored four goals in a match again and, more important, his Dad had successfully negotiated every staircase, if not many business deals. Until now.

Graham, his younger brother, was already there with his perfect wife Mimi and their less than perfect children Kent and Hunt. Graham was unarguably good-looking, and a sufficiently successful bond dealer to be fronting up a hedge fund. Graham was smart, sartorially and mentally, and Graham could drive. Stirling was the flip-side. Despite having to pick up their Mum and drive twice the distance, Graham had beaten them to the hospital by a couple of minutes. Stirling's Mum – short, blonde, still ditzy after all these years – was sniffing lavender and humming Andrews Sisters numbers, and after Stirling had nudged her she kissed him somewhere near his left ear lobe.

They were all ushered into an unoccupied office in the Radzinowicz Neuro-Surgery Unit where they sat and swapped brave little grimaces. They took it in turns to ask Mum if she was OK. They drank their cups of tea with six sugars. Stirling looked at the doodles on the desk. 'How many vegetables does it take to . . .' 'A vegetable walks into a pub . . .' 'What do you call a vegetable who . . .' He needed a cigarette.

The senior consultant walked in, a bad sign, accompanied by the country's top neuro-surgeon, a dreadful sign. 'Your husband has suffered a brain clot.' Pause. 'We need your permission to carry out brain surgery.' Pause. 'Do you grant that permission?'

Graham responded first, asking the necessary questions about odds and percentages and chances. The questions that had to be asked to glean the information upon which an informed decision could be made. The questions that Stirling didn't have it in him to ask.

'If we don't perform the surgery, he will die,' said the neuro-surgeon. 'If we do, he has limited chances of recovery. At best, he might leave the hospital in a wheelchair with his mental faculties intact, or be able to walk out but with his brain impaired. More likely, he will be reduced to a vegetative state. It's impossible to tell.'

Stirling's Mum stopped humming 'Boogie Woogie Bugle Boy' and started howling to God for help.

'Again, again, I can't believe it's happened again,' she said.

'I'm sorry?' asked the neuro-surgeon.

'There was a fall thirty years ago. It's not relevant,' said Graham.

'What would you do?' asked Stirling's Mum, having turned her attention from the ceiling to the experts.

'I can't answer that question,' said the neuro-surgeon.

She looked at the side-kick.

'What would you do?' asked Stirling's Mum.

'I can't answer that question,' said the consultant.

'What would you do?' said Stirling's Mum.

Stirling stared at the doodles. And then at the 'No Smoking' sign.

'Can we have a moment to discuss it?' asked Graham.

'Of course,' said the neuro-surgeon.

'Of course,' said the consultant.

'How long have we got?' asked Graham.

'If we're going to operate, we need to do so quickly,' said the neuro-surgeon. 'Fifteen minutes?'

Stirling blew five of them having a cigarette. He blundered out of the ward – Bach's *St Matthew Passion* for some reason ringing through his head – picked up the family on the way, exited the hospital, and in the little time available between drags he tried to make some sense of things to B as Charlie and Nancy gambolled in the flower-beds pretending to be fairies.

The decision was swiftly made. There was no decision. Even if everything was pointless, something must be done. Even if there was no God, they had no choice but to rely on one. After all the little failures and small disappointments, perhaps now, near the end, Dad's luck would finally come good.

He shuffled into the neuro-surgery unit to have one last look at his father – immobile, tubes everywhere, face pink, big and unmoving – and then Dad was wheeled away to have his brain cut open. Stirling muttered an 'I love you' as the inert form was trolleyed past and then got the hell out of there. He had always hated hospitals.

No one rang Stirling to say they had a relative who had died in the same unit. A few people telephoned to talk about their own family medical miracles. Mothers who had had the last rites delivered and were now in pretty good shape considering they were seventy-three – eight years older than Dad – and brothers who'd come out of comas after three days or three weeks or was it three months. Difficult as they were, these conversations were helpful in providing Stirling with encouraging precedents to pass on to his mother. He knew what would happen, and Graham knew what would happen, and even Mum knew, but no one was letting on. Least of all to themselves.

They booked into a hotel. They tried desperately to remain positive. They concentrated very hard on continuing to talk about Dad in the present. They conned themselves that no news was good news. They sat around waiting for the phone to ring and jittered like hell when it did. They took it in turns to sit by the hospital bed. They all felt numbingly tired.

Stirling, who had always found his father the easiest person to talk to, didn't have a clue what to say. Each time he visited he would guilelessly start a conversation with the bulbous form – 'Hang on in there', 'You're going to be OK', or 'It will be all right, Dad' – but having tried to be positive he would be hushed at once by the inanity of what he was saying, the immobility of the body. There was only a diabolical breathing sound created by the machine that was keeping him alive while the surgeons determined how much of him was truly left alive.

The pair of them incapable of conversation, Stirling was left with his thoughts. He remembered a late afternoon on Lytham sands playing football. Dad, dressed in light blue canvas shoes and polka-dot golfing hat but minus the nearly always present tie, was the Blackpool side from the Matthews final. Stirling was Peter Bonetti. The game played with a golden plastic ball. The goal a shaft of rock face in the sand. Time after time Mortenson, Matthews and Perry dribbled through the Chelsea defence and aimed shots at the goal. Time after time Bonetti saved them, hurling himself from side to side and laughing uncontrollably as Dad launched another attack with an accompanying commentary.

There were the annual beach cricket Test matches. Dad's Dead XI against Stirling's Alive XI to be played for two hours a day, weather and Dad's patience permitting, for the entire fortnight. One-a-side cricket. W. G. Grace batting with the sea lapping at his ankles as Lillee ran through the surf to bowl. Washbrook completing the first century in the series with a trademark dab to third man which Stirling, who had just come off a twenty-yard run-in (in the early days he mistakenly packed his side with quicks – Holding, Hall, Lillee, Thomson, even Willis), would have to jog the length of the beach to field. Year after year, his excitement mounting as they selected their twelves in the car on the drive up and, having inspected the beach in the morning, decided whom to leave out. Until one year father had retired just a bit earlier than son was expecting and, disappointed, Stirling had spent the holiday playing

Howzat on his own, day after day rolling the dice, re-enacting an imaginary County Championship.

The horse-racing. The days of glory. A box at Ascot for Grundy v Bustino. The race of the century. The prodigiously successful businessmen – soon to be disgraced, bankrupted or imprisoned – deserting Lester for the first time and piling on Grundy. The finish so ferocious that neither horse ran well again but who cared, because at the finish Grundy was ahead by a neck. The celebrations – champagne for the adults, yet another bitter lemon for Stirling, who was made giddy by a quinine high. The sense of possibility. The happiness. The certainty nothing could go wrong. And later, during the fallow years, when although Dad was betting far lesser sums he was gambling so much more. Hanging around for days at the track before plunging heavily on just the one two-year-old, knowing if it lost he would have to ask Mum for a loan, or wait for another relative to die. The silences on the way back if a treble-star nap had failed.

The three-day meeting at York, the best in the calendar. Their first holiday together. Dropping in on Nan and Dot, still on £2 a week after forty years' service, and staying up all night working his way through the boxes where Nan had stored every press-clipping about her only child. The headlines, the promise, the grandiose predictions, the faded photo from another age. The headlines, the bankruptcies, the public admissions of failure, the same photo. They had talked it over for the first time. And Stirling, who was proud of the achievement rather than shamed by the falls, had perhaps offered his father comfort. It was only money. Better to have your moment than grind your way to a cottage in the country. They had bet like men. Dad had nearly broken even. Stirling had trebled his money on Tuesday, shipped a bit on Wednesday, and lost the lot on Thursday.

Best of all, there was football. They had started going in the early Seventies. The ritual was always the same. Meet Dad's mates for a few pints before the game in the thrillingly grown-up world of the pub. Stirling looking up at the men, only speaking when spoken to, wearing his colours and sipping his bitter lemon. Then off to the match, scurrying to keep up as they struggled to make kick-off. Prime seats. The adults taking the piss. Stirling rapt. Praying to his eleven-year-old God that Osgood, Cooke or Hudson might score. The journey back listening to *Sports Report* in the traffic. Every Saturday when Chelsea were at home.

The first game they had seen together was the 1971 Charity Shield. Chelsea lost. A pattern was established. In the twenty years of going together Chelsea failed to win a trophy, unless you counted the Second Division Championship or the Auto-Windscreen Trophy or the Leyland Daf Trophy, negligible achievements which even Stirling, stuck in puberty, was too grown up to pretend to take seriously.

Chelsea were crap, the football was crap, but the violence was top-of-the-range. A riot at Tottenham, sitting in silent fear at West Ham, running away from Leeds. When the away fans weren't up for it the police stepped up from the bench. 'Harry Roberts is our hero, Harry Roberts is our hero, he kills coppers,' the fans would chant. The police would flail in, truncheons out. After the match, in a fenced-off area behind the flash stand which would bankrupt the club, a twenty-a-side affair between the faces on either side. It was the days before Hillsborough and Heysel. Hooliganism was something that you watched for as long as you dared and then ran away from.

It was nowhere near as upsetting as a string of duff FA Cup results: Chelsea 2, Crystal Palace 3; Chelsea 1, Leyton Orient 2; Chelsea 0, Wigan Athletic 1; Chelsea 2, Millwall 3; Chelsea 1, Oxford United 3.

Throughout it all, Stirling and his Dad had kept going. Football providing a comfortable talking-point whenever either was too bashful to mention something more important. Always always start with the football. The idea of opening a conversation any other way was as alien to either as interrupting it to say, 'I love you.' Over the years Stirling's views began to resemble his Dad's, a decade of defeat helping to change him on matters Chelsea from a God-fearing idealist into a faithless cynic. Dad suddenly stopped going, Chelsea started winning, and Stirling stopped going too.

He was a little disappointed that his bedside recollections should be exclusively centred on sport, deflated that they should be so irredeemably trivial. He was watching his father die and his mind was filled with childish ephemera. His Dad was probably dead and all he could recall of their time together was pretending to be Peter Bonetti.

He yawned once again, took a slug of multi-sugared tea, said a 'See you tomorrow', kissed the juddering and very pink and slightly engorged head, said 'I love you' and exited the Radzinowicz Neuro-Surgery Unit with the *St Matthew Passion* clanging, once again, through his head. Fuck off, Bach.

The end, when it came, was farcical. The results, such as they were, had been promising, as far as they could be, or, to be more exact, not unpromising. Dad wasn't clinically dead, or so they said. Mum and Graham had decided to go for a walk. Stirling had offered to drop in on the hospital before going to London to pick up some clothes for Mum – by his family's standards a foolproof plan. Except when Stirling arrived at the hospital a nurse had cleared the waiting-room – a family with an eighteen-year-old daughter in a two-weeks-and-counting coma, a bloke from Birmingham with a wife on a life-support machine, a young couple with an irreparably brain-damaged three-month-old, all in all not a great room – made him a cup of tea, six sugars, and said calmly, 'Your father's dead.' Stirling had stared at the blank *Times* crossword, trying to focus on the text as the nurse had gone through her consoling patter. Finally, quite incapable of seeing the words through the tears, he had jumped from the chair, said 'Thank you', half-hugged the nurse, said 'Sorry', and hurried out of the hospital. Round and round he had walked, desolate, smoking and bawling to B down his mobile.

Once he had gathered himself, a task not entirely assisted by a confusing visit to the on-site church, he had returned to the waiting-room to find out what needed to be done next and been told by the new duty nurse, 'But your father's not dead.' That threw him.

There had been an error in communication. The corrected consensus that emerged informed Stirling that although things were no better, and in that sense marginally worse, they weren't irredeemably so. Time was running out but there was still time. With this established, he had returned to the section of the car park where the mobile worked, rung B to bring her up to date, made another confusing visit to the on-site church, walked out, seen his mother and Graham bustling through the hospital and realised he had a problem. If they saw him, they would assume the worst. Which might be the proper assumption, but might be the wrong time to make it. Stirling should be in London, trains permitting. His presence could only signify bad news.

What to do? There was a hairdresser's, but for once he didn't need a haircut. There was a newsagent's, so he bought a copy of *The Times* and re-stared at the crossword. It wasn't getting any easier. He failed to untangle an anagram, and reckoning what will be will be, went back to the Radzinowicz Neuro-Surgery Intensive Care Unit.

'Jimmy, what are you doing here?' said his mother and burst into tears. It reminded him of the rare times when, being the eldest, he had interrupted them making love. Graham consoled his mother. Stirling thought about consoling Graham, moved unsteadily forward, and thought again. Incapable of providing a halfway decent explanation for his presence, thoroughly bamboozled as to what, if anything, was going on, he hung around making 'What can I say? What can I do? Not my fault' gestures.

For the first time in his life he was relieved to see a neuro-surgeon. The top man herded them out of the ward, evicted their new friends in the waiting-room and explained the state of play.

'The drugs we gave him to enable us to perform brain surgery have now worn off and there has been no reaction whatsoever, which . . .'

'I knew when I saw Jimmy he was dead. He's dead, isn't he?' said Stirling's Mum.

'He is being kept alive by the breathing apparatus. If we remove it then nature will take its course. He may be able to breathe of his own accord, he may not.'

'Oh, I just knew it. I just knew it when I saw Jimmy . . .'

They all looked at Stirling, improbably and unhappily cast as a harbinger of doom.

'We do obviously require your consent before we can remove the apparatus,' continued the neuro-surgeon.

It struck Stirling as they briskly deliberated that his Dad had already been downsized from patient to bed-blocker. He didn't share the thought.

They gave their consent. His father convulsed horribly, once. And then he was dead.

There were over a dozen photographers, a trio of film crews (both national and local) and a couple of representatives of the working press hanging around outside the hospital. Stirling had half expected them. True, his Dad had had a quiet few decades of late but he had had his moment. It was right and proper that he should be recognised, and entirely appropriate that the industry Stirling worked in should record his passing.

He walked towards his peers, sombrely, pensively, fast-editing sentences in his head. No one blocked his path. When he was a couple of yards past he stopped and turned back.

'What's the story?' he asked.

'Nicky Butt.'

'Nicky Butt?'

'Yeah, he fucked his hammy against Leicester. The consultants are checking it out. We should know in a couple of hours if he'll be fit for the Leverkusen game.'

He was a long way from appreciating a fundamental tenet of his job, namely that he was meant to report the news rather than be the news. Couldn't quite get his head round the fact that, boringly, he wasn't the story. Couldn't see it at all.

4

'Silvinho doesn't know the meaning of goal-side! He's got a mental block, he can't tackle,' said Derrek Junior, sitting at his father's desk and staring intermittently at Sky Sports News, which was on the thirty-six-inch screen.

'I love Silvinho, but I'm worried about him. Ashley Cole though!' said a callow individual whom Stirling didn't recognise. Must be yet another work experience.

'Ashley Cole . . . Good shout,' said Derrek Junior, pausing for a few seconds and flicking something out of his right ear.

'I'm dreaming about the Cup Final now. I wasn't but now I am. It'll be great,' said the work experience.

'Liverpool will be tired, tireder than us,' said Derrek Junior. He yawned and, demonstrating the talent for the obvious that made him such a moderate captioner of pictures, added, 'I'm tired too.'

'Yep,' said the trainee, probably for the first time experiencing how fatiguing even the shortest of conversations with Derrek Junior could be, 'so tired . . . I was supposed to be interviewing Paddy . . . fell through.'

One name and Derrek Junior was enthused. 'Paddy's a superhero.' There could be no greater praise.

'Ohhhh,' said the trainee. 'Greater than that, a demigod, a black Pegasus.' There could be greater praise.

Derrek Junior stared into the mid-distance, usually, but not always, a sign that he was doing some deep thinking. 'Misses Manu.'

'Misses Manu, yep,' confirmed the work experience, playing the Phil Neal role to Derrek Junior's Graham Taylor.

'Manumanumanu . . . my Emmanuel,' ejaculated Derrek Junior.

'Paddypaddypaddy,' said the workie. 'Untwinned, separated before their time, Paddy's soulmate dispatched to Barcelona to sit on a bench.'

'Life's a bench . . .' said Derrek Junior.

'. . . and then you die,' whispered the work experience before regaining his confidence.

'Stepanovs, eh! Useless cunt . . .'

'Cost us the title . . .' said Derrek Junior.

'Who is Paddy?' asked Stirling.

'Oh, hi, Jimmy,' said Derrek Junior. 'Didn't see you come in. Who's Paddy? Ha, ha, ha.' And then to the work experience, 'Meet Jimmy Stirling. Quite the wind-up merchant, doesn't support The Arse, but not a bad football writer all the same.'

'Pleased to meet you. I've read some of your stuff. I'm Rob Parsons.' The short man with the weasely face, who was wearing loafers and had done something to his hair, extended his hand. Stirling let it dangle.

'Who is Paddy?'

'Patrick Vieira, you dumb cunt,' said Derrek Junior and paused. 'Sorry to hear about your old man. Must have been a bit of a blow.'

'Yeah, well, it was, is,' said Stirling. He wasn't ready for this.

'Anyhow,' continued Derrek Junior, 'about Saturday. The old man has you pencilled in for Blackburn v Leicester. Doesn't look great on paper, but if Blackburn fail to pick up maximum points, Ipswich pull off a shock at Liverpool and Middlesboro keep up their excellent run then the boys from Ewood Park might, right at the death, find themselves embroiled in the relegation fight. Too good to go down, you might . . .'

'Blackburn's terrific,' said Stirling and pointed at Rob Parsons, who had slunk off to try and make friends at the water-cooler. 'Who's the workie?'

'That ain't no work experience, Jimmy, that's Rob Parsons. He's our new football writer. Brilliant story gatherer and all-round truffle hunter. Friends with Frank Lampard, Ray Parlour, Darren Anderton. Used to edit *Shoot*.' He paused. 'Respect and all that.' Derrek Junior did something funny with his right hand. 'But we could use the odd story.'

The Fat Man was right. In ten years in newspapers Stirling had never broken a news story. He had reacted to other people's news stories adequately and promptly, but as to actually truffling one out – never close. To be frank, he hadn't the first clue as to even the rudiments of story gathering. He supposed it involved making phone calls. Ringing up, say, Rio Ferdinand and asking him . . . what? There were no questions he wanted to ask Rio Ferdinand, nothing he had to say to the undeni-ably young centre-back. 'Hello, Rio,' and then he'd have to put the phone down. And Rio would 1471 him, painstakingly write down his number, and report him to the police as a nuisance caller. Why make the call?

'Thought I might do a profile of The Professor.' Parsons was back.

'Nice,' said Derrek Junior. 'Jimmy wrote a piece on Wenger

a fortnight ago but, in my book, you can never have enough on El Maestro.'

'Yeah, you could do a book on the man. Easy. But I thought I'd go for a little essay. Is he the new Herbert Chapman? That kind of thing. Bit of history, some stats, throw it forward, wrap it up. I'd need about twenty pars.'

'Lovely. Howwld it.' Derrek Junior whacked up the volume on the remote. 'Storytime.' A bright red News Alert Aston was flashing away along the bottom of the screen permanently tuned to Sky Sports News. The text read: 'CREWE TO LEAVE GRESTY ROAD. PRESS CONFERENCE LIVE AND EXCLUSIVE 3.00 P.M. ON SKY SPORTS NEWS.'

'Phhewww,' said Derrek Junior. 'Crewe, hey. That could be right up your street, Jimmy.'

But by the time the Fat Man had turned round, Stirling was gone.

Stirling sat in the top tier of the Pavilion at Lord's watching Mike Atherton bat. He had thought it might be a suitable place to grieve because his father through all the ups and downs had clung on to his MCC membership. When officeless his father had reacted to his straitened circumstances by putting on a suit and tie and travelling in to Lord's to use their facilities for his rather fluid business meetings. He could, more often than was seemly, be spotted trying to flog the Far Eastern rights to his beloved chip machines in an impromptu office he had constructed round the back of the Real Tennis Courts. Or approaching the unwary in the bar at the top of the Warner stand with flashy prospectuses for Canadian oil companies. Or, on quieter days, just hanging around the Pavilion checking the share movements on Ceefax on the small telly in the

Library. No one, in the two centuries history of the MCC, had made more use of their membership.

As for Atherton, his father had long appreciated dour Northern opening batsmen. From Hutton to Boycott to Atherton he had applauded every dot ball. Stirling had learned from him. The combination of Atherton and Lord's might even have granted him some peace, except that all around him were fathers and sons, sons and fathers.

The patriarchy was in suits, or tweed jackets and slacks, and wore bacon-and-egg ties; the juniors settled on smart but casual, striving for a suitably deferential look. All of them were pattering away, the conversation seemingly about cricket but every so often veering towards something verging almost on the personal. By the close of play sufficient would have been said to reassure both of them that nothing was too wrong with the world. Father OK, Son OK, and didn't Atherton bat well. A ritual observed, another day comfortably wasted.

'I must say I'm not a Hussein fan. Very Essex man,' said a young man with a sharp nose and a Nigel Havers haircut.

'He has those bright blue eyes,' replied his bald father, cracking his worryingly large knuckles.

'Yes, odd mixture.'

'And very odd choice for captain.'

Stirling retreated to the Bowlers bar. Two buffers blocked his way to the counter.

'Did I see you yesterday?' said Buffer A.

'Indeed, you did. We had a long conversation,' said Buffer B.

'Did we?'

'About golf.'

'Do you golf?'

'No.'

'I seem to be spending most of my life at the golf club.'

'You told me,' said Buffer B, and drained his pint and, without ado, vamoosed.

Buffer A, florid of face, navy blue of blazer and wearing what might have been cavalry twill trousers, looked at Stirling quite shrewdly considering how pissed he was.

'Do I know you?'

'I don't think so.'

There was a pause. The Buffer continued to stare beadily at Stirling, who in turn tried to stare engagingly at the reluctant barman. Suddenly The Buffer slapped him quite hard on the shoulder.

'Stirling, isn't it?' Stirling nodded. 'Knew I'd get there in the end. You must be Charlie Stirling's boy.'

'Yes.'

'Where is Charlie? You can usually count on bumping into him here. Not ill, is he? Everyone seems to be these days.'

There was no dodging the question. 'He died ten days ago.'

'Bugger.' The Buffer steadied himself on the bar. 'Poor you.' He wiped his right eye with a vivid silk handkerchief and then blew his nose thoroughly. 'What are you having?'

'Whatever,' said Stirling.

'Good man. Peter, a bottle of your second cheapest claret, if you will? And two glasses.'

Peter moved. The Buffer and Stirling made their way to a table that afforded a view of the cricket, sat down, watched Atherton and waited for Peter. Atherton had added seven to his score by the time Peter had filled their glasses. The Buffer drained his opener in one and spoke.

'Cancer, was it?'

'Sorry?'

'Or his ticker?'

'No, no, he fell down the stairs.'

'Bloody typical. They keep telling you you'll die from this or that and then you miss a poxy stair and that does for you.'

Stirling took out his cigarettes.

'I shouldn't, but may I?' asked The Buffer.

'Of course.'

The old man lit his cigarette and refilled the glasses.

'That's better. Good man, your father. Very kind man. Quite definitely not an s, h, one, t.'

'He is, was, kind.'

'Shame he never quite cut it in business.'

'His projects did have a tendency not to come off.'

'Kept pitching them though.'

'He was nothing if not an optimist.'

'That he was. Not an s, h, one, t, but definitely an . . .'

'Yeah, anyway . . .' Stirling looked away at the cricket, then turned back.

'Are you bearing up OK?' asked The Buffer.

'Not really, no.'

'Not easy. Not at all easy.'

They both turned to watch the cricket. Atherton left a ball, left a ball, blocked a ball, played and missed, left a ball, ran a ball down to third man for a single.

'Did he leave you anything?'

Stirling laughed, for the first time in a while.

'A little over a fiver.'

'That much.'

'It was sort of funny, actually . . . Another bottle?'

'Of course.'

Stirling went up to the bar. He was no longer invisible to

Peter now that, via The Buffer, he had established his credentials. What was he doing unburdening himself on a man he had almost certainly never met? Why was he on the verge of telling an anecdote to someone with no name? Because it was a good anecdote, he supposed. And if he didn't start talking it was long odds on that The Buffer would start detailing his illnesses. Since his Dad's death he had become a magnet to the over-sixties, who, if not terminally ill, couldn't help themselves telling him how they had cheated death. He couldn't face another bottle's worth of that.

'As you were saying, Dad was an optimist. So a couple of weeks before he dies, after what must have been a particularly good lunch meeting, probably about his beloved chip machines . . .'

'The chip machines I know about.'

'He drops in on this lawyer he knew from the old days who is now a senior partner in some hotshot firm and tells him he needs to make a will. The lawyer, who one assumes owed him a favour, says fine, and Dad is at his most grandiose. It's all how can we evade this tax and how can we avoid that death duty and he generally comes across as a man intent on making a hefty bequest. So the lawyer begins to take an interest, what with there being something in it for him, and a few days ago we are invited in to see him at his swish office to discuss the contents of the will.

'His secretary ushers us in and he's sitting behind this desk piled high with inheritance tax textbooks and there's this horribly keen young thing called Giles next to him with his pen poised to take a note. Sleek as you like he asks what have we got for him. Not much is the answer, but I couldn't quite say that. He prompts us. "Bank statements, perhaps?" These I

44

have and I hand over a couple of pages of Alliance and Leicester headed paper containing thrilling debits such as Oddbins £9.98 and Esso £9.99. The lawyer studies them quickly and says, "Not a lot of movement. Any share certificates?" These, too, I have. I place on the desk some grimy certificates indicating ownership of stock in long-defunct Canadian oil companies. The lawyer files them away. "Right, let's get down to business, where's the beef?" Well, of course, there isn't any. "That's it," I say. The lawyer, who must be shit-hot, barely flinches. "House?" he asks. "Mum's," I answer. "Car?" "Just failed its MOT." "Pension?" "Not really his style." "In that case," and he turns to Giles, "I think this is what we call a one-pager."'

'A one-pager, yes, very good. I've been on the receiving end of my fair share of them,' said The Buffer. 'One minute you think you're set up for life, the next you realise that you've barely covered your tube fare.'

They returned to Atherton, who played out a couple of overs without incident before The Buffer spoke again.

'About those chip machines . . .'

Stirling laughed. 'Bonkers idea. Press a button and this powdered potato is meant to miraculously transform itself into a punnet of edible fries.'

'That's the one.'

'Can you believe I invested in them – the Far Eastern rights or something. Just to give him a fillip when everything was getting him down.'

'Me too.'

'You didn't?'

''Fraid so, what with bumping into Charlie over the years at Lord's and him being quite persuasive.'

'Sometimes.'

'It has to be said I wasn't always at my sharpest, and anyway my accountant rings me last week and apparently I've got a controlling interest in the company.'

'Oh, fuck. I'm sorry.'

'It's hardly your fault.'

'No, but I mean, Dad shouldn't have sold you so many shares, I mean . . . I don't know what I mean. Do you want me to buy them off you?'

'Why in the name of buggery would you want to do that? They're almost certainly worthless.'

'Yes, of course, but . . .'

'Relax. Even under these socialists you're not liable for the old boy's debts.'

'No, but . . .' said Stirling, uncertain as to what the law and who the socialists might be.

'I shouldn't have mentioned it. It's just I bumped into Charlie here a month ago and he took me over to the corner of the bar and he gives me his usual hush-hush on the q.t. line of patter.'

'Unhuh.'

'And whispers, "Chip machines heading north. See you in sunnier climes. You never know, we could be on a winner."'

But Stirling did know, knew how many times he'd had this conversation with his father, how many times he'd become carried along with his father's enthusiasm for a project where the bubble hadn't so much burst as failed to leave the ground and he'd had to cope with the latest dashed hopes. It was too many times.

'I'd better be getting back to Norfolk.'

'Norfolk. Why do you want to go there?'

'I live there.'

'Ah, well. Take care.'

'You too.'

The cricketers were coming off. Atherton had batted all day and was seventy-two not out.

5

For a longish while Stirling seriously considered sitting on his arse and doing nothing, but thinking what the hell, and anxious to avoid an unnecessary argument when there were so many necessary ones pending, he sluggishly rose to his feet and 'impeccably observed' a minute's silence for some nugatory member of the extended royal family. It was the third time he had paid his respects to one of the nation's greatest drinkers in the last week. Throw in a recent couple of quiet minutes for some bloke from FIFA, sixty seconds for a sometime host of *World of Sport* and a baffling silence for Glenn Hoddle's Dad before a Spurs reserve game and it was hard not to conclude that this paying of respects was getting out of hand. It was as if those who ran Brand Football were so proud of their customers' new-found ability to stand for a minute without swearing that they couldn't resist the most trivial excuse to showcase it. Look at us. We respect the dead, no royal too minor.

The problem as ever with football, thought Stirling, was that by pushing some practice to excess they were rapidly robbing it of meaning. They'd have to open up the top end. If the man who linked the TV coverage of the 1966 World Cup Final received a minute, then logic demanded that the players who actually played in the game should be awarded –

what? – double the accolade. By that token, there was a compelling case for Sir Geoff (was he really a Sir?) Hurst to take up three minutes of everyone's time. And as for Sir Bobby Charlton, well, how long have you got?

Stirling awarded the silence – under a dozen coughs, four mobiles – an eight out of ten. The newspaper never printed these marks but that was beside the point. Allowed to speak again, a sizeable minority chanted 'Two World Wars and One World Cup', which clearly confused the twenty-five visiting Swiss fans at whom it was directed. England v Switzerland. At Pride Park, Derby. Friendlies don't come any bigger. The first chance – before their next chance – for Paul and Graeme and Phil and Gary and Darren and Darius to impress the new manager. Which of them would take this opportunity to play himself into contention/force his way into the manager's calculations just like Sir Geoff Hurst did back in . . . oh, not him a-fucking-gain.

Stirling switched on his laptop and made a belated attempt to watch the game. Was that really Nicky Butt in the England midfield?

There had been a time, back in the days when old-style journalists had been united in willing England to lose, when covering the national team had appealed to him. There were reasons for this. 'We are crap' stories were so much more entertaining to write than Rule Britannia drivel. There was the undeniable buzz to be gained from watching someone who'd dicked you around for two whole years lose his job so publicly. And it was less work. If England didn't make it to a major Championship, nor did most of the football writers. Stirling could merrily spend the summer half-watching on telly at home and making up some unverifiable nonsense about a Uruguayan schemer. He was spared the stress, strain and mortifying tedium of hanging around a team hotel in the company of football writers.

Now the bright young pups, New Patriots all, openly cheered on the rare occasions when England scored. After Michael Owen had scored his goal against Argentina they queued up to touch his football, waited in turn to cop a feel of his golden bollock. It was verging on the paedophilic. In Albania, when David Beckham, an hour after the game, had wandered past the press box, they had all risen and given him a standing ovation. 'Well played, mate,' said Blue. 'Fucking exceptional,' said Brown. 'Simply magnificent,' said Pink. Beckham had looked confused. The culture of complaint had been replaced by a culture of compliance. Frankly, he would rather be in Halifax.

Stirling wasn't a complete cunt. He had once supported England – when he was six. Staying up late to watch Banks save from Pele, England beat Romania, and Peter Bonetti let down by chaotic central defending. But then the trail had gone cold. Any sane pre-teen couldn't fail but be impressed by Tomaszewski in the Poland goal. By the time England played again in an international competition Margaret Thatcher was in power and the hooligans had taken over the stadium. He had found it impossible to disassociate the team from the support, the country from its prime minister, and had swiftly become ambivalent about the fate of the national side. When Maradona punched the ball past Shilton he had laughed, but not out loud.

His ambivalence had been ratcheted into loathing by the emergence in the Nineties of the new fan. Every DJ, cultural commentator and game-show host latched onto parochial England as Stirling adopted an increasingly global position –

Anyone But England. He had started with Ireland then Holland and Scotland before adding Spain, Italy, France, Greece, Portugal and the entire Eastern bloc. Within months he had tacked on Scandinavia, the Americas, Africa and the whole of Asia. Wales and Germany gave him pause, but not for long. And by the 1994 World Cup England would have needed to be drawn in a group containing New Zealand, Canada and South Africa for Stirling to be even neutral. As it was, on a funnier than usual night in Amsterdam, they blew it.

'Yyyesssss,' screamed Brown, struggling to his feet and tipping Stirling's laptop to the ground. Stirling scrambled around for the various leads, extensions and battery packs that made his working life so much easier. By the time he had reassembled his equipment England had scored again and Stirling was two goals behind the game. It was no way to write a match report.

'Seven bottles of Pinot Grigio, four vindaloos, two rogan joshes, a . . . chicken masala. Twenty-eight poppadoms, fourteen onion bhajis, as much chutney as you can lay your hands on, six pilaus, seven nans, four sag aloos, and all the veg that's fit to eat,' said White, reading from a note on his match programme with the same easy style he usually reserved for the auto-cue.

Stirling had yet again, and against his better judgement, found himself in a curry house. He had been snookered between Brown and Blue when the 'Ruby, anyone?' call had gone out and then got caught up in the rush as Britain's finest football writers chugged their way to The Bombay Garden. No one seemed to mind that he was there – not even Stirling, really, as he was weary of eating dinner alone after major sporting events.

51

When a man is bored of his own company he'll derive a poppadom of comfort from the following dinner-party line-up:

White (fat and white): A fighter not a writer. £300,000-a-year man plus global club class travel. Host of *Totally Football* – an extraordinary live TV show in which men in suits sat around eating breakfast and talking about football with a seriousness more befitting high-stakes poker or no-limit diplomacy. There was no other programme that Stirling found so objectively funny and so subjectively sad.

Green (fat and white): Racist, sexist, homophobic. And homicidal. Married four times, more often than not to one of his secretaries. Looked like a publican, talked like a publican, was a publican. In his spare time.

Brown (fat and white): Very dim. The ghostwriter's ghostwriter, author of thirty-seven books, conspicuously more than he had read.

Pink (gaunt and white): Grand Old Man of British Sports Writing. Convivial-ish when sober. Achingly nostalgic when pissed. Like an expensive claret, best appreciated alone.

Blue (conventionally good-looking): Worst of the lot. Younger than Stirling, better-educated than Stirling, paid more than Stirling. Nasty habit of opening pieces with quotes from Roman poets, presumably in a showy and leaden attempt to allude to his Oxbridge education. Considered being a football correspondent as 'the best job in the world'.

'Butt's the missing piece,' said Brown. 'The Beckster must play on the right, the boy Dyer looks more comfortable with every game wide left. Which leaves your middle pairing. Little Stevie Gerrard, obviously. If fit. And then Scholesy or the Butt-man. And call me a cunt if you must but the ginger-nut is too flaky for me at international level. Butty, though, can run all day for you, terrific engine, solid distribution over the shorter distances, knows exactly where to stand on a football pitch. He won't win a game for you but you can rely on him not to lose one. And at World Cup level it's the defeats that hurt.'

'Obviously,' said Blue. 'But I can't help feeling that if you put yourself in, say, the manager of Argentina's loafers, for a moment, and Sven hands over the team-sheet and its got Butt's name on it, the first thing that crosses your mind is that The Three Lions will settle for a draw. In that sense, it's a retrograde step. It places the Argentinians in the ascendancy, and we all know how dangerous they are going forward.'

'Lethal,' said Green.

'The eternal dilemma of being Nicky Butt,' started Pink. 'The humble artisan chosen so that others might look better. A selfless man condemned to ply his trade in selfish times. An unlikely hero. A working-class hero, if you will. A player who evokes memories of Brian Greenhoff and . . .' He paused to recall a name and noticing he had lost his audience changed tack. 'What do you think, Jimmy?'

Stirling hesitated for a moment. 'Couldn't you play both of them?'

'Oh for fuck's sake,' said Brown. 'There's only eleven players on a team.'

'Very true,' said Stirling. 'But perhaps Sven could experiment with five in midfield . . .'

'Leaving precisely who to plough a lonely furrow up front?' asked Brown.

'Michael Owen,' said Stirling, relieved to have finally been asked a question to which he knew the answer.

'Bollocks,' said White. 'You win nothing with midgets. When was the last time England enjoyed a sustained period of success without a Big Number Nine?'

'Gary Lineker?'

'Six one, mate.'

'Was he? Looks smaller on the box.'

'Television does that to you,' said White definitively.

'How about three at the back?' asked Stirling desperately.

'And waste the greatest talent this country has produced in the last decade at right wing-back? Ask the greatest crosser of a football in the world bar none to concentrate on furrowing back? I don't think so.'

'You're dead right. It's an insane suggestion,' said Stirling, conceding defeat as rapidly and completely as he was able and reverting to his barely touched masala.

Brown picked up from White. 'Early doors, I know, but what I can't help but like about this Swede is that he's set out his stall to play 4–4–2 and then gone out and done precisely that in his debut game. Does wonders for a team's morale, knowing what they're doing. No fannying around with continental nonsense. No messing. Back to basics. Play it the English way. 4–4–2. The ironic thing is that it took a Swede to work this out.'

'It's a funny old . . .' said Green.

'World,' said Stirling.

'Game,' said Green.

There was a lull. Pinot Grigio was drunk, curries consumed, side-dishes wiped clean.

'How many Nevilles?' asked White, mid-bhaji.

'Sorry,' said Pink.

'Gary and Phil? Gary not Phil? Phil not Gary? Neither Phil nor Gary?' said White.

Jesus, thought Stirling, not the Neville debate. This could take hours. There was no more complex subject in the modern game than the conundrum posed by the two sons of Neville Neville. Any top football writer could talk at length about the inherent contradictions and logical implausibilities of accommodating both Nevilles in a back four. Over the years the debate had been waged, that much was now common ground. Everything else was up for grabs. The discussion might last beyond Christmas.

Stirling survived by turning the evening into a game of snooker between the left side of his brain and the right. Every time one of the Tarantubbies used a cliché it counted as a pot with Green scoring three points, Brown four, Blue five and Pink six. However, if White committed a cliché the break came to an end. The cue ball was deemed to have gone in off and four points were awarded to the other side of his brain, which was then given its chance to come to the table. It passed the time, left leading right by four frames to two in the current season thanks, in part, to a record break in the high three hundreds after White had, uncharacteristically, fallen asleep. The score was 68–47 to the left side of his brain when the argument ended predictably.

'I'm not fucking having it,' said Green, banging the table with his knife. 'I don't have to fucking sit here and take that kind of shit about Rosa from a cunt like you.'

'You want some, pally? You want some?' said White, rising to his feet and belching quite menacingly. 'Because believe me, sonny, I'd love to give you some.'

'Don't start something you can't finish, prannock,' said Green, prodding at White with his fork. He always defended his secretary's honour.

White lunged for the piece of cutlery, managed to gain himself an above-average hold and enjoyed the better of the opening exchanges in what someone would one day try and sell as impromptu fork wrestling. Stirling had twenty quid on White. Seconds later, White retired with a suspected severed artery and, muttering 'slag', took himself off to hospital.

'Cunt,' said Green.

'Compadre, six more double brandies,' said Pink to the waiter.

After the violence, the mawkishness. Green, flush with victory, was the first to produce photographs of his children.

'Far left we've got Diane. Only twelve but a phenomenal ballerina. On the right, Joe Junior, whose golf handicap matches his age. Which wouldn't be worth mentioning, but is going some when you take into account that he's only nine. And started playing at Easter. In the middle, Ronnie, or Pride and Joy, as the girls call him behind his back, who is considered by many good judges, not just me, to be the most promising left-sided midfielder to have come out of the West Midlands in many a year. Villa want him, Albion want him, Brum want him but both his mother and I have been quietly impressed with the quality of the youth set-up at Stoke City. So he's going to stay at Victoria Road until he's done his GCSEs and then we'll see what the big clubs bring to the table.' No one said a word. 'How many kids you got, Pink?' he continued.

'Two, darling. Both flown the nest. Jocasta who took a double first in PPE at Oxford, enrolled at Harvard Business

School and is now researching a book on a commune in Herefordshire. And Lysander, who is a late developer from whom we expect great things.'

Before Stirling could ask Pink to be more specific, Brown produced an entire photo-album from the fake leather Burtons hold-all he carried everywhere. Before Stirling could react, Brown had opened it in front of him.

'You see at the front Anthea's written "In praise of Chloe"?' said Brown, choking a little and then choking some more as a double brandy went down the wrong way. 'And the first few pages . . .' He coughed and wiped some moisture from his eyes. 'Sorry. The first seven pages are filled with every scan they took of Chloe. There are so many of them, not because there was anything wrong with Chloe, or anything like that, God, no, but because we went private. The Portland, as it happens.'

Stirling, still squeamish after all these years, had never looked at scans of his own children, let alone someone else's. He moved quickly through the album.

'Stop there, Jimmy. That there is the proudest moment of my life. Second only to Coventry winning the Cup. And I'm not shitting you.' He knocked back a stray glass of Pinot Grigio. 'It's all recorded for posterity. You'll notice that there are two midwives on the job. Better to be safe, I always say. I mean, you wouldn't fly in a plane with just the one pilot . . .'

Stirling was drunk, but not drunk enough to pass comment on pictures of Brown's wife giving birth. He flicked on until Chloe and Anthea were safely out of hospital.

'And now as you can tell from the date and' – Brown moved from his seat and positioned himself behind Stirling – 'that Week One written there.' He pointed at the 'Week One' written at the top of the page. 'We have a double-page spread dedicated to each week of little Chloe's life.'

'How old is she, again?' asked Stirling.

'Six months.'

'That old,' said Stirling, and quickly, 'Lovely age.'

'Lovely age,' repeated Brown.

Stirling worked his way through the album, all twenty-six double-page spreads. Staying awake by counting the photographs, all 356 of them.

'Amigo, six more double brandies with the bill,' said Pink. 'And, then, my friends, I think we might retire to a passable club where I happen to be a member.'

There was the usual kerfuffle over receipts, everyone asking for a separate copy so they could make a tidy profit on the evening. Then it was into a single cab, more receipt action, and, after a small dispute, a table was secured at Panthers of Derby, one of the few venues in the United Kingdom where not even Green bothered to ask for a receipt.

Stirling had no interest in paying Derby's finest a tenner a song to remove their clothes but was relieved that the others were less reticent. With their attention diverted from football or fighting or their kiddies he finally achieved some peace, settling back to listen to bad pop music and drink warm supermarket-brand lager.

As he approached forty Stirling found he was doing some of his deepest thinking in lap-dancing bars. Tonight was no exception. The trick, as he saw it, would be to reinvent himself. To somehow come up with a way of writing about football that was acceptable to his employers and, crucially, didn't involve watching any football. He must move fast. If he had to cover another season he would most surely go mad. Football writers were, at core, Public Relations executives with poor clothes sense. They were nothing more than paid cheerleaders. And Stirling had stopped cheering long ago. It was as the pundits said 'a simple game'. For once they were right. There were only so many ways you could score a goal and Stirling had seen them all. He had exhausted the permutations and was consigned to a life of repetition. More goals, more games, more of the same. It wasn't exactly chess.

He could, he realised, use the stock of football knowledge he had involuntarily accumulated to pepper his reports with references to matches from the past and give the appearance of competence by padding his copy with nostalgia. The readers appeared to enjoy such backward-looking nonsense and the appetite for football's past was as gross as that for its present. It would be the natural career path for a football writer of his age. And after ten years of e-mailing it in they might start referring to him as a doyen. Whatever that meant.

But, no, he couldn't do it. For a start, the more he watched the less he remembered. The last European Championship, which he'd spent a month in Belgium covering, was now a haze. France won it. England didn't. The Portuguese were very upset. And that was it. If asked to name a team of the tournament he could come up with Desailly, Zidane and, he supposed, Shearer, but he made a point of never picking Shearer, for personal reasons.

Green was haggling: 'Look, petal, this isn't the West End, you know. There, maybe, if you were better-looking, you might be able to get away with three figures. But we're in Derby, love. I've already said there's a twenty on the table. The question you have to answer is "What does that buy me?" Comprendez?'

Pink was singing.

> 'Three little maids from school are we,
> Pert as a schoolgirl well can be,
> Filled to the brim with girlish glee.
> Three little maids from school!'

And Brown and Blue were arguing about the Nevilles.
'Gary.'
'Phil.'
'Gary.'
'Phil.'
'Gary.'
'Phil.'
Stirling ordered himself another lager.

6

As the 2000/01 football season finally wore to a close Stirling stood in the express checkout queue at the Budgens in Bungay calculating how long it would be before he was out of there. Six people: three over seventy, two over sixty, one, surprisingly, could be in her thirties, each with an average of six items in their basket, and Bethan working the till. In principle Stirling believed in positive discrimination – inequalities ought to be levelled by affirmative action – but his belief was always tested in the Bungay Budgens. Laudably, the company employed its fair share of the less advantaged, but it could make for some very slow shopping. And Bethan, who might uncharitably be described as the special needs' special need, didn't have the tools, either literally or metaphorically, to deal with express shopping. Not only slow, she was talkative, and further hampered by the store's most notoriously faulty pricing machine.

Only once, in a year of shopping, had Stirling seen the machine correctly price up an item, and on that occasion Bethan had been on the till and was so overcome that she had had to call for assistance. Which, in the fullness of time, had arrived. Usually the procedure was as follows:

1   Punter hands over intended purchase.

2   Bethan, or deputy, slowly moves product over laser.

3   Nothing happens.

4   Bethan, or deputy, slowly moves product over laser.

5   Nothing happens.

6   Bethan, or deputy, slowly moves product over laser.

7   Machine makes noise more regularly associated with failed answer on Les Dennis vehicle *Family Fortunes*.

8   Bethan, or deputy, painstakingly types serial number of product into the computer.

9   Bethan, or deputy, makes mistake.

10 Bethan, or deputy, has another crack.

11 Success.

12 Bethan, or deputy, carefully moves product to end of till, picks the next product out of basket, returns to step one.

A twelve-step programme craftily devised by some higher power to adjust you to the pace of country living. The Bungay Budgens – the Waveney Valley's number one spot for confronting Anger Management. It was an inducement wasted on Stirling, whose mind was more preoccupied by Anger with Management.

At the front of the queue, a deaf seventy-year-old with too much time on her hands was scrabbling in her handbag and every once in a while depositing a coin on the counter. The bill for a sliced loaf of Sunblest, two tins of cat food, and a reduced – in price not size – lemon meringue pie came to £2.27. There was (Stirling was too far away to compute the amount exactly) approximately £1.80 piled on the counter, and she was down to coppers. It was long odds on a shortfall. Followed by a stark economic decision. Would she jettison the bread, cat food or pie? Meanwhile,

'How's the garden?' asked Bethan.

'Who?' replied the loose-change artist and, taken by surprise, she missed the counter with her tuppence. The entire queue looked on as the coin rolled towards the understocked fresh fruit and veg section. Stirling reacted quickest. Before the coin had come to a halt he had cupped it and handed it back to the grateful pensioner. He might have seized the moment and subbed the woman forty odd pence, but he knew the gesture, supposing it was heard or seen, would have been misinterpreted.

They were suspicious of flash in these parts, a discovery Stirling had made early on when he was spotted disembarking from a cab for a PTA meeting. The appearance from the taxi had not been a statement but a necessity. Despite weekly two-hour lessons it had taken him over a year to convince various examiners that he could drive an automatic car without serious error. The tests had come, the tests had gone. Colchester (poor clutch control from the off); Clacton-on-Sea (collision with pedestrian walking on the promenade); Peterborough (road-rage) – he had failed them all. A lifetime of disappointing interludes at the Driving Test Centres of Great Britain – Galashields, Golspie and Isle of Tyree, Lochgilphead and Rothesay (Bute Island) – stretched ahead of him. He had consoled himself with the thought that he could write a Pevsner-style guide to these oft-overlooked monuments to the English way of doing things. But it would take some thirty-five years to compile and might not find a market.

Finally, only last week, he had struck lucky in Spalding. Driving magnificently, he had skilfully avoided a drunken cyclist – some you hit, some you miss – and completed the examination to the required standard. 'Eighteen years, seven tests, thank you,' he had gabbled. The examiner had paused, looking like a man who had just made a decision he feared he and others would live, or conceivably not live, to regret.

Before that historic increase in his mobility he had been reduced to the PTA. He had joined not for any of the usual power reasons but from a more humane longing – to make friends. The meetings provided a once-a-month opportunity to get out of the house and talk to other people who lived some-where near him. The topics of conversation, while arguably trivial – the state of the curtains in Class One; the cost of plac-ing a notice in the local newsagent's (a very reasonable 10p a week); could now be the time for the long threatened redesign of the school book-bags? – were reassuringly uncontroversial. And by fence-sitting his way through the various debates Stirling had shrewdly limited his chances of falling out with his new friends.

None of whom, and this was a first for Stirling, drank, nor, not a first, did they offer to buy their round. This burden fell exclusively on Stirling, who spent long periods during the meetings up at the bar ordering 'a pint of bitter, two cokes, both diet, a St Clements, that's an orange juice and lemonade, yes, same glass, a bottle of sparkling water and a half of tap water with a splash of lime', or more regularly 'a quick pint in there, thanks, pally'. Because although his friends were soft-drinkers they were also slow drinkers, and with a pre-booked taxi offering him only two hours' drinking, Stirling often found he had to set his own pace. As lads' nights went, making allowances for the fact that there were no other lads present, they were all right.

And then, while Stirling was up at the bar ordering a sneaky pint, he had missed a vote on which he would most definitely have had an opinion. On his return to the table he was informed by the Co-Deputy Chairperson, Charlotte – smug and unattractive, always dressed for the stable – that smoking had been banned with five voting in favour of the motion, one abstaining, and a lone absentee. He took it well. He might have argued that now was perhaps the time for the PTA committee to discuss issues of mortality; to be made aware that whether they charged £1 or a change-problem-creating £1.50 for a glass of white wine at the forthcoming Quiz 'n' Chips night they would still die; to be told, forthrightly, that whether they passively smoked or not this was inescapable.

Instead he had said, 'But this is a pub.'

'Not in this corner,' a husky-wearer with a terrible haircut had replied. 'Look at it this way, if we were holding these meetings in the pre-school classroom would you be smoking?'

'No, but this is a pub.'

'Which we use because of the facilities provided,' said the husky-wearer, glancing at a largely untouched vol-au-vent and chicken wings combo platter. 'If we are to be taken seriously we must take ourselves seriously.'

'Yes, but this is a pub.' Stirling was becoming confused. Perhaps the bitter was off. He changed tack. 'Putting smokers' rights to one side for the moment, does anyone else think the school's letting in too many Protestants?'

That divided the Catholics from the faux believers, the hypocrites from the hypergamists. There was, uniquely in his limited PTA experience, uproar.

'I can't believe you just said that,' said Charlotte.

'My husband's a Protestant,' said bad-hair.

'I'm not sure I completely agree with Jimmy, but he has raised something which I have been meaning to raise for some time,' said a woman who, now Stirling looked at her again, was quite foxy if you stared hard enough. Blonde-ish, trim-ish, wearing a jumperish dress, she was, in fact, something of a revelation. 'St Olaf's was established as a Catholic school to propagate the faith to young children living in the area. That remains its primary purpose. Sometimes when we discuss the arrangements for the Quiz 'n' Chips night I feel we are in danger of losing sight of this.'

Stirling briefly allowed himself to consider how she might look taking communion. Kneeling, supplicant, arms outstretched with cupped palms, mouth open.

'Some of us are working very hard to make this Quiz 'n' Chips night a success, Bella,' said Charlotte. 'And our jobs would be a lot easier if certain members of the committee stopped criticising all the time and pulled their fingers out.'

'Anyone want a top-up?' asked Stirling.

He had gone to one further meeting but found, what with ordering drinks for himself and having to go to the other side of the pub to smoke, he might as well have been drinking alone, something he could very easily do at home without the bother and expense of ordering cabs.

The Budgens queue had shifted. Pensioner number one had traded in one tin of cat food to meet her debts and received a 17 pence dividend.

'Something to put aside for a rainy day,' Bethan had said.

'He's dead,' the pensioner had shouted.

Next up at the counter had been a ballsy number with dyed lilac hair wearing a pink nylon cardie that didn't quite cover her diaphanous top. Displaying commendable briskness, she had completed her purchases (a bottle of Asti, two sponge cakes, some low-quality mince, a tub of ice-cream, twelve cans of Orange Fanta, some air-freshener and sixty Consulate) without error. Only for the next customer to create a hiatus by attempting to buy a tube of Chewits and a pack of Handy Andys with her platinum Barclaycard. Credit cards were not Bethan's strength. There was much faffing around, consultations with colleagues both on hand and in head office, an aborted phone-call to a credit control company in Northampton, before the 61 pence transaction was okayed.

Three down, two to go, thought Stirling, looking at the exit door with some optimism. Oh, bollocks . . . the last of the high rollers. A jockey-sized man dressed in a flat cap, charity shop three-piece suit and wellington boots – clearly a farmer brought down by swine fever? mad cow disease? incompetence? – had deposited a plastic bag on the counter and like a bad children's entertainer, with an ever-decreasing flourish and to no one's astonishment, produced from inside it lottery ticket after lottery ticket. To be fair to Bethan she was crash-hot on the lottery machine, rattling through a dozen tickets and confidently stating that each one 'was not a winner'. Flat Cap didn't like it, but he had to lump it. The loser.

Having bombed out of the PTA, Stirling had finagled his way into the Waveney Valley Book Club. It hadn't been easy. The WVBC was something to which class-ridden people aspired. It had cachet. Stirling had waited patiently on the substitutes bench, ringing up on the first Sunday of every month to see if he would be invited on the first Monday of the next month to discuss a book someone else had chosen for him to read. Time passed. During the summer holidays he made it to first reserve, and at the height of an autumnal influenza epidemic he finally reached high table. The book under discussion was Siegfried Sassoon's *Memoirs of a Fox-Hunting Man*. But Stirling had supposed this was just a blind. The intensive vetting procedure, the long waiting period, it had to preface something a little more exciting than sitting around discussing an outdated memoir. And it was Stirling's hunch that that 'something' was wife-swapping. Why else would he have made all those calls?

B had no intention of going to a poxy book club, even, or especially, after he had explained that it wasn't a book club but a 'book club'. Was it socially acceptable in Norfolk to go to a wife-swapping party without a wife? What happened when the wives were divvied up? Problematic, the whole thing, especially as Stirling, on his debut, had possessed neither car keys nor car. And from his wide experience of wife-swapping – the novels of Jilly Cooper – these were fundamental props. Ah well, there was nothing he could do about it at such short notice. He'd have to wing it.

The evening had started promisingly with a little light literary name-dropping. Someone thought they had spotted Louis de Bernières entering the pet-food shop in Harleston. Someone else was almost certain they'd nearly been run over by Elizabeth Jane Howard approaching the recently opened Poringland roundabout. A third was convinced he had seen W. B. Sebald skulking out from the UCI cinema complex in Norwich, a conviction that was dented not a jot by his wife claiming to have read an obituary of said Sebald in the *Eastern Daily Press*.

Having exhausted, and indeed exhumed, the local literary celebrities the conversation moved on to the book, briefly, and then ineluctably to horses. Boy, did these chicks love their ponies. Poppy, Dingle, Maude and Freckle – they were all passionately remembered. The thrill of the chase, the consummation that was the hunt. For an ugly moment or two Stirling wondered if he'd misguidedly come to a pony-swapping party.

The food, the little there was of it, came and went. Port was served. The women stayed in the room. Let this be the moment, thought Stirling.

'Do you hunt?' asked the Sebald-spotter.

Stirling paused. He had pony-trekked once, when he was eleven and short of things to do on holiday in Wales. Never again. But did the man mean hunt or 'hunt'?

'I have been known to,' he had replied, sounding rather more leery than he intended.

'You're not one of those anti-blood sports chappies, are you?'

'Not at all.' It was true. He didn't give a fuck about animals. Couldn't care less how they died.

'Because, if you'll forgive me for pointing it out, you certainly look like one.'

'Sorry.'

'Vote Labour, do we?'

'Sometimes.'

'Never met anyone who voted Labour. Don't suppose it will happen again.' And, as Stirling lunged for it, the man had reacted quicker and decamped to the other end of the table with the bottle of Graham's Non-Vintage Port. Stirling's role in the conversation had rather petered out after that.

Stirling suffered a pang of guilt in Budgens. For forty-seven minutes he had been wondering why the woman in front of him in the queue, a lost-looking soul, was buying a two-pint container of milk, a one-pint container of milk and a half-pint container of milk, thereby ensuring that Bethan would have to attempt three transactions when by purchasing a six-pint container, only 27 pence more expensive, she could third the amount of time she had to spend at the counter and, as a side-benefit, nearly double the amount of milk purchased. Now, as she produced a book of milk tokens, Stirling felt shabby. It wasn't classy to sneer at those below the poverty line. As the woman walked out, he put ten pence in the Panda charity box for disadvantaged children. Christ knows, there were enough of them around locally.

'All your Marlboro Red, please, Bethan.' When Stirling shopped at Budgens, Budgens stayed shopped.

'Is this a hold-up?' squeaked Bethan.

'No. I've got the cash.' Stirling always went to the cash-point first to save Bethan the hassle of dealing with his Switch card.

'A packet of Marlboro Red, was it?'

'Twenty.'

'A packet of twenty?'

'Twenty packets of twenty.'

'Twenty packets of twenty?'

'Yes, please, Bethan.'

Stirling snuck into the house and, undetected by the family, made it up to the east wing of the attic. His office was a mess. The intention had been to keep unopened mail in one corner, newspapers in another, books in a third and paperwork in the fourth, but things had become confused. Every time he spent over an hour looking for something he vowed to sort it all out, but in the immediate aftermath of wasting so much time there was always something more pressing to be done.

What to do? There was a Gary Mabbutt interview to be

written up, but he wasn't in the mood. He logged on and checked his e-mail. There was the usual array of 'all-users' nonsense from the office. Someone had found a fiver in the Gents Loo, someone else was asking if anyone had some tooth-paste, and the features editor urgently needed a number for Andrew Neil. It was all happening down there. He scrolled down looking for some correspondence he could kill some time replying to, but there was nothing, so he moved on to his hypothetical share portfolio, which was down a staggering seventy grand. He joined a chat-room to find out what was going on. 'I shorted this company again last night,' he typed. 'Selling 100,000 shares at an average of £13.10 in the belief that the fundamentals in this company are all out of whack, the p/e ratio beyond nonsensical, the management, so I hear, crooked, and in the certain knowledge it could only go south. What happens? On light trading and on a flat day for the Footsie it rises nearly 8%. So come on, you cretins and clowns who are ramping this stock. Explain yourselves.'

Feeling better, he lit a cigarette, and took a bottle from the mini-bar in the paperwork corner. Moderate rapture.

'Daddy, I didn't know you were home.'

'Where have you been?'

There were two little faces peering round the door.

'Budgens.'

'But that was hours ago,' said Nancy.

'Yeah, Bethan was on the counter.'

'Are you working?' asked Charlie.

'Erm,' Stirling looked at the screen, 'not really.'

'Great,' they said together.

Charlie looked at Nancy. 'You ask.' Nancy looked at Charlie. 'You ask.'

Charlie composed himself and then asked, 'Will you come and do the Play?'

Nancy waited anxiously on his answer.

The Irrefusable Double Act.

'It's show-time,' said Stirling. They clattered down the stairs. B was standing on the far side of the island near the Aga holding something very burnt in her hands.

'Any phone calls?' asked Stirling.

'No,' replied B.

It was their private joke.

'Right,' said Charlie. 'I'm Jesus.'

'And I'm Mary,' said Nancy.

'And I'm . . . ?' asked Jimmy.

'Pontius Pilate,' said Charlie.

'And King Herod,' said Nancy.

'And maybe also Saint Peter,' said Charlie.

They scrabbled around for costumes. Charlie, ever the perfectionist, had to have everything just so. Nancy was only happy if Charlie was happy. To avoid a double tantrum Stirling constructed a makeshift crown from an economy Cheerios packet, conned them that one of his Dad's old silk dressing-gowns was a robe and, for a sceptre, pulled a nine-iron out of an otherwise empty golf bag. Charlie put on the bottom half of his sister's tutu.

'What are you wearing, Charlie?'

'A loincloth,' said Nancy.

'Just like Jesus,' said Charlie. 'We read about it at school.'

'Fine.'

'Music,' ordered Charlie, who was not only Jesus but also the director.

Stirling whacked on Handel's *Messiah*. He was ordered

by the director to stay in the kitchen while the twins went into the TV room. There was much wailing from the other side of the door. Concerned there had been some kind of ghastly incident involving a nine-iron, Jimmy disobeyed the script and entered stage left. Charlie was standing on the rim of the sofa with his arms outstretched, his legs together and his head lolling awkwardly. Nancy was licking his feet.

'What are you doing?' Stirling shrieked, allowing a little more alarm into his voice than he intended.

'Duhh, Dad, I'm being crucified,' said a now alert Charlie. 'Can't you remember where we were in the script?'

'Charlie's about to ascend to heaven,' said Nancy.

'And, Daddy, we need to find a way for me to go through the ceiling and up to your office.'

'Christ, is that the time?'

'Bad word, Daddy,' said Nancy.

'Come on, it's bedtime.'

'But Daddy, we can't leave Jesus here,' said Charlie.

'We'll have to, you've got school tomorrow.'

'You promised, Daddy,' said Charlie.

'Mummy says you should never break promises,' said Nancy.

'She's right, but . . .'

'Bad Dadda,' said Charlie.

'Bad Dadda,' said Nancy.

'Look. Let's skip the bath. If you're in bed in five minutes I'll continue the story.'

They scuttled off. He had bought himself five minutes. He poured a beer and lit a cigarette. He needed to think. The story had haemorrhaged badly. What had started as a simple plagiary of Harry Potter had escalated into an impossible mélange as, keen to keep abreast of their interests, he had introduced Hercules, Monsters Inc., Scooby Doo and Johnny Bravo into the plot only to discover he had neither the imagination nor the discipline to sort it out. He ploughed on regardless.

'That wasn't very good,' said Charlie as Stirling, noticing his beer glass was empty, signed off with a 'That's all, folks.'

'Daddy?'

'Yes, Nancy.'

'You said Stuart Little was having a Scooby snack with Shaggy.'

'Yes.'

'But in chapter two he was squished by Fluffy.'

'He's better now.'

'Daddy?'

'Lights off. Now. I'll put a tape on. Do you want Heidi, Danny or Marnie?'

'Dadda, we haven't said our prayers yet.'

'Sorry.'

The twins held hands and prayed to their God, Charlie leading Nancy in a prayer for Anne Robinson, Nancy for Chris Tarrant. As ever ending, 'God Bless Papa who is in heaven. Thank you for a lovely day. Amen.'

The reference to his father retained the capacity to jolt him. He waved a hurried goodnight to the twins, feeling proud, guilty and confused, but before he could get downstairs for another beer he was called back.

'Daddy?' said Charlie.

'Where will you be?' asked Nancy.

'Kitchen, TV room, Blue loo, bed.' It was a familar litany which eased the fears of his fretful children.

'OK,' said Nancy.

'See you tomorrow,' said Charlie.

'Yup, no, damn. I better go into work tomorrow.'

'Why do you have to go to work?' asked Charlie.

'Good question.'

'Why do you have to go to work?' asked Nancy.

'To earn money to pay for videos and toys and books and . . .'

'You better go then,' said Charlie.

'I'll be back as soon as I can.'

He moved from beer to wine, ambled into the TV room, and punched in Ceefax page 101.

Page 104: Record numbers expected to watch Cup Final.

Page 105: The Neville brothers seek nation's 'forgiveness'.

Page 109: The Emlyn Hughes verdict.

Page 110: 39 feared dead in Hebron.

What a complete failure of perspective. Even the normally reliable Ceefax was now hopelessly out of kilter. What system of priorities ranked a football match higher in news value than the death of nearly forty Palestinians? It was yet another sign that football was omnipresent and omnipotent. Which, given that Stirling was technically a football writer, should have been just cookie. But he was prodigiously, comprehensively and overwhelmingly bored by football, by its inanities and irrelevancies, its pomposity and presumptuousness, and he knew only too well that that which makes you bored you swiftly come to hate.

7

The office was becalmed. Derrek Senior was out at a Sport England buffet. Derrek Junior was staring up at Sky Sports News, drinking it in. And Rob was on the phone: 'Look, Maxie, love, we're travelling over old ground. You have your job to do and I have mine. Either we rub along together and everything's A OK. Or it's curtains. Finalissimo. Your call, sweetheart.' It was either his third wife or some PR. Either way it was unconscionable.

Both of his fellow employees were wearing suits. Rob probably had an interview elsewhere, but Derrek Junior? There was really no need to wear a tie to watch Sky Sports News for eight hours straight. Stirling looked at the time on his computer – 'Tue 3.27.43pm'. He looked at the screen. 'Gary Mabbutt: Suggested Headline: Adding insulin to injury. Main Text: For the majority of his career Gary Mabbutt was famous for two things. One, being a diabetic. Two, getting injured. But a long afternoon spent in his company at his palatial, yet understated, Box Hill home demonstrated that those who have categorised him in such a way are guilty, at best, of hastiness; at worst, malevolence.' He hit word count. 56. Time to jack it in for the day.

The Butt of Lewis made working for the newspaper bearable. It was almost entirely without facilities. There was no jukebox, pool table or big-screen TV, just a curmudgeonly fruit machine. The decor was shocking, a universal fading dun-brown wallpaper unleavened by posters or special offers. The management didn't believe in promotion. There were no karaoke nights, quiz evenings or darts extravaganzas. You went there to drink and they provided drink. There was no call for anything else.

The fixtures were dangerous. A whorled carpet whose stick-iness soon found out those presumptuous enough to wear crepe soles; banquettes in such disrepair that even experienced drinkers occasionally sat down carelessly and buggered them-selves on a protruding rusty spring; stools so short that only the very small could use them without coming over all knees and elbows.

The food was DIY. On the corner of the main bar a Breville sandwich maker sat next to a loaf of Mighty White, catering packs of processed ham and cheese, and a tub of margarine. Behind them was an honesty box and a sign, 'Ham or Cheese £1; Ham & Cheese £1.20'.

The toilets were unsanitary. For some months Stirling had been concerned that he had contracted genital nits because whenever he used the facilities, which was often in the days before permanent dehydration set in, tiny lazy insects appeared at groin level. But at the end of a long afternoon and stretched for things to say he had mentioned the ailment to a personal finance journalist who had assured him that the fault, and potential liability, lay with The Butt of Lewis.

The establishment was run by David, a genuinely award-winning journalist. He had covered Vietnam, returned to break the Thalidomide story, jetted off to share a Pulitzer for his articles on Watergate and on returning from the States had moved sideways into pub management. This, he would graciously explain, allowed him to enjoy the company of journalists without the bother of journalism. It was also considerably more lucrative. He had bought a pub within twenty yards of the tradesmen's entrance to a national newspaper and let natural causes take effect. The paper hadn't moved, nor had he.

'Afternoon, Jimmy. Guinness?'

'Why not?' It was May, it was warm, lager weather, but he was hungry and didn't fancy a toastie.

'Still playing the market?'

'Hypothetically. I'd short the fuck out of it if I had any money. All those idiots piling in, talking nonsense about boom following boom, suckers for perpetual growth, the Footsie going to 10,000. Wrong, wrong, wrong, wrong, wrong. All you have to do is bet into them and wait for the market to crumble.'

'It's one thing knowing they're wrong, quite another working out exactly when it will dawn on them that they are wrong.'

'That's the problem with stupid people: unless you're brilliantly stupid it's almost impossible to quantify how stupid they are. You think you've nailed the limit of their stupidity and then they go and do something out-of-the-box dumb.'

He took his pint to the main table. It was more Drunks Demos than Algonquin, but no less entertaining for that. Towards the end of the week, when there was mild pressure on everyone to produce a Sunday newspaper, departments tended to huddle together, but on a Tuesday or Wednesday it was usually a mish-mash of disciplines. At the top of the table sat Terry, the paper's chief colour writer. Possessed of hyperacute hearing and incapable of being rendered fall-over drunk, he was the man the paper relied on for assessing the mood of the nation. Tuesday through Friday he practised in The Butt of Lewis and on Saturday he was dispatched to pubs in an area in the news to subtly overhear what people were actually saying out loud. If the Queen Mum died, he'd be drinking in Windsor; rise in illegal immigrants, Dover; rise of the BNP, Oldham; rise in paedophilia, Portsmouth. He was employed to drink in some pretty dreary pubs but he was paid well.

On Terry's right, the seen-it-all political correspondent. For eleven years Ian Drury with two 'r's had railed against Thatcher, for seven years he had belittled Major, and he was now six years and counting into slagging off Blair. To be fair, his column published on 4 May 1997 and phoned in the night before from Casualty had been pretty upbeat. But a few days later Blair had done something to irritate Ian and in so doing 'forfeited the support of every right-thinking person in the country'.

Opposite Ian sprawled Malcolm, the gardening correspondent, who had joined the paper after the Second World War and was coming to the end of a career in which he had written at some stage or another, and often serially, every single column on the paper. It was presumed that gardening would be Malcolm's last beat – he'd been struggling a bit since moving into a mansion block – but after a cigar or two he wasn't above putting the wind up the shopping correspondent or alternative health guru by talking loudly about the 'need for a new challenge'. Thanks to writing his own contract – he'd been pally with the thirteenth-last, and arguably best, editor – he was unsackable. The newspaper was obligated to publish a column of his choice, and if the muse took him he couldn't be prevented, legally, from writing the second leader. This led to the newspaper adopting some fairly contradictory positions, but as the new budget advertising warned readers 'to expect the unexpected' there were no grounds for complaint.

There were no women, there were never any women. They went to the wine bar down the road. There had been a time when there were women but, strangely, all of them had moved on to better jobs with better-funded papers. The men had stayed put, all of them in the habit of dropping into The Butt of Lewis on the way in to work. If someone was in, fine. If no one was in, but they had a book, magazine or crossword on the go, also fine. If it was empty and they didn't feel up to playing the fruit machine then, and only then, would they make their way up to the office, check their e-mails and wait for something to happen.

'What is the point?' said Ian, cadging a cigarette off Stirling. If they were on to futility they had been here a while. 'What is the fucking point? Fuck Twat [The Deputy Editor], Double Fuck Fuckwit [The Editor]. What do those goons know about democracy? Surely I am not alone in thinking that there is vital work being done on some of the Select Committees? And what do Twat and Fuckwit want me to write about?'

'Fox hunting,' said Terry.

'Fox fucking hunting,' said Ian. Either it was an inspired guess by Terry or they were on a loop.

'Wouldn't have happened in my day,' said Malcolm. Something of a catch-phrase.

'And what day was that?' said Terry. The correct response.

'Well,' said Malcolm, gearing up. 'I was political correspondent, briefly and famously, during Suez. There was another stint during the Sixties, I think. I can remember having to write about the three-day week and the Oil Crisis and the IMF, all quite complicated and time-consuming. And then, of course, I came back and used the column to campaign for Roy Hattersley . . . which . . .' He looked momentarily confused.

'Did they ever ask you to cover fox hunting?' said Ian.

'Not in that capacity, no,' admitted Malcolm.

'Thank you. It's ridiculous. Didn't they see me on Channel 4 News the other week?' Point made, he struggled over to buy himself a drink, disguising his meanness by stopping on the way back to pile the money he might have better spent buying the others a drink into the fruit machine.

Parsons entered the pub – a bit forward for an ex-editor of *Shoot* – and even though every other table was empty elected to sit at their table, which was beyond brazen. There was an irritating beep-beep sound.

'Bingo,' he said, staring moronically at his mobile phone. 'So which lovely lady sent me this?' He handed the contraption to Stirling.

On the screen was written: 'U R GR8 C U 4 T X.'

'Why are you showing me your car registration number?' said Stirling.

'Get real, Jimbob.' Jimbob? 'It's a text from Nell McAndrew,' said Parsons.

'Who?' said Stirling.

'Bollocks,' said Terry, who considered himself the most attractive man in the pub. Now, in the unlikely shape of Parsons, there appeared to be competition. 'Throw me that phone, Jimmy.'

Stirling lobbed the phone.

'Careful, Jimbob. I might want to save that,' said Parsons.

'There's no proof this is from Nell,' said Terry.

'Of course it is.'

'She's not clever enough to use GR8.'

'She's not as stupid as she looks.'

'Malcolm,' shouted David. 'Phone.' Jimmy nudged the septuagenarian awake. 'Phone.'

'What day is it?'

'Tuesday.'

'Tuesday. Tuesday. Ah yes, Tuesday.' He moved smartly to his feet, signalled to David to make him a half-pint of Gordons gin and tonic, and picked up the pub phone. 'How kind of you to call . . . Just polishing the pay-off line . . . It will be with you within the quarter-hour . . . Thank you once again for your forbearance.' He put the phone down, picked it up, and dialled the one number he knew by heart. 'Is that Copy? I have a thousand words for the magazine. Author's name: Binney. Title: Gardening. Copy starts . . . Forgive me if I return to the subject of my beloved . . . b-e-l-o-v-e-d window boxes but spring is a challenging month for the urban gardener . . .'

At the main table, Parsons had made the mistake of going to the toilets without his mobile. Terry was onto it in a flash, tapping away expertly. 'I'll give him Nell McAndrew,' he said, showing Stirling the product of his labour. 'Y R U STALK-ING MOI, U *FUCKER. LIFE. A. GET. PS R U HIV+.' He pressed reply. And placed the phone exactly where Parsons had left it.

At the jukebox Ian was having difficulty achieving closure. 'The people read my column. The people need my column. They don't want to wake up on a Sunday morning to a rehashing of the arguments raised in The Belstone Fucking Fox. There are limits. It can't go on.' Pint in one hand, fag in the other, he stepped back from the machine to calculate how to maximise the seven nudges he had been awarded. Parsons caroomed into him. Lager went everywhere.

'Twat,' screamed Ian.

'You backed into me,' said Parsons.

'What are you doing in my pub if you can't even fucking

drink?' He looked down on the hapless football writer, removing his beer-stained glasses and wiping them on his shirt. All the while, the nudgeometer ticked away.

'And, more importantly, little fuckwit, what are you doing in my paper when you can't fucking write?'

Parsons had a choice. He could either chin Ian or ignore him. Thinking he had a tea-time date with Nell McAndrew he picked up his mobile and left without further comment.

'Wanker,' said Ian, sitting back down at the main table. 'Didn't even buy me a pint. Whose round is it?'

Stirling got to his feet, happier than he had been in a long time. This was the life.

The afternoon wended on. Malcolm, his week's work complete, toddled off to the London Library for a snooze prior to an early dinner at the Irish Club. Terry and Stirling listened to Ian on Ian. It was the same old story: the paper was crap these days, no one appreciated him, it was all puff and nonsense, he had half a mind to go and tell them, fuck it, when he had finished this pint he would go and tell them. In this he was heartily encouraged by Terry and Stirling who, by now, were running out of anything to say to Ian about Ian.

To be fair to the big man, and unlike the rest of them, he usually carried out his threats. Barrelling around the open-plan office with a copy of last Sunday's paper and filleting it as he went he would leave sections on the desk of each and every editor detailing how miserably they had performed. 'What were you thinking of?' he would write over a multi-alliterative headline. 'Get a grip' underneath the main leader. 'Under no circumstances should this mental defective ever be employed by this paper again' over one of Parsons's weaker efforts.

'Work of a pygmy' in bold capitals on the front of the stand-alone broadsheet travel supplement. Having marked the eight sections of the paper he would turn on his computer and rifle off a series of regrettable e-mails. Ian's problem was that he cared too much.

The suits sat and took it. In part because, as with every left-of-centre newspaper, management were paid considerably more than the workers. In part because even they realised that without Ian there would be a political, moral and critical vacuum at the heart of the paper. It would be indistinguishable from *Heat* magazine. And while this was a main plank of the long-term strategy they were currently financially constrained from pursuing such a course. Buying in celebrity interviews wasn't cheap.

'It's show-time,' said Ian, finishing his pint of Import, stubbing out yet another of Stirling's cigarettes and heading for the exit. But before the political correspondent could come to Fuckwit and Twat, the editor and deputy editor came to him, making a rare patronise-the-troops appearance in The Butt of Lewis.

'Nice piece on Sunday,' said the editor.

'Can I get you a drink?' said his deputy.

Peter and Gareth were an unremarkable pair, but they possessed sufficient nous to be able to defuse a drunken journalist.

'Errr, yes, Import, pint, thanks,' said Ian, his fuse momentarily snuffed by his muse.

'Which piece?' he asked the editor.

'All of them, comrade. Splendid effort,' said the editor. 'We should pay you more.'

That's fucked him, thought Stirling, who had been hoping that Ian might thump the editor and take him out of the conversational equation. Stirling became confused when talking to authority figures. However much he prepared, his nerves, lack of self-esteem, whatever, always intruded and he ended up not only not getting what he might have wanted but also somehow what he expressly didn't want.

'Behind you, Jimmy,' said Terry.

Coming through the far door were Derrek Senior, Derrek Junior, Jeff McKenna (a perma-tanned Nationwide League manager from Cumbria who was one of their star columnists), Mrs Jeff (a hyper-tanned ex-page-three girl who hadn't kicked on) and Phil Davies (an ever-present in the Welsh national side and bit-part player for Bolton who was their other star columnist). Authority to the right of him, football heads to the left, Stirling was trapped. He stared into his pint, hoping everyone would go away.

The editor walked straight past him and clapped McKenna on the back. 'Great column about Nicky Butt. Top-notch.'

'Thanks, ed.' Ed? Who the fuck did he think he was? 'Can I introduce you to Mrs Jeff and Phil.'

'Delighted.'

While Stirling buried his head in his hands the editor prostrated himself before three of the four least intelligent people ever to have entered The Butt of Lewis. Unbelievable but understandable. So delinquent were the times that Phil and Jeff were easily the best-paid contributors to the paper. They received £2 for every word written by someone else; a Nobel prize winner would be lucky to be paid a quarter of that amount for a précis of his life's work.

Derrek Junior, the fourth member of the Hall of Fame thick quartet, plonked himself down on the banquette next to Stirling.

'Aggh,' he squealed. Fat Boy had hit a spring. Rubbing his

arse with one hand and stealing one of Stirling's cigarettes with the other he asked, 'What are you wearing?'

How literal could the man get?

'A shirt, a pair of serge trousers . . .'

'I can see that, you moron,' said Derrek Junior with a sigh. 'I meant where's your whistle?'

Whistle? Was that why everyone was here? For a long and arduous debate on refereeing followed by a practical test.

'Whistle and Flute – Suit.'

Hard to credit, what with all the football matches he crammed in, but Fat Boy obviously had time to spare to watch *Minder* on UK Gold.

'I neither possess nor have need of a suit,' said Stirling, irritated.

'You do for the Football Writers' Dinner,' said Derrek Junior, smirking at a rare conversational triumph.

Oh fuck, thought Stirling. That's why he'd come into the office. That's why everyone was dressed up – The Football Writers' Dinner. Four of the more dispiriting words in the English language.

By the time Stirling had borrowed a jacket from his sort of friend in personal finance, purchased a tie from the Sock Shop in the tube station, found a cab, got snarled up in traffic, debated with the cabbie whether it would be better to walk, decided against it, wrongly, finally won a long argument with the pedant working security over whether his name was on the list, and hurried into the George III dining suite at the Royal Lancaster Hotel, everyone and anyone in his profession was standing by their appointed seat listening to Sir Bobby Robson say grace. Stirling paused, muttered an 'Amen', and walked slowly to his table.

In such company it was impossible to have decent placement, but nonetheless he had been badly drawn between Derrek Junior and Phil. How much of his personal space was Junior going to invade? How much more of his life was Junior going to waste? As for Phil, talking to him once a week for the last year in order to ghost his column had confirmed within minutes that the footballer had nothing interesting to say. Now he was side-by-side with the Welshman. Thankfully he didn't appear capable of putting two and two together.

'Phillo, meet Jimmy Stirling, one of our top men,' said Derrek Junior, performing the preliminaries and blowing Stirling's anonymity.

'Jimmy Stirling?' asked the Welshman darkly.

'Yes,' Stirling answered quietly.

The Welshman repositioned his cutlery.

'He ghosts your column,' said Derrek unhelpfully.

'Thought it rang a bell. Good to meet you in the flesh.'

'Great.'

'Have to admit I never read it.'

'I wouldn't bother,' said Stirling. Which wasn't wholly self-deprecating. Stirling relied on his subject not reading the words he put in his mouth. It was the golden rule of ghost-writing. If the midfielder had an inkling of the ways in which his life, in Stirling's hands, had taken a severe turn for the worse he would lamp him. And then sue him for libel. If, indeed, it was possible to base an action on something purported to be written by yourself. Perhaps not, thought Stirling. Self-libel didn't sound right.

Derrek Junior, as was his wont, kept the conversation moving along: 'Phillo, what's your take on the Arsenal back four? Generally agreed to be showing signs of wear and tear, but how do you go about replacing the irreplaceable?'

'I don't know if you can, Derrek.'

Stirling gently pushed himself back from the table to allow the pair to talk round rather than through him. There was a slab of melon on his plate. Stirling didn't eat melon. He looked at the menu for sustenance. Main course: Chicken à la King – a couple of overcooked drumsticks covered by a warm sherry sauce. Pass. Dessert: Death by Chocolate. Stirling didn't eat chocolate. And he wasn't allowed to smoke. The wine was Pinot Grigio. The wine was always Pinot Grigio. There had been a time, back in the early Nineties, when Frascati had been the football writing fraternity's Italian white wine of choice, but now they only drunk Grigio. It was easier to mispronounce.

His dinner companions were stuck on Lee Dixon. Stirling blotted out their white noise and concentrated on what his elders and betters were saying on the other side of the table.

'You don't see many nig-nogs in management these days,' said Jeff, a decibel or two louder than he might have done.

'The paper is doing all it can to increase minority representation but . . .' The editor wasn't to know that Jeff never talked about anything other than football.

'Mark my words, the day of the jigaboos will come. When I was a player a lot of good judges questioned their commitment when it got cold, but they proved they could guts it out on a wet Tuesday night in Shrewsbury along with the rest of us.'

'Yes,' said the editor, sneaking a glance at his watch.

'It'll be the same with managing. No earthly reason why they shouldn't be up to it.'

'Yes,' said the editor, pouring himself a further glass of wine.

'Do you ski?' asked the deputy editor, desperately.

'*Mais bien sûr*. Lynn may not look it' – Jeff pointed at his wife – 'but she's a very special skier. I wouldn't be at all surprised to see her attempting black runs before too long.'

Stirling enjoyed the editorial discomfort. How beautiful was their game now they were at the thick end of it, and Jeff hadn't even finished his melon. They could be there for hours. Stirling, unhindered by food or conversation, drank steadily. If he didn't say anything he couldn't make a fool of himself. He restricted himself to a brief 'It's nothing' in reply to a 'Cheers, buddy,' from Junior after he had gifted him his Death by Chocolate. The noise level rose. At a nearby table Pink, dressed in unhired black tie (he was either showing off or he had actually won something), was, Stirling estimated, a mere bottle away from Gilbert & Sullivan. Green was chatting to his secretary, his hands very much under the table. White was surrounded by footballers' daughters and Andy Gray. Brown and Blue were catapulting peas at each other. Pathetic. Were there no depths to which Blue would fail to sink in his efforts to show he was one of the lads? Stirling surveyed them all with contempt. What did they know about football that only football knew? Mind you, what did he know about football when he rarely watched a game?

Finally, David Pleat rose to his feet. Stirling speed-smoked his first cigarette and promptly lit another. Pleat had been turned over by those seated in the George III dining suite throughout his tortured career. If he was ever to take his revenge . . .

'How lucky we are to be working in the football industry at a time when so many talented writers are on hand to record our exploits.' (Bottle job, thought Stirling.) 'If you will forgive a flight of fancy, we are merely Boswells, and you are our Johnsons.' (Wrong again, David, thought Stirling. Johnson? Isn't that rhyming slang for love-stick? thought Derrek Junior.) 'And what Johnsons. Might I suggest a front five that would stand comparison with the greats from any era. On the right wing, obviously, the man we have come to call Mr White. White and nearly always right, I often think to myself whenever I finish reading his well-thought-out journalism.'

The host of *Totally Football* raised his glass of Pinot Grigio. The footballers' daughters cooed.

'At centre-forward who better than John Brown? He is, as his byline states, quite simply The Man the Players Read.' (Or more accurately, The Man the Players Who Can Read, Read, thought Stirling.) 'At inside-left, providing a touch of class from the quality end of the market, ladies and gentleman, the Bluester.'

There was perfunctory applause. It was very much a tabloid occasion.

'At inside-right, in these politically correct times it's important to have one for the ladies, so let's get it up for Mello Bilton.'

'Slag,' shouted Jeff.

'And completing the line-up, on the left-wing' (did it really matter to Stirling what David Pleat thought of his journalism? Not really, but . . .) 'Rob Parsons, who we remember fondly for his spectacular job of work at *Shoot* and who may well at the end of the day come to be regarded as the voice of his generation.'

'Great shout,' shouted Derrek Junior, prematurely levering himself to his feet.

'Shame,' shouted Pink, who hated losing.

'Without further ado,' continued Pleat, 'it is my great pleasure to hand over to the man who you the football writers voted your Player of the Year . . . Mr Robert Pires.'

Stirling had never seen him play.

'El Piresidente. Yess,' screamed Derrek Junior, the only man standing.

There was whispering at the high table. Pleat returned to his feet.

'Unfortunately Robert cannot be with us here tonight, but he has sent us a short message which I will now read: "I am honoured by the great honour, thank you, Yours, Robert."'

Pleat sat down. Everyone else – bar Stirling, Green and his secretary – started to mingle. This is where Stirling had unravelled in the past, mingling neither wisely nor well, and upsetting people who became violent when upset. But if he stayed silent at his table until he was drunk enough to be able to sleep in a hotel bedroom, calamity might, God willing, be averted. For twenty minutes he cut a solitary but sane figure. A few more glasses of Grigio and he'd be able to call it a night.

'Wotcha, buddy.' It was Junior.

'Hello, Jimmy No Mates.' It was Rob.

'Top news about the Robmeister making it onto Pleaty's all-time forward line,' said Derrek Junior before disappearing to find his father, probably to ask him if he could stay up late just this once.

'Sorry, Rob, I should have said something. Quite an honour.'

'Thank you, mate, thank you. No idea it was going to happen; no idea, at all. Ironically I was on *Talk Sport* yesterday morning with Pleato giving it a bit of large on *Breakfast with Brazil* and he didn't let on at all. He's a sly one, all right.'

'So I've heard.'

'Can I get you a mineral water?'

'A what?'

'Carbonated water, Jimmy, it's what the professionals drink.'

'Bollocks.'

'Take a look around you.'

It was true. None of the current players appeared to be drinking Grigio. No one under forty appeared to be drinking Grigio. Stirling was a dinosaur. He rose from the table and staggered over to an unoccupied table to snag a three-quarters-full bottle.

'Why don't you drink?' he asked, in a spirit of genuine inquiry but rather aggressively nonetheless.

'It doesn't agree with me.'

'Can you sleep at night?'

'Depends how many lovelies are under the duvet.' Parsons smiled.

'How did it go with Nell McAndrew?'

'The slit stood me up.'

'Now there's a surprise.'

Parsons gave him his trademark evil look. Stirling yawned. Parsons looked round the room.

'Isn't it great to be here?'

'No, not really.'

'When I was editing *Shoot* I dreamed of the moment when I would be in the same suite as the big boys, my heroes, shoulder to shoulder, and now it's happening and . . .'

'It's a crushing disappointment.'

'It's one of the highlights of my life.' Parsons paused for thought. 'Have you ever thought about retiring?'

'I'm not even forty.'

'Aren't you?'

Stirling was momentarily more perplexed than usual. He

had always considered himself young for his age – it was one of his plus points – but it had been a while since he had looked in a mirror.

'Truly, Jimmy, I believe that football is the new . . .'

'Rock 'n' Roll?'

'Religion.'

'Don't be silly.'

'Think about it, Jim. We have our own cathedrals: The Theatre of Dreams, The Stadium of Light, Pride Park . . .'

'The Reebok Stadium.'

'We worship star players such as St David of Beckham, St Michael of Owen, St Rio of Ferdinand . . .'

'St Gary of Neville.'

'With our own hymns which are passed down from generation to generation, and all the while we the scribes are writing the Gospels of our time for all time.'

'Sorry.' Stirling was overcome by a vision of the Gospels according to Green, Brown, Blue and Pink founding the basis for some horror sect that would bring nothing but harm to the world.

'To many Bill Shankly was God, and what is Sven-Goran Eriksson if not a Messiah?'

'A middle-aged Swede with thinning hair.'

'Don't be snide, Jimmy. Football has so much to offer. For instance, I can't believe it was total coincidence that we buried the family dog on Cup Final day. It certainly helped us all cope with our loss.'

'I thought Arsenal won.'

'I'm talking about the dog.'

'You're mad, Rob.'

'I'm a believer, Jim.'

'In what?'

'Football.'

'OK, keeper of the faith, what does football have to say about what happens to us when we die?'

'Football is more important than life or death, you know that, Jimmy.'

'What does football have to say about morality?'

'Everything I know about morality I owe to football.'

'What does football have to say about free will?'

'Every man his own football.'

'For fuck's sake stop talking in T-shirt slogans.'

'But they are T-shirt slogans. Philosophy Football T-shirt slogans. I've bought the lot.'

'Of course you have. However, there's an inconsistency here. First you tell me football's the new religion, now you're saying that it's a new branch of philosophy.'

'Religion, philosophy, what's the difference?'

Stirling paused. 'I'll get back to you on that. There's someone I have to talk to.'

It was true. Peter and Gareth were on the verge of leaving the building. If he didn't catch up with them now it could be another year before he could have a sensible discussion about his future. He bounded across the George III dining suite imbued with purpose. There could be no doubt that being marooned in Norfolk had been a hindrance to his career. He was out of the loop. People forgot about him when it came to doling out the less taxing jobs.

Serendipitously, he reached the editor and deputy editor before their lift arrived. Coordinated when he needed to be, he placed an arm round each of their shoulders.

'Peter, Gareth, I just wanted to say what a tremendous job

you're doing. It's a great product and a truly great read. I wouldn't work for anyone else.'

'Thank you, Jimmy,' said Peter.

'But if you really pressed me I'd say that the paper needed some more humour.'

'Sorry, Jimmy, but that's our lift,' said Gareth, disengaging himself from Stirling's half-hug and moving to what was unarguably a ready and waiting lift.

'Yes, but . . .'

Peter joined Gareth in the lift. The doors closed.

'Couldn't you at least have waited for another lift, you cunts,' said Stirling to the elevator doors. The sudden burst of exercise had brought all the Grigio to his head. 'Ten years I've given to your fucking newspaper and you won't give me a cunting minute. Fuck you and your fucking awful newspaper. Full of celebrities with nothing to say and lifestyle consultants no one wants to read. Fuck the lot of you. I wouldn't read your fucking newspaper if you paid me to.' He gave the finger to the lift doors, which opened to reveal a pair of Derreks. He plunged the offending finger into his right ear lobe.

'Not leaving, are you, Jimmy?' asked Derrek Junior, who was well used to disgusting acts of personal hygiene and, on this subject at least, no hypocrite.

'It's time for the quiz,' said Derrek Senior.

Not the quiz. Not hour after hour of football questions. Questions to which he neither knew, nor wanted to know, the answer. Anything but that.

'I'm just going up to my room to freshen up and I'll be right with you,' he said, tacking round the Derreks and into the lift.

After the doors had closed he checked himself in the mirror.

Did he look nearly forty? It was hard to tell. He reached the seventh floor, exited and paused. What was his room number? He patted his pockets for one of those silly credit-card-style keys. Nothing. He checked his wrist, where his watch might be if he ever had need to wear one and where he usually wrote his room number down just in case things became complicated. Nothing. Bollocks, he would have to go and ask the receptionist which room he was in. He waited patiently at the lift. Sod them if they didn't appreciate him. He didn't have to work for people who hid behind lift doors or tried to press-gang him into football quizzes. There were grown-up people downstairs, working for proper newspapers. It was time to let them know he was available.

He re-entered the George III dining suite cautiously. There was no need. The Derreks were so absorbed that they wouldn't have noticed if Robert Pires had bothered to show up.

Uninvited, he took a seat at the main rival's table and struggled to put a name to their main man's face.

'Hi, Big Man. How's it going?'

'Jimmy, long time no see. Drink?' said one of the three men in the room in a position to offer him a job. There were fifteen national sports editors, of whom ten didn't speak to him and two, including his own, only spoke to him to remind him he was a cunt.

'Love one.'

'To what do we owe the pleasure?'

'Just wanted to say what a terrific job I think you're doing. Great product. Great read.'

'You want a job.'

'No, no, no, yeah, why not?'

'You know we can't afford you, Jimmy.'

96

'Oh, come on, big fella, don't pull that one. I'm the second cheapest football correspondent in the country.'

'Who's the cheapest?'

'Tristam, Tristan, Tristram . . .' He was fucked if he was going to dignify him with his nickname even if he couldn't ever remember his first name.

'Doubt it. We tried to poach Mr Blue and they came back with an extra twenty grand to keep him.'

'They paid twenty grand more for him?'

'Apparently.'

'Extraordinary. Sorry, did you say you tried to poach him?'

'Absolutely.'

'May I ask why?'

'He's a good writer.'

'Not really.'

'Won a lot of awards.'

'Haven't we all?'

'Have we?'

'Whatever, that doesn't explain why you approached him.'

'We needed another star football writer.'

'But last Sunday he started his interview with that advertising bloke at the FA with a quote from fucking Tacitus.'

'It was a good interview.'

'Didn't read it.'

'Good quote, too.'

'Have you got my new Norfolk number?'

'The one you gave me a year ago?'

'That's the one.'

'Yes.'

There wasn't much more that could usefully be added. 'Good to see you again . . . Big Man. Stay in touch.'

'See you, Jimmy.'

One down, two to go, both of whom worked for right-wing daily tabloids. Could he work for such people? Probably not. He wasn't good enough. If you worked for a paper that people read you had to know your stuff, go to three or four live games a week, even break stories. On a broadsheet things were simpler. You read what the tabloids were saying, wrote the opposite and trusted that no one noticed. Working on a tabloid would mean spending more time with White, Brown and Green than he did with his family. But what was the alternative? When they offered him a job he could always use it as a lever to prise more money from Peter and Gareth.

He surveyed the room. The sports editor of the *Daily Mail* was up at the bar listening to Pink. He didn't need to be standing so close, for Pink was in good voice:

> 'For he himself has said it,
> And it is greatly to his credit,
> That he is an Englishman!
> For he might have been a Roosian,
> A French, or Turk, or Proosian,
> Or perhaps Ital-ian!
> But in spite of all temptations
> To belong to other nations,
> He remains an Englishman!'

It would be difficult, if not impossible, to pitch for a job to such an accompaniment.

The sports editor of the *Sun* was . . . the sports editor of the *Sun* was sitting at a corner table talking, apparently intently, to Tristan, Tristam, Tristram, whatever his fucking name was.

Stirling shimmied straight over, sat down, and poured them all a glass.

'Hi, lads.'

'Jimmy, it's not . . .' said the potential employer.

'Great quote from Tacitus.'

'Thanks.'

'Did the *Oxford Dictionary of Quotations* fall open on that page or did you spend days leafing through it?'

'You're so funny, Jimmy.'

The other two men at the table appeared extremely bored.

'I can see you guys are busy so I'll keep it brief. It just struck me what with the *Sun* taking its wholly admirable line not to be homophobic any more you might be able to steal a march on those lippy counter-jumpers at the *Mirror* by employing the first openly gay football columnist.'

'And . . .' said the editor.

'Well . . .' said Stirling.

'Are you gay, Jimmy?'

'Christ, no. I mean, of course not. But I'm sure I could wing it. There's probably a bit of gay in all of us, isn't there, Tristan, Tristam, whatever?'

'Oi, pal,' said Mr Blue in his best mockney.

'Sorry, sorry. It was only an idea. You get back to your important conversation. Catch you later.'

He made for the bar. Where did that come from? Britain's first gay football columnist? The Man Who Gives It To You Not So Straight?

Had he really said 'Catch you later'?

8

Stirling checked his wing mirror, checked his front mirror, looked over his shoulder for the illusionary blind spot, turned on the ignition, methodically placed the gear stick in reverse and began ever so carefully to attempt to extricate the red car from Diss station car park. All the warning lights on the dashboard flashed at him, as per usual. Within yards, the engine packed in. He tried again and gained a couple more yards. Reversing had become like a game of American football. Could he move the car ten yards in three attempts? Or would he be forced to give it up as a bad job and kick it? Something of a queue was beginning to develop. Stirling sweated a bit, thought about lighting a cigarette, checked his mirrors again. Just because he'd passed his test it didn't mean he could drive. He added an apologetic gesture of thanks to the check, look, check again routine and at some pace and with great good fortune the red car was free. Stirling restarted the engine, waved at the vehicles stacked up behind him and chuntered off.

The events of the previous evening were slowly recollecting in his mind. Surely not? Could he possibly? Stupid, stupid, stupid. Thus engaged it was perhaps inevitable that he would forgo a series of his regular mirror checks and fail to spot the white car that had patiently been following him and flashing its headlights. As soon as he did, he tapped the left indicator to alert other road users to his intentions, and, on finding a convenient and safe parking spot, utilised it.

The female member of the Norfolk Constabulary was brisk. 'Are you aware how badly you have been driving?'

'Sorry, I was just following the car in front.'

'What car in front? You were veering all over the road.'

'I'm sorry. I'm a nervous steerer. What can I say?'

The policewoman had no answer.

'I'm pretty new to this driving lark,' he continued aimlessly.

The policewoman stepped closer to him. It had been a while since a woman had been so forward.

'And to be honest,' Stirling kept continuing, 'the red car was a terrible buy. Safe, possibly; but very unreliable and, now you mention it, the steering probably needs looking into.'

'Could you just breathe in my direction, sir?'

'Certainly.'

The policewoman staggered back.

'Have you been smoking, sir?'

'Of course. I always smoke when I drive. Helps calm the nerves. Or so I find.'

'Have you been drinking, sir?'

'No,' said Stirling, surprising himself that he could give such a truthful answer at six in the evening.

'Then you wouldn't mind taking a breath test?'

'No,' he replied, less positively.

The policewoman confronted him with her breathalyser equipment. 'Have you seen one of these before?'

'No,' said Stirling, lying through his teeth. He had always suspected that being passed fit to drive might interfere with his drinking, but not to this extent. Twice in the last week he

had been breathalysed. Three trips to and from Diss station –
two tests. He was operating at a phenomenal 66 per cent
breathalysation rate. On any given drive he was more likely
to be interrupted and required to take a breath alcohol test
than not, a chaotic and potentially dangerous state of affairs.
Stirling was a bad enough driver as it was without having to
worry about being nabbed by the police at every turn. Surely
if he concentrated exclusively on his mirrors he was statistically certain to hit something straight in front of him. It was
another example of rubbish policing. And, worse, victimisation.
Why him? There had to be drunker drivers on the roads.

He failed the test. 'I have to inform you that you are under
arrest,' said the policewoman.

Arrest, thought Stirling.

'You have the right to remain silent but anything you say
may be used as evidence . . .'

Fucking arrested, he thought.

'Have you anything to say?'

'How much Grigio did I drink?'

'Can you repeat that?'

'How . . . no.'

The policewoman turned her attention to her dictaphone:
'The suspect was initially apprehended for driving erratically
and having a broken left rear indicator light. On being
questioned it was noticed that his breath smelled of alcohol,
therefore . . .'

Tiddlydee, tiddlydum, thought Stirling.

'. . . having failed a roadside test he was placed under
arrest,' said the policewoman, wrapping things up with the
dictaphone. 'Have you anything valuable in your car?' she said

to Stirling. Tricky question. The car had no street value but the contents. 'You may not be returning to it for some time.'

'In that case, there's a few things I'd better pick up.' He lugged out a battered plastic Carling 'Follow England' hold-all which contained an idiosyncratic laptop and enough receipts to bankrupt his newspaper. On the front seat there was a Threshers bag containing two bottles of red wine which he had bought during an idle moment at Liverpool Street station. Quite decent red, in fact, certainly by Threshers standards.

On his return to the cop car he was surprised to see the policewoman had a side-kick to do her driving for her – perhaps she was over the limit, too. If he was going to sweet-talk his way out of this one it might require a threesome, thought Stirling, the bottles clashing rather loudly at his feet. Three hurried calls established that Norwich nick was full, Thetford nick was understaffed and Diss police station was being refurbished. Against her better judgement the police-woman rang Lowestoft police station. Bingo. Bad news all round: Stirling could be accommodated, the policewoman had lumbered herself with a shelf-full of cross-county paperwork, and the side-kick, having driven reliably in the wrong direc-tion, was suddenly required to pull off a U-turn on one of the less safe stretches of the A143. If he hadn't been under arrest for drink driving Stirling might have made some tart back-seat observation re The Highway Code.

Instead, he kept his counsel, which became grimmer the more he silently deliberated. That he was guilty he had no doubt. He might have been sixteen hours and counting between drinks, but such were his consumption levels that he might have rendered himself permanently over the limit. If you could drink yourself sober it was probable that you could sober yourself drunk. A five-year ban seemed the most obvious outcome. He wouldn't be able to do the school run until the twins were on the verge of leaving. He'd better phone B.

'Can I ring my wife?' he asked, arguably blowing the three-some option.

'No,' said the policewoman.

'Please,' said Stirling.

'No,' said the policewoman.

Thanks to a truck full of aggregates overturning near Kirby Cane they didn't reach Lowestoft until nearly seven o'clock. He was escorted to the front desk and instructed to place his belongings upon it, which he did carefully, mindful of the Threshers red.

'Are you on medication?' asked a bearded man whom Stirling was almost certain he had seen on *Look East* directing police inquiries in a most lethargic fashion.

'No.'

'Have you taken any illegal substances in the last twenty-four hours?'

'No.' If there had been any drugs available at the Football Writers' Dinner no one had been sufficiently public-spirited to offer him any. Thank heaven for small mercies.

'Are you depressed?'

'Good question.'

'Have you been diagnosed with clinical depression?'

'No.'

'Date of birth?'

'24/7/61.'

'Occupation?'

'Football writer.'

'Really?'

'Sadly.'

'What do you think of George Burley?'

Was it a trick question? What was that about anything he said being used in court against him? He prevaricated. 'Who?'

'George Burley. The Ipswich gaffer. I don't know about you, but I think he's doing a fantastic job. You've got to fancy our chances in the play-offs.'

'Absolutely,' said Stirling, pulling himself together. 'Tidy little club. Family values. Play a neat, flowing, attractive game. The Tractor Boys deserve to grace the Premiership if only because they demonstrate what can be achieved on a well-managed shoe-string. Arnold Muhren, hey?'

'Most naturally gifted playmaker it's been my privilege to see.'

'Kevin Beattie, hey?'

'Indeed.'

'Commander Mick Mills?'

No comment.

'Little Eric Gates?'

'If you could go with WPC Christie she'll take an inventory of your possessions.'

'Not a problem.'

The WPC was dismayed by both the extent and disparity of the receipts that Stirling unloaded onto the formica table in the waiting cell: train tickets (c 150), bar bills (c 114), snack bills (c 71), Travel Lodge bills (27), restaurant bills (7), Novotel bills (3), Euros (70), forged annual newspaper account (1).

'What the hell are these?' asked WPC Christie.

'I really need to get my filing in order.'

'I can't deal with this now. We'll face it if you're detained overnight.'

'Something to do.'

'If you'll just come this way, sir.'

She led him past an occupied cell to an upright piece of machinery the size of a fruit machine, the centrepiece of which was an outsize keyboard.

'OK, Mr Stirling, we are now in a position to conduct the second part of your breath-alcohol test. If you could just disengage the breathing apparatus from the left side of the machine, sir.'

'Oh, thank Christ for that, for an awful moment I thought you were going to ask me to write something.'

'Why would we want to do that, sir?'

Stirling pointed at the keyboard.

'That's for professional use, sir. Now, take a deep breath, would you, and exhale slowly into the tube.'

'Adnams?'

'Thanks.'

The barmaid pulled the pint, computed his change and gave both to Stirling.

'Thanks,' he said again, and made his way to the table near the corner window that offered a framed view of the cash-point machine. There wasn't much action in Never Pullham on a Saturday night, but such as there was revolved around the out-of-hours banking facility. He settled himself down. The whole point of going to the pub was to be able to kid yourself that you weren't drinking alone. But the illusion was difficult to sustain in The Hare and Greyhound when it was just the barmaid and you. There had been a time, before the barmaid had worked out that Stirling only ordered Adnams, when they had talked more. But those days had passed.

Did he fancy her? Almost certainly not.

Yet she was unarguably the most conventionally attractive barmaid in the Pullhams (Little, East and Never) and always made the effort to dress with a tarty availability. But Stirling, a month shy of forty, still had a problem finding conventionally attractive women attractive. This had caused rows in the days when he had killed time working on men's magazines and swathes of editorial conference time had been given over to compiling top 100 shag-lists. When pressed for a contribution Stirling could only ever come up with three names: Fanny Ardant, Sandra Bernhard and Hanna Schygulla. The first and third they'd never heard of and the second was 'almost certainly a muff-diver, mate'. None of his fellow contributory editors could fathom why he couldn't get excited over Darryl Hannah and/or Y and/or Z in a jacuzzi, despite him explaining that it was all to do with possibility. Unless he was able to inject the remotest shard of reality into his fantasy the unsteady construct tended to collapse. Which left the barmaid.

Could he have another pint? He studied the breath-alcohol test record which WPC Christie had so kindly given him and did some maths. The line between guilt and innocence was drawn at 36 ml. Exactly seventy-two minutes ago Stirling had scored a 24 ml, followed a minute later by an eyebrow-raising 23 ml. Yet an hour and a half before that he had been sufficiently over 36 ml for that bitch to place him under arrest. All of which meant he was shipping the Grigio out of his system at a minimum rate of 12 ml per hour, which further meant that if, as was statistically likely on current form, he was breathalysed on the four-minute drive home there might be a few too many traces of Grigio remaining for the roadside test but by the time they had all made it to Lowestoft nick for an encore no sign whatsoever. Therefore only the beer came into the equation, and as 2 pints of Adnams = < 36 ml he could most certainly have another pint.

'Adnams?' asked the barmaid.

'Thanks,' said Stirling.

The lack of chemistry between the pair was palpable.

Borderline embarrassing, thought Stirling, as he sat down and watched a youngish couple take, guessing from the look of them, ten pounds from the cash-point machine. Bored, he turned his mobile on. 'Bring bring, bring bring.' He tapped in his security code (1234) and brought himself up to date.

Message One – Derrek Junior: 'Jimmy, where are you?'
Message Two – B: 'Jimmy, where are you?'
Message Three – Derrek Senior: 'Jimmy, where the fuck are you?'
Message Four – Derrek Senior: 'Ring me, you cunt, your job's on the line.'

He rang his wife.

'Hello.'

'Babe, sorry I'm late, the lawyers got all arsey over the Mabbutt interview. No matter, I'm bearing down on Brockdish. Christ, what are the twins doing?'

'I'm at the PTA cheese and wine evening.'

'Oh, right, I'll see you there.'

'Have you remembered the wine?'

'Of course I have. Love you.'

He was finding himself doing more and more things subliminally these days. Buying something or going somewhere and only later discovering a reason for his actions. It could be dislocating. A couple of weeks ago he had found himself at the Hawthorns at midday and had had to ring Kath to ask her, without alerting either Derrek, to discover why he was in West Bromwich on a Thursday lunchtime. Good old Kath had hacked into the Fat Man's computer and phoned him back to tell him he was down for a one-on-one with Gary Megson. Which was a start, although he had had to blunder his way through a number of non-Garys before finding his man and been forced to open the interview with the rather weak: 'So, Gary, how, in your own words, would you describe what you do?' And followed up with: 'Talk us through, if you will, how the last fortnight has treated Gary Megson.' Not very well, it transpired.

He finished his pint, placed it on the counter and, with a parting gesture to the barmaid intended to convey that, far from having no friends, he had to rush off to a cheese and wine do, made for the exit and hit the road again.

Anecdotes, anecdotes, anec – what the fuck was he going to talk about? In London he could talk about Norfolk and be guaranteed a laugh, but previous C & Ws had taught him that this strategy didn't work in reverse. Nor could he wax lyrical about police harassment. There had been some funny moments – his 'Thank you for the salutary warning, officer' had amused Stirling if not the bearded Ipswich supporter, and the tirade of relieved patter he had kept up as a convictionless WPC Christie drove him back to the red car had not been lacking in nervous laughter from the back seat – but bragging about drink-driving had ceased to be fashionable even in East Anglia. If not that, what? Pigs, perhaps. He wasn't uninterested in pigs, and there were bound to be a few pig farmers in the house. Rain, of course. Persistent drizzle or intermittent downpours: which posed the greater threat of flooding? And why? Chickens always worked. Throw in some light flirtation – 'That's a lovely Puffa jacket you're wearing, Mrs K. Did you get it from Bonds in Norwich? Personally, I can't get enough of their light furnishings' – and it might be quite fun. More entertaining, with luck, than a night in Lowestoft police station sorting through his receipts.

B was standing outside the Wortwell Community Centre (built with Lottery money to commemorate the millennium and opened by Bernard Matthews on 14/2/00) having a cigarette as Stirling cautiously parked the red car.

'Thank Christ you're here, Jimmy,' she said. 'Have you got the wine? The stuff here's undrinkable.'

'A bottle each, darling.'

'Great. There's this bloke you must meet.'

'Why?'

'Because he may be the most appalling person I've met up here. You know what he said to me just now?'

'No.'

'As a parent I've always thought you're only as good as your last spanking.'

'You're joking.'

'No.'

'He was joking?'

'People don't joke round here.'

'Too true. Do you think he spanks adults as well?'

'You never know your luck.'

The venue usually given over to badminton players, tae kwan do, and rudimentary first-aid classes was packed with worthless worthies and pillocks of the community. On one side of the gymnasium there was a large trestle table, encumbered with boxes of Slovakian Merlot and Slovakian Riesling and a cheese collection sufficiently unappetising to stump even Derrek Junior. B sashayed through the middling crowd until they arrived at the flagellist, who was sitting at a table on his own.

'I must introduce you to my husband,' said B.

'Met him already, thanks.'

'Have you?'

'Book club,' admitted Stirling.

'Oh dear,' said B. 'I'll just go and get some,' she looked around, 'cheese.'

The women having departed, Spanker, as he had been brought up to do, effortlessly turned the conversation towards politics.

'Voting Labour again, are we?'

'Christ, no.'

'Good man.'

'I thought I'd vote Lib Dem.'

'Didn't know there were any of them round here.'

'There may not be,' conceded Stirling.

Bring bring, bring bring.

'What's that infernal racket?'

'Sorry,' said Stirling, patting his pockets. He located his mobile, pressed the green button, and said, by way of explanation, 'It's my mobile.'

'Why does the fact that you have such a contraption not surprise me?' said Spanker.

'I know it's your fucking mobile,' said Derrek Senior down the phone. 'What I want to know is why it's been switched off on a Saturday. The newspaper pays for your mobile so we can contact you in an emergency, not as some fancy fucking fashion accessory.'

'I was held up,' said Stirling.

'What do you mean you were held up?'

'I was driving along and I was pulled over and it's not important. What's the emergency?'

'Brian Moore's dead.'

'Brian Moore's Head Looks Uncannily Like the London Planetarium,' said Stirling, instinctively. 'Cult song by Half Man Half Biscuit and title of Gillingham fanzine.' He might have forgotten everything he knew about football but he was still up to speed on trivia. And how typical of Derrek to intrude on his Saturday night needing the answer to a quiz question. Hadn't he anything better to do?

'Dead, not head, you idiot. Brian Moore is D for Dead, DEAD,' screamed Derrek.

'That's a shame,' said Stirling.

'And not just for his close family. We've got a gaping big hole needing filling with an appreciation, and thirty minutes to fill it.'

'Not a problem. How many words?'

'Eight hundred.'

'I'll bang it straight over.'

Stirling pressed the red button. 'Sorry, work,' he said to Spanker.

'Remind me what it is you do again?'

'Football journalist.'

'Rugby or Association?'

'Association.'

'Stop me if you've heard this before, but I've always thought rugby to be a hooligans' game played by gentlemen whereas football . . .'

'Heard it before,' said Stirling, and bustled out of the

112

Wortwell Community Centre dialling 'Copy' as he went. He found a bench, lit a cigarette, took two drags and hit call.

'Some copy for the sports section. Writer: Jimmy Stirling. Subject: Brian Moore. Copy starts: The name Brian Moore, with an e, cannot fail but evoke, in the minds of men of a certain age, memories of crisp winter Sunday afternoons spent playing football in the park. The roast had been finished, *Big Match* had been watched, and off down the road we hurried for pick-me-up games of football with jumpers for goalposts and hoi polloi for opponents. So it was we happily spent our Sundays, Moore's commentaries ringing in our heads as we rounded the goalkeeper to score the "last goal wins". Yesterday he died. How many words is that?' Stirling lit another cigarette off the one he was holding. 'And with him died our childish dreams. It would be no exaggeration . . .' Stirling blundered on – 'a man not given to hyperbole who understood that less could be more, one "o" . . .' and on – 'He was a gentleman and a football scholar . . . How many words is that? . . . Great. We'll lose the football scholar, replace that last "and" with a full point and leave it there. Thanks.'

'What are you doing?'

Bella was standing by the bench, smoking a Dunhill and looking at him with some curiosity.

'My job. Brian Moore died and they needed an impromptu obituary so I was just phoning one in.'

'You write obituaries?'

'Once in a while. Usually I watch football.'

'I hate football.'

'So do I.'

'Something of a handicap in your profession.'

'Probably.'

'Richard would love your job.'

'Your son?'

'My husband. Football, football, football. I came out here to escape. They keep talking about three brothers called Neville, Gary and . . .'

'Phil.'

'That's the one. Unbelievably boring.'

'The worst. I'll take care to avoid him.'

There was a pause.

'Your phone,' said Bella.

'Yes.'

'How old is it?'

'I've no idea.'

'Can I look?'

'Sure.'

Bella tapped away on the phone.

'What are you doing?'

'Just bringing it up to date. You don't mind?'

'Not at all. It's just the last person to play with it – a bloke called Parsons – did something to the phone which meant it was all Greek. Literally. And I didn't notice until I was halfway to Norfolk and had to go all the way back into London to take it into IT to get it fixed and, anyway . . .'

'I'd better be off.' She handed the phone back. 'Will you be in church tomorrow?'

'Should I be?'

'Not yet,' she said with a smile. 'See you, Jimmy.' And blowing him a kiss she disappeared into the darkness surrounding the Wortwell Community Centre.

Odd, thought Stirling, she didn't look pissed. He dialled the office.

'Jimmy, here. Just checking everything's OK.'

'You can't half be a cunt at times.' The Fat Man appeared to have a cold. 'But this piece is magnificent. I tell you, Jimmy, I'm in bits here.'

'Sad times.'

Sniffle, sniffle.

'I'll ring you next week, big fella. Better put the kids to bed,' said Stirling, pressing the red button and noticing the time was 23.45. Shockingly late for that excuse but Derrek wouldn't register. He was in bits over the death of a football commentator, the mawkish fool. The Fat Man needed to get a grip.

He had spotted his bottle of wine in the corner and was bearing down on it when he was diverted by the father of his children's only friend.

'Ah, Jimmy, I was just saying to Charlotte how good it was of you to have Esme to tea so often.'

'It's a privilege.'

'I've seen how much she can pack away. It must cost you a fortune.' Roland laughed. He worked as a management consultant and never strayed too far from the bottom line.

'I've never added it up,' said Stirling. 'But anything, or rather anyone, who encourages the twins to eat has to be worth while in the long run. The food we waste.'

'Tell me about it. As a cost-cutting measure I've suggested that Charlotte pour unused milk from the children's cereal bowls back into the container, but does she listen?'

'Ahh, my ever-generous husband,' said Charlotte, appearing like Satan at her husband's shoulder, albeit a Satan dressed in one of Roland's old school hockey shirts and plus-fours. 'Nice to see you again, Jimmy.'

She had obviously forgiven him for his rebel stance on the PTA smoking vote.

'Lovely to see you, too, Charlotte.'

'Would you believe my beloved husband has started marking the milk to check how much dear Esme and I use?'

'Better the milk than the gin bottle,' said Stirling.

'Don't you start,' said Charlotte.

'Sorry.'

'It's all right for you to make little jokes living in your huge mansion but because of "difficulties at work",' said Charlotte, forefingering her own inverted commas, 'we have to make do with a town house. Little wonder dear Esme's so dim when she doesn't have the space to express herself.'

'I wouldn't say she's dim,' said Stirling, kindly.

'And I know that journalists aren't known for being observant, but even you might have to agree that ten is rather old to be still reading *Swallow and Amazons*.'

'Perhaps,' said Stirling.

'Don't you think so, Roland?' said Charlotte.

'Well,' said Roland.

You didn't need to be a marriage guidance counsellor to predict which way this one was going. But what could Stirling do? Esmerelda, dim or not, was the twins' sole friend, and while he was happy enough to totter around friendless it was important that Charlie and Nancy, of all children, met someone to divert their attentions away from each other. At the end of every schoolday Stirling asked them who they had played with during break, and every time Charlie said Nancy and Nancy said Charlie. He sort of guessed that it was crap parenting to emphasise daily their lack of social success, but, given the national curriculum, you could only ask 'How was PE?' once a week.

He looked round for B. She was asleep with her eyes open, an old trick, being talked at by a man who looked as if he had played a lot of rugby in his youth and, if Stirling remembered correctly, was a South African who had left his mother country the morning after Mandela had been released.

He snuck a look at his mobile. An hour and a half to go. It was not the least of their social problems that taxis had to be ordered a fortnight in advance, requiring an ante-party prediction to be made on when the event might become unbearable before you even knew the runners and riders. They had plumped for 1 am. B had dipped out early. Stirling had a long wait.

'The least you could do is get me a drink,' demanded Charlotte.

'Of course,' said Stirling, returning to the real world.

'Of course,' said Roland, happy to escape that selfsame world.

'There's a decent bottle of burgundy hidden behind the floral print curtain,' said Stirling.

'Thanks,' said Roland.

'Do you like these bashes?' asked Charlotte.

'To plagiarise John Belushi in *The Blues Brothers,* I like two types of party. Cheese. And Wine,' said Stirling, and laughed.

'Who's John Belushi?'

'Fat bloke. Funny once. Dead now. Not important.'

Charlotte moved closer.

'Let me ask you a question.'

'Unhuh.'

'Father Vernon, Bella, Mabel and me were discussing the purpose and meaning of confession and guess who piped up, "Anal sex isn't a mortal sin, is it?"'

'Father Vernon.'

'Don't be cheap.'

'With the Father out of the equation that leaves you, but no one is so selfish as to be the answer to their own trivia question. Bella or Mabel? Mabel or Bella. I'll go with Bella.'

'Interesting.'

'Potentially. But correct?'

'That's for me to know and you to find out.'

'Oh, please, don't say that. You can't begin to know how irritating I find that phrase.'

'Tough.'

'And that word. How exactly am I meant to find out? I can't sidle up to Bella and say . . . whatever I would need to say to elicit that information.'

'Why not?'

'Because it would be, I don't know, intrusive for want of a better word.'

'And since when were you journalists interested in being polite?'

'Since . . . I don't purposely set out to be rude.'

'Don't you?'

'No I fucking don't.'

'I win,' said Charlotte, and gave him a look almost as patronising as the one she directed at the returning Roland.

'Your wine, darling,' he said, and smiled a smile so small and full of loathing that Stirling almost felt sorry for Charlotte.

'I'll leave it for later, thank you, Roland. Now, Jimmy, do you find little Charlie so unattractive that you can't bring your-self to ask her for a dance?'

That explained the strange behaviour in the far corner, where Spanker was moving unsteadily from foot to foot and goggling at someone else's very static, very frightened and, from a distance, only arguably teenage daughter. The tinny speakers played Abba.

'Yes. No. Of course,' said Stirling. 'Would you like to dance?'

'And I thought you'd never ask,' said Charlotte, offering her hand which Stirling, ever the gentleman, accepted. With a jerk like she might use to rip a hare from the mouth of a coursing greyhound, Little Charlie dragged him to the makeshift dance floor. Stumbling, he looked round for his wife. She was still asleep, which had allowed the chancy South African to place his arm around her. Steady, pally. He'd have to deal with him after he'd extricated himself from his dance partner.

'Watch out, there's a commie about,' said Spanker, welcoming Stirling to the dance floor. The, at close quarters, clearly pre-teen looked round, her thick glasses unable to mask the fear in her eyes. Stirling gave a sympathetic shrug but had no knowledge of the social protocol required to extract a youth from such a predicament. Besides which Little Charlie had gripped both his wrists and was jitterbugging, the flaps of her fawn and blue quartered shirt bopping up and down to reveal a thermal vest.

Stirling flailed.

'Put some life into it, man. This is meant to be fun,' she shouted, louder than was needed to make herself heard above the still small voice of Agnetha singing 'The Winner Takes It All'. Several people turned to stare, including the South African, who raised his wineglass, as if in appreciation of a cracking racist joke, and moved his other hand ever closer to B's left breast.

'Fucking yarpie,' muttered Stirling.

'Sorry,' shouted Little Charlie.

'This is lovely,' said Stirling.

'Isn't it just,' whispered Little Charlie, manoeuvring Stirling closer to her bosom. He was an inch from a clinch and possible suffocation when his lack of hygiene kicked in.

'What's that smell?'

'Sorry.'

'Eeuggh, it's your hair. When did you last wash it?'

'Last week,' Stirling lied.

She released him and retched loudly, thereby alerting Spanker to her availability. The flagellist moved quickly.

'Mind if I cut in, old boy?'

'Be my guest.'

Spanker placed a fully extended arm round Charlotte's stomach and proceeded to waltz his delighted partner around the Wortwell Community Centre to the jaunty backdrop of 'SOS'. Stirling looked at the probably nine-year-old and opened his arms to signify the absurdity of the adult nation. She misinterpreted his gesture and held his hands.

'Where are your parents?' asked a concerned Stirling.

'Over there,' she said and turned her head in the direction of the South African. The yarpie smiled broadly and cupped B's left breast. She woke up quickly, brushed the offending mitt aside, asked the yarpie what in fuck's name he thought he was doing and, noticing that her husband was dancing to Abba with a nine-year-old, asked, with rather more urgency, what in fuck's name did Stirling think he was doing.

It was at that moment their pre-booked cab arrived.

'The children have few enough friends as it is without everyone thinking you're a paedophile,' said B, continuing the argument in the back of the cab.

'There's a lot of it about round here. Not enough to do, if you ask me,' said Cedric, Stirling's least favourite depressed cabbie, from the driver's seat.

'Thank you,' said Stirling, and turned to his wife. 'How many times do I have to explain that I wasn't dancing with her? Charlotte had stopped dancing with me on account of my hair smelling,' the cabbie unwound his window, 'and Spanker, that bloke from the Book Club who you were talking to earlier, and if anyone's a child abuser it's that fat freak, whisked her off and left me standing with a young girl.'

'So you admit she's a young girl,' said B.

'Over ten?' asked Cedric.

'Since when did you get so fucking chatty?' said Stirling.

Cedric pulled the cab over to the side of the road. 'Out.'

'Sorry,' said Stirling.

'I will not tolerate foul and abusive language at my work station.'

'Sorry.'

'This is a no-swearing cab. Particularly when ladies are present.'

'I'm sorry. That's what I meant. Not sorry I didn't understand you, but sorry for swearing.'

'And the lady.'

'I'm sorry for swearing, darling.'

'Don't fucking darling me.'

The cabbie restarted the car and Stirling changed the topic of conversation.

'Who was the yarpie?'

'He's got a name.'

'Hansie?'

'Richard.'

'So that's Bella's husband.'

'Who's Bella?'

'Short, quite sexy, doesn't mix much in the playground. On the PTA.'

'Her. He's married to the Queen of Bungay society. No wonder he's so full of himself.'

'An uppity South African, well I never.'

'He wouldn't stop talking about his fast car and his fast helicopter and his Chechen au pair with, as he put it, "humungous breasts".'

'And still he wants more.'

'At least he isn't a paedophile.'

'As far as you know.'

Stirling didn't tip Cedric or ask for a receipt. When B and he reached the TV room they found the babysitter asleep in the armchair. Charlie and Nancy were sitting on the sofa, holding hands, giggling and watching *Basil the Great Mouse Detective*.

'What are you doing?' asked Stirling.

Both Charlie and Nancy made 'ssshh' sounds and looked at the babysitter.

'It's one thirty in the morning,' said B.

'Way past your bedtime,' said Stirling, taking the hint.

'I was scared so I woke Charlie up,' said Nancy.

'And because Bouchie girl was scared I was scared,' said Charlie.

'So we came downstairs to see if you were back,' said Nancy.

'And put a video on,' said Charlie.

'On mute so we wouldn't wake . . . her up,' said Nancy.

'You deal with the babysitter and I'll put them to bed. Come on, you two.'

They fell happily into line.

'Night, Big Dadda.'

'Night, Big Dadda.'

'Night, darlings.'

He approached the babysitter carefully. His only experience with waking women was provided by B, who reacted violently even if you weren't feeling her up. It would help if he knew her name. Then he could repeat it over and over again until she stirred. But he hadn't a clue. Could he just shake her? But what if she misinterpreted the wake-up call and incorrectly thought he was making an intentionally clumsy pass? Or worse, what if he mistakenly damaged her? Given his current luck she probably had a faulty cranium. One shake and she'd be paralysed for life and he'd be known as a babysitter batterer.

He retired to the kitchen, poured himself a whisky, walked back into the TV room and barked his kneecap horribly on the side of a heavy metal occasional table.

'Aagggghh, fuck.'

The alarmed babysitter woke up.

'Who are you?'

'Jimmy.'

No bells rang.

'Charlie and Nancy's Dad. Can I get you a drink?'

'No thanks. I'm driving.'

'Very wise. How were they?'

'Perfect. Didn't hear a peep from them all night.'

Stirling sat down and looked at the TV. A beaky and shifty animated mouse was playing a violin while a chubbier mouse sat in a comfy armchair drinking port.

'What are we watching?'

'I'm not sure.' She picked up her white handbag. 'I'd better be going.' She opened her handbag.

'How much do we owe you?'

'I'm not sure.'

Stirling pulled a wedge of notes from his back pocket and peeled off a fifty.

'Thank you,' said the babysitter, examining the note with the same caution Budgens' Bethan devoted to a fiver. Just because he was from London they all assumed he was a forger.

'Night,' said the babysitter, hurrying out before Stirling could ask for change.

He drained his Scotch, placed the glass in the sink and lumbered up to bed. Charlie and Nancy were sleeping where he should be sleeping. He snagged a pillow from under their pretty heads, picked up a sleeping bag off the floor and made his way to one of the spare rooms. He was exhausted. Whatever the mid-market papers might say, not many people found themselves on the receiving end of a drink-driving charge and a paedophile allegation on the same evening.

9

The end when it came for Derrek Senior was swift. One minute he was forcing an extra serving-spoonful of coleslaw onto his crowded plate at a Sport England buffet, the next he was dead. Trevor Brooking, noticing the Fat Man's collapse, had called for an ambulance on his mobile, but to no avail. They had cancelled the lunch as a mark of respect.

Stirling, sitting at the back of a Presbyterian church on the outskirts of Pontypridd, wished they had cancelled the funeral. The hymns – 'Bread of Heaven', 'Land of Hope and Glory', 'Abide with Me' – had been unexceptional and now Derrek Junior was saying a few words.

'The Gaffer, Big Man, Boss, Skipper, Fella, these were some of the names my father answered to. But for me, in or out of the workplace, he was Dad.' Derrek Junior paused. The congregation – 60 per cent journalists, 30 per cent friends and relatives, 10 per cent locals with nothing better to do – looked at their shoes or coughed and shuffled or stared at their hymn-sheets.

'My Dad, The Gaffer, Big Man, Boss, Skipper, Fella, will be remembered by us all as a great lover of sport. He ate sport, he drank sport, he slept sport until at a Sport England buffet attended by Trevor Brooking, the Vice-Chairman of the British

125

Athletics Association and the Deputy Shadow Minister for Sport, he no longer breathed sport. Sport, ladies and gentlemen, has lost a friend.'

There was a clearing of throats.

In a sense, it was very brave of Derrek Junior to attempt an appreciation. Stirling certainly hadn't been up to it at his father's funeral and had read instead, haltingly and with little conviction, a brief passage from the Bible, all the time staring high above his father's friends for fear that if he caught any of their eyes he would be unable to continue.

'On the bright side,' continued Derrek Junior, 'he has left us with a locker-full of great memories. Who can forget Dad and Bertie Mee dancing on a table at the White Elephant on the River as Pat Rice and Peter Storey sang along to "Chirpy Chirpy Cheep Cheep" by Middle of the Road on the night Arsenal won the double in 1970/71? I was two at the time.'

'Fuck. He thinks he's doing a Best Man's speech,' whispered Terry.

'All we need now is mention of the high jinks on his . . .' replied Stirling.

'Or his stag night. I wasn't there, for obvious reasons, but I've heard tales and seen pictures which suggest it was a belter of an occasion. Anyway, enough already. The thing about my Dad is that he was a great bloke, a great sports journalist, and last, and very much not least, a great Arsenal fan. No one loved the Gunners quite like Dad. He was the complete Gooner. And as a mark of respect to Dad and the greatest football team the world has ever seen I'd ask you all to join me in chanting his all-time favourite song.'

The organist started to play the tune to 'You've lost that

loving feeling'. The crowd rose to its feet and with Derrek Junior conducting from the lectern they sang as one:

> 'We've got that Double feeling,
> Ohh, that Double feeling,
> We've got that Double feeling,
> Cos it's on, on, on.'

'Please God I never have to do that again,' said Stirling when it was over.

'Oh, I don't know, it makes a change from "Dear Lord and Father of Mankind",' said Terry.

They hustled out of the church and stood in the corner of the graveyard, smoking and watching the journalists file out. They'd go anywhere for a free drink, thought Stirling, even Wales.

'Britney Spears,' said Terry.

'Where?' said Stirling.

'It's an anagram of Presbyterians.'

'Very good.'

Invited back to the Derreks' family home, Stirling sought refuge in the sports video library. He had always suspected that it might be a mistake to come to the funeral of a man he had loathed. A man about whom he had often said he would gleefully piss on his grave. A man who had sent him to Coventry, Halifax and beyond. It was the first funeral he had been to since his Dad had died.

Then, he had drawn comfort from his father's eclectic group of friends, their evident grief allowing him to evade confronting his own, their happy anecdotes allowing him to think that his

Dad might not have wasted his life. The rituals had helped. He knew exactly how he was expected to behave and could do so unthinkingly. Having to think of others allowed him to dodge thoughts of loss and mortality. There would be plenty of time for grieving later, on his own.

Now, the rituals irritated him. The words which had carried meaning and solace when applied to his father seemed empty and false when used to describe Derrek Senior. Platitudes such as 'a great loss' were triter than ever when uttered with solemnity by people who usually used the phrase on hearing that the Manchester City left-back would be out until Christmas. Everything was out of kilter.

There was only one book in the video library (a hardback edition of the latest *Rothmans Football Annual*), so Stirling turned his attention to the room's primary purpose. The tapes were arranged alphabetically from Arsenal 4, Aston Villa 1 all the way through to West Bromwich Albion 0, Arsenal 1, hundreds of football matches taped and filed away and every one an Arsenal victory. They looked used. Perhaps, after multiple help-ings of Sunday roast, the two Derreks had retired to the library to sit on their matching beanbags and rewatch games whose score they already knew. Madness, but there was fuck-all else to do. He chose Arsenal 2, Charlton 1, put it in the machine, poured himself a glass from his name-tagged bottle of Pinot Grigio, sat on a convenient beanbag, pressed mute to avoid Richard Keys's hyperbolic introduction, and stared into space.

The tears came quickly. After three decades of pretending to be stoical he had started crying again around about the time the twins were born. Not at the actual birth – that would have been clichéd – but a fortnight later when watching an *Only Fools and Horses* Christmas special. The high concept of Del Boy becoming a father had put him on edge. During the birthing process he had become sweaty and throaty and when Del Boy had cuddled baby Damien and taken him over to the window overlooking London and said 'One day, we'll be millionaires, my son' Stirling had been tipped over the edge. B had looked at him suspiciously – they were watching a populist sitcom, after all – and then the confusion had been broken by the sound of one twin crying, followed, seconds later, by the other one joining in.

After his father's death new fronts had been opened up in the battle against tears, and television continued to catch him out. *Frasier*, *The Sopranos*, anything with John Thaw in it, all of them might leave him feeling momentarily bereft. It was pathetic and it was self-pitying, but the only programmes he could confidently watch with no chance of being struck by a crying jag were *Newsnight*, *Countdown* and sport. Lost, confused and uncertain, it was becoming a struggle to stay on top of things. He tried to concentrate on the game. The team in red were attacking, ineffectively. The other team took their time over a throw-in.

'What the fuck are you doing?' said Terry.

'Watching Arsenal against Charlton.'

'Why?'

'I haven't a clue.'

'Come on, Jimmy, it's a funeral, for Christ's sake pull yourself together. If you stay in here everyone will think you thought he was a cunt.'

'But I still think . . .'

'Which is exactly why everyone expects you of all people to be out there pretending he wasn't. Just for fucking once stop seeing everything from your point of view. How do you think his wife feels? Or Derrek Junior?'

Stirling had never met Derrek's wife, wouldn't recognise her at her own husband's funeral, but Terry was right, it couldn't be easy for Derrek Junior. If Stirling wasn't over his father's death yet, how bad must Fat Boy be feeling?

He followed Terry through the kitchen, complete with Arsenal FC calender above the Neff oven, and on to the red and white checked patio. The wake was in full swing. An entire hog was being roasted. Two hired staff, complete with chef's hat, aprons and trousers, were lopping meat off, inserting it into unbuttered baps and adding large dollops of iridescent apple sauce. People happily queued for the product. Over by the leylandii the motliest of crews, including a man in a plaid suit who had to be Brown and a bloke in reflector shades who was probably Green, were singing 'The famous Tottenham Hotspur went to Rome to see the Pope'. Derrek Junior, tie undone, was reclining on a sun-lounger next to the all-weather pool table sipping Stella Artois.

Stirling perched himself on the baulk cushion.

'Are you bearing up OK?'

'Bit fluey but nothing to moan about, thanks, Jimmy. You look like shit.'

'Yeah, well, I drove down.'

'No fun.'

'No.' Stirling lit a cigarette. 'I was very sorry to hear about your Dad.'

'These things happen, Jim.'

'Yes, but . . .'

'And what a way to go, hey? Having a laugh with Trevor Brooking and, swoosh, that's your lot. It doesn't get better than that.'

'No, I suppose not.'

'I was chatting to Gareth earlier. Brainstorming how the paper might mark the Gaffer's passing, and we reckoned a double-page centre spread could do the trick.'

'Seems appropriate.'

'Big photo-montage in the middle and all around it some words of appreciation from our star writers. Including you, my old friend.'

'Not a problem.'

'You've ye olde cartey blanche to write as much as you feel comfortable with. A couple of hundred, couple of thousand words, whatever you reckon you need to make it come alive.'

'Fine.'

'Good man.' Derrek Junior sniffed. 'Sorted. Now what I could do with is a drop more amber nectar. Can I get you anything, Jimbob?'

'No, thanks. Where's your Mum?'

'M/Cing the hog roast counter.'

Stirling thought it best to wait until the queue had died down before offering his condolences. He moved slowly to the drinks counter. Ouch. Someone had crept up behind him and punched him unreasonably hard in the left bicep area.

'Jimmy. Surprised to see you here,' said Parsons.

'Derrek and I go back a long way,' said Stirling, massaging the small bone between his elbow and shoulder.

'Like right,' said Parsons. 'And during most of it you were at it hammer and tongs like Paddy Vieira and Tim Sherwood on a late Nineties Monday night North London derby at a windswept White Hart . . .'

'Appearances can be deceptive.'

'So, are you going to go for it?'

'A drink?'

'The job, you old piss-head.'

'Rob, I hardly think it's appropriate.'

'Bollocks. You have to move fast in this business. I was talking to Gareth . . .'

'Does he ever take a day off?'

'. . . and he thought you had been a bit restless recently and would be an outside contender if you stepped up to the plate.'

'Relax, Rob. I have no more intention of applying for the sports editor's job than the idiots who run the paper have of ever giving it to me.'

'That's good to know. What about me?'

'What about you?'

'Am I too inexperienced?'

'No one could be too inexperienced.'

'Give youth some head and all that. I take it I can count on your support?'

'Whatever for?'

'As a senior man it might help to have you on board. *Entre nous,* I was thinking of forming a dream ticket with Derrek.'

'He's dead.'

'Derrek Junior, dipstick.'

'Derrek Junior,' Stirling said with some surprise. The prospect, genuinely, had never entered his mind.

'He's not as thick as he looks.'

'Well.'

'And what I have to decide is who should be the Presidente and who the Veep.'

'What?'

'On the one hand, Del's the more experienced man and his knowledge of minor sports is, at times, breathtaking. Added to which he probably has a stronger support base within the office. On the other hand, he has weaknesses. Words, for one. And, if we're going to be brutally honest, pictures also. So it might be better, all round, for him to stay at deputy level. But I can't completely gloss over the fact that over a ham and cheese toastie in The Butt I promised Del he could have first crack at the leadership if his Dad suddenly passed away or became medically incapable of holding down the job. Which is a problem. I kinda know how Tony Blair felt.'

'Now you're really losing me,' said Stirling.

'For Big John Smith read The Boss. For Brown and Blair read Fat Boy and myself. For The Butt, Granita, the trendy Islington eatery fraternised . . .'

'I know what Granita is.'

'Good. So what would you do?'

'What would I do? What would I do? I always wake up thinking I know the answer to that one but by the time I've had a coffee and read the papers . . .' Stirling paused.

'What would you do if you were me?' Rob explained.

'Panic.'

'Very funny. Can't you take anything seriously?' Rob sped off in search of a better opinion. Stirling ambled off, via the free bar, to a deckchair. The queue had receded in front of the hog roast but Stirling was anaesthetised by lack of grief. There was nothing for him to say to the widow aside, perhaps, from offering condolences for her front lawn, which Brown and Green and friends were routinely trashing with a game of touch rugby, journos v locals, twelve a side, much caterwauling.

Strange the way death affected some people, thought Stirling. And who was to say the muddied oafs were wrong? If Derrek Senior were looking down, or rather up, he'd probably be delighted that people were so obviously enjoying his funeral. Life's for living, he would say, even if he himself was prevented from joining in on account of being dead. As for what he would have made of the reluctant guest sitting in the corner of his patio and drinking his wine and mourning someone else – that was easy. He'd have said, 'Will you look at that miserable cunt? Why can't he pull himself together?'

'But what do you do in No-folk?' Terry asked Stirling. They had left the funeral as soon as it was no longer impolite to do so and dropped in to the first pub on the way to the centre of Pontypridd. The Fleece was, if possible, grimmer than The Butt of Lewis, but Terry and Stirling had long ceased caring what a pub looked like. They did, however, keep a watching brief on the collection of over-muscled and under-employed youths who were killing time with some friendly arm-wrestling in the lounge section of the pub.

'Nothing much,' said Stirling, sipping his keggy bitter. 'But the funny thing is I seem to be pretty busy.' He killed the soapy aftertaste with some Scotch.

'Who do you drink with?' said Terry, half-drunk and semi-interested in country life.

'No one.'

'So what do you do in the evenings?'

'I still go to the pub, only two or three times a week, with a book or something.'

'And during the day?'

'In the winter, I don't know, I might make a bonfire. Which takes time. Gathering the wood, piling it up, lighting it, relighting it and waiting for night to fall when you can wonder at the majesty of flickering flames in a dark, dank Norfolk field.'

'And you do that every day.'

'No, two or three times a week.'

'And . . .'

'There's always fires to be lit inside,' Stirling said. 'I find I enjoy watching the way different logs burn and inhaling the different aromas they give off. I've even thought of laying them down. I could fill one shed with 2000 oaks, another with a batch of fruity 1998 pine, a third with . . .'

'Jimmy, you're boring.'

'A sad and lonely pyromancer, which is a fairly pointless form of idolatry. What's a fire ever done for me?'

'Kept you warm.'

'There is that. Same again?'

'Yup,' said Terry, stubbing out a cigarette early and placing the half-finished Bensons in a jacket pocket.

Up at the bar, the amateur arm-wrestlers registered Stirling's presence before the barman.

'You a bum boy?' shouted a man in tight jeans and T-shirt watching over two similarly dressed men grunting and groaning and straining and staring deep into each other's eyes and moving their lips oh so slowly closer together at a pace that would have tested audiences who thrilled to Trevor Howard and Celia Johnson in *Brief Encounter*.

'Sorry.'

'You a gay boy?' said the umpire's friend who, understandably losing interest in the arm-wrestling, seemed to be up for a conversation.

'No.'

'You sure look like a bum boy, gay boy,' shouted the umpire.

'I've got two children.'

'So what?' said the umpire's friend.

It was a fair point. 'I'll have two pints of Best and two double Scotches and whatever you want for yourself,' he said to the barman.

The umpire's pal lugged his muscles towards the bar.

'So where you from, faggot?'

'Norfolk.'

'Where?'

'Norfolk.'

'Is that near Shrewsbury?'

'Near enough.'

'What you doing here then, bandit boy?'

'Funeral.'

'Who?'

'Derrek William.'

'The Derrek William?'

'There's only one Derrek William.'

'What a man, hey?'

'Yes.'

'No one would ever call him a bum boy.'

'Not now. Can I get you a drink?'

'Steady, sonny. I know your type. You'll be wanting to stick a frozen orange up me arse, next. But since you asked.'

'And a pint of . . .'

'Import.'

'Import for my new friend,' said Stirling to the barman.

The steroid abuser was placated by the unexpected gesture. He wouldn't have minded a fight but a pint would do. Stirling went back to his corner table.

'Do you find young men keep coming on to you and taking the piss out of you for being gay?' he asked Terry.

'No.'

'It's happening to me all the time. At the pub in Liverpool Street station, on the beach at Great Yarmouth, at a meet-the-players afternoon with Cheltenham Town, all these fit, in the well-built sense of the word, young men keep calling me a "poofter" or a "homosexualist" or the equivalent. Why?'

'Are you gay, Jimmy?'

'I doubt it.'

'All those Saturdays spent watching lissom-thighed athletic men running around for your delectation. Are you sure you don't become the teeniest bit excited?'

'Not yet.'

'Which means all those fit young men must be mistaken. Statistically improbable, but if you give your word . . .'

'I'm forty on Saturday.'

'Hard luck.'

'And I still can't make sense of my father's death.'

Beep beep, beep beep.

Terry searched his pockets for his mobile, rescuing a dozen half-smoked cigarettes which he placed on the table.

'It must be yours.'

Stirling took a similarly long time to unearth his mobile. It was vibrating.

'What's going on?' he asked, handing it over to the IT expert.

'You've got a text message.'

'Impossible. I don't get text messages.'

'You have now.'

'What does it say?'

'R U UP 4 IT? C U IN NCP AT 8 X B.'

'For what? See you where? 8 X B? I really don't need to be stalked by a crazed text messenger.'

137

'Jimmy, is there something you haven't told me?'

'Not as far as I know.'

'Have you got a secret admirer?'

'Not as far as I know.'

'Who's B, then?'

'My wife.'

'She wants to see you at 8, which gives you less than an hour to bomb down the M4 . . .'

'But B doesn't have a mobile phone.'

'She could have borrowed one.'

'Who from? The twins don't have one either.'

'So who is B?'

'I honestly don't know.'

'And why is she sending you kisses and asking to meet you in . . . must be a National Car Park?'

'I don't know. I didn't even know there were any NCPs in Norfolk apart from the one near the Castle Mall shopping centre in Norwich which shuts at 5.30 . . .'

'Come on, Jimmy, who are you shagging?'

'No one.'

'No one?'

'My wife. Sometimes. That's it.'

'No one else.'

'No one.'

'Maybe B's not a woman but one of those fit young men you keep meeting. Brendan, Boris, Bertie, Binky, ring any bells?'

'Christ, it must be Bella.'

'Bella?'

'She was playing around with my mobile at the PTA Wine and Cheese do on Saturday.'

'Very fruity.'

'But she's the Queen of Bungay society. What would she want with me?'

'Fuck anything that moves these country housewives, in my experience. Possibly including you.'

'What on earth do I do now?'

'Move pubs,' said Terry, looking up at the entrance to The Fleece. Brown and Green and their groupies had entered, singing.

> 'Cockney boys,
> We are here,
> Shag your sheep
> And drink your beer.'

The arm-wrestlers stopped arm-wrestling.

'Whatcha, Jimmy? Magic funeral,' said Green.

'Wonderful.'

The umpire and his friend noticed the interaction between them. He had been drawn, unwillingly, into the conflict.

The drunken football writers moved inexorably towards the steroid-abusing local youths. The former sweated. The latter's veins popped. It was a difficult one to call, the experience and weight advantage of the football writers providing an intriguing contrast to the desire and fitness advantage of The Fleece's finest. It would, as ever, thought Stirling, probably come down to who wanted it more.

'Even money the football writers,' said Stirling.

'I'll have twenty to win sixteen on the locals,' said Terry.

'If you must.'

Stirling's new friend continued to stare at Brown. A couple

of the youths detached themselves from their group, moved over to the pool table, inserted thirty pence and smiled at the sound of fifteen pool balls becoming available. Not flying pool balls, thought Stirling, trying to edge, Grandmother's footsteps style, towards the exit. The barman spotted him before he had reached the end of the banquette and, with something approaching a flourish, locked all the doors.

Stirling had never been brave, had never had the physique to be physically courageous, had always said sorry or run away or both to avoid being hit. And until now this mix 'n' match policy of appeasement and withdrawal had served him well. However drunk he became, he had never been thumped, he had only ever injured himself. Irritatingly, while sober enough to feel it, his lucky streak seemed certain to come to an end in a pub quite near the centre of Pontypridd.

'Cockney boys, We are here,' Green chanted, again with feeling. The Welsh boyos, never taking their eyes off the opposition, reached into the innards of the table for ammunition. One of them managed to single-handedly come out with four pool balls. Fuck, his hands were big, thought Stirling.

Before Green could move on to sheep and beer and inevitable mayhem, the umpire finally made the connection.

'Didn't I see you on *Totally Football* last Sunday?'

'Certainly did, boyo,' replied Brown.

'Wicked, you must know Jimmy Hill.'

'Certainly do.'

'What's he like?'

'Personal friend of mine, actually,' Green butted in. 'We go way back . . .' Saved by the chinny one. The evening passed peacefully enough. A relieved Stirling didn't even mind too much spending most of it discussing Welsh football. Ryan Giggs – bum boy; Robbie Savage – bum boy; Vinnie Jones – man's man. The journalists bought the drinks – on expenses – and the youths drank them. There was an arm-wrestling contest, which Stirling, struck down by tennis elbow, agreed to co-umpire, and, then, de rigueur these days, there was a visit to a lap-dancing club. Embarrassingly, the lads, over-proud of bumping into Brown and Green and, by association, Stirling, were anxious to show off their new friends to the regulars at Zeta's. They continued to chat Welsh football. Terry removed himself to the bar and listened out for any colour he might be able to cram into an overdue and under-researched piece for the magazine on Sex and Alienation in Modern Britain. Everyone had a high old time. Perhaps too high in the case of the umpire and his friend who, rather missing the point of Zeta's, treated everyone to an unscheduled pole dance. 'Not what the doctor ordered,' said Brown.

Stirling disappeared to the Gents, pressed reply on his mobile, and composed his first text message. 'SSS6MM 50M WYXX, he typed in before mistakenly pressing send. He thought about sending another message to explain any confusion created by the first one but realised, correctly, such a process might become Sisyphean.

Finding a quietish corner table out the back, Terry and he discussed their midlife crises. Until Zeta's closed and it was time to make their way to the Travel Lodge.

'What the fuck are you doing?' Stirling screamed at the bloke in a silver car who had come out of the Happy Eater exit at speed and forced Stirling's red car to veer into the middle lane, where he never felt comfortable. The silver car positioned itself right up his arse, making him so fretful that he jagged into the slow lane and was a whisker away from totalling a blue car which, thank God, despite being in a slower lane was moving faster. There was much hooting and finger-giving and general wanker signs. Stirling tried to remember if it was illegal to drive on the hard shoulder in such circumstances. He had still to traverse Suffolk and he was twitching badly. Surely the roadworks at Stansted couldn't be far away, with their 40 miles per hour speed restrictions and the opportunity to light a cigarette. A manoeuvre, a handful of bills from the local garage had taught him, best attempted at speeds not in excess of 30 mph. He was not sufficiently ambidextrous to be able to fiddle with a lighter with his left hand while steering with his right. He found it difficult borderline impossible to concentrate on two things at once. That's why he drove automatics. He checked his mirrors twice, slowed down to 45 mph, and turned on the radio. It was stuck on the award-winning Five Live.

'Coming up after the News the start of a new series in which John Inverdale interviews footballers with hinterland. Tonight on *Thinking A Good Game* the thoughts of Wales and Bolton midfielder Phil Davies.' Should be a laugh, thought the man proceeding in a cautious fashion down the M11. Had Invers done his research? And, if so, had he believed it? Was it possible that he had fallen for the litany of lies Stirling had written about Davies? Surely Inverdale would spot so obvious a spoof. But if he had, what was Davies doing on the show? He wasn't going to talk for an hour about sitting on the Bolton bench, was he? Not at the start of a series . . .

'Phil, good evening.'

'Evening.'

'It strikes me that your interest in literature was sparked by reading Sebastian Faulks . . . Which of his novels struck a particular chord . . . *Birdsong*?'

'Sorry, John. You're losing me a bit here. I don't think I've ever met anyone called Sebastian.'

'Not even at the Bolton Amateur Dramatic Society where you perform in the close season?'

'Not sure about that, John. I think if you asked the lads about amateur dramatics at Bolton they'd point the finger at Dean Holdsworth. Quite a card, Deano, both on and off the pitch.'

'I bet he is.' Inverdale paused, presumably to look at his notes. 'Here's Lindsay with the travel.'

Stirling laughed. All the travel bulletins in the world wouldn't be able to save this interview. They were only a minute in and Davies had already used up his only anecdote. The footballer had nothing to say for himself. That was why Stirling was employed to say it for him. The travel bulletin segued into a seven-day international weather report.

'Phil, during the break, and can I apologise for the some-what extended weather bulletin, during the break, Phil, you mentioned that despite winning thirty-nine international caps for Wales you consider your life to be a failure?'

'Well, the thing is, John, I'm thirty next week and although it's been a great honour representing your country and all that, if you look at the stats and all that, as I did last week, we've only won three of those games.'

'Three.'

'Yeah, and I was substituted in all of them. The thing is, John, Wales have never won a game which I've finished.'

'I didn't know that.'

'Not a lot of people do. It's not something you like to have in the general domain. Here I am nearly thirty, John, and what am I doing with my life? Sitting on the bench at Bolton, that's what.'

'Is there a future for Phil Davies?'

'To be blunt, John, I don't think so. On my agent's advice we issued a come and get me plea last January and . . .'

'And . . .'

'No one came.'

'No one. How does that make you feel?'

'Like shit, sorry, John, family show. Pretty, erm, well, down, frankly, John.'

'Let's have some travel.'

How come Davies had never opened up to him like that? Bastard. He cranked the red car up to near the 55 mph mark.

After a nine-and-a-half-hour drive he arrived home to find Richard and Bella drinking wine with B in the kitchen.

'Hi, babe,' said B. 'How was the funeral?'

'Boring.'

'Richard Westerhoven,' said Richard Westerhoven. 'Lovely to really meet you properly.'

Stirling shook the man's hand.

'Hiya, Jimmy,' said Bella with a little wave.

'Hi, Bella,' said Stirling, without a wave.

'Charlie and Nancy are waiting for you,' said B.

He poured a glass and went up to say goodnight to the children. They were on the same bed. Charlie was lying on his back with his legs in an O shape balancing a book between his feet which Nancy, kneeling in front of him, was reading.

A position more appropriate for Sting and a partner than six-year-olds, thought Stirling.

'Charlie, Nancy, what are you doing?'

'Reading *The Prisoner of Azkaban*,' said Nancy.

'We love each other,' said Charlie.

'I know you do, but . . .'

At least there were no tongues. The other Sunday the twins had been caught snogging during children's liturgy and there had been whispers at the post-Mass coffee. Fuck 'em. Better by far for the twins to have their tongues down each other's throats than be at each other's throats. The Twins Handbooks might disagree, but it made for a quieter life.

'Read us a story,' said Charlie.

'No,' said Stirling.

'Please,' said Nancy.

'OK,' said Stirling.

He picked up a copy of *Watership Down,* which he had never finished as a child and had no intention of completing as an adult. 'Two pages.'

'Dad,' said Charlie.

'It's nearly ten o'clock. Two pages or nothing?'

'Nothing,' said Nancy.

'Four pages, then.'

'OK,' said the pair of them, grudgingly.

Stirling rattled through the text, surprised to find himself slurring. The drive, obviously, had taken its toll, but there was something odd going on between alcohol and him. The less he drank, the more drunk he felt; the more he drank, the less drunk he became. It was a complex equation. He was neither never completely drunk nor ever entirely sober. He was always somewhere in between.

Down in his kitchen, the yarpie was showing off.

'Jimmy, I was just saying to B that the pair of you must come up in my plane for a spin?'

'No thanks.'

'We could pop over to Paris, park the old Spitfire, and take in some sights.'

'I'd love to, Richard, but I'm scared of planes.'

'But you're a fully-grown man.'

'Particularly tiny ones flown by enthusiasts.'

'Whoa, Jimmy, why the anger? I was only trying to see how we could all hook up.' The South African poured Stirling's wife some of Stirling's wine, a gesture that necessitated him moving to B's side of the island and left Bella and Stirling stranded on the other.

'You don't look the type to be frightened of a little plane ride.'

'Not in the slightest,' said B.

'Bingo. We must go for a ride, then. If you'll excuse the pun.'

'What pun?' Stirling asked Bella.

'The obvious one.'

'Fine,' said B. 'As long as Jimmy can look after the kids.'

'Whatever,' said Stirling.

'I'll e-mail you,' said Westerhoven.

'I don't have e-mail,' said B.

'Dicky'll sort it,' said Dicky.

A twin started crying. The Stirlings looked at each other.

'I'll go,' said B.

Having humiliated his host, Westerhoven came over all pally. 'So, Jimmy, what do you guys do for fun?'

'I don't know.'

'Come on, you must enjoy some leisure pursuits.'

'I quite like cooking.'

'Anything, how can I put this delicately, more manly?'

'Such as?'

'Parachuting, abseiling, duck-shooting, Norfolk's made for outdoor activities. And an extra benefit of having a live-in Chechen au pair with huge jugs is that you can take full advantage of them.'

'I'm more of an indoor man.'

'Squash?' asked Bella, obliquely.

'I've played squash, yes.'

'Double bingo. Bel's been looking for a squash partner ever since Harold was relocated.'

'I'm game if you're game,' said Bella.

'Pun excused,' said Stirling.

Was that how it was done? You invited yourselves over for a drink, chucked around spurious 'leisure activities' until you found a match, and then hooked up. It was all rather stark. Did B know what was going on? She must do. And why not? After all, they'd been fucking each other for decades so she, of all people, deserved a break. But why the yarpie? If he'd been in any respect attractive Stirling might not have minded. Might even have been quite excited by the prospect. Might have asked to join in. But this bloke was a horror-show. The type of man who loved sports changing-rooms. A man who took his underpants off first and would loiter around with his dick hanging out talking to all and sundry about the batting order. A man never happier than when standing bollock-naked under the hairdryer while everyone else sat around fully dressed waiting to go home.

'I think this calls for another bottle,' said the man who

loved changing-rooms. Stirling realised that by agreeing he would in some way be sanctifying the arrangement. As ever, his need for a drink took precedence over other considerations.

'Be my guest.'

The South African, axiomatically, plucked a bottle of red Stirling had been saving for a special occasion – his fortieth, perhaps, if it panned out OK – from the stack. He opened it, poured himself the largest glass, and insisted they all clink glasses.

'B was telling me – where is B, by the way?'

'Asleep, probably. She often nods off when soothing the twins.' Or in your company, he might have added.

'And what kind of a name is B?'

'Quite a sensible one if you were christened Bernadette.'

'Anyway, B was telling me you're a football writer. Jeez, that must be a fun job.'

'For some people.'

'Have you met Arsène Wenger?' asked Westerhoven at the same moment as Stirling asked Bella, 'Who buys the drinks at the PTA?'

The husband answered his own question before his wife could answer hers.

'He's just got to be the most intelligent man in the business. What the Professor doesn't know about football could be written on the back of a kaffir's pay packet.'

'I'm sorry . . .'

'One of the companies that I advise hired an executive box for the Leicester game last season and I had the privilege of watching his multi-talented outfit go through their paces at first hand and it struck me . . .'

Stirling let him drone on, wondering if people would ever

stop talking at him about football. Not in the short term at least: the man had latched on to his subject and his unwilling audience of two were powerless to stop him. Bella gave him a wistful look. She wasn't unattractive, although he could have done without the wistfulness. Stirling patiently finished the bottle and then before the South African could snaffle more wine he did what he always did when guests had outstayed their welcome. He turned on BBC Radio Norfolk.

'Hello, again, to Gill from Swaffham.'

'Hello, Adrian.'

'So, Gill, what have you to share with us as we approach the midnight hour?'

'I'm ringing about that gentleman who said he'd once eaten frogs' legs . . .'

'Michael.'

'Yes, Michael. And how he claimed that they tasted of chicken.'

'Yes . . . Have you ever eaten frogs' legs, Gill?'

'Certainly not, Adrian, but I was in Cromer once, looking for some wet fish . . .'

The Westerhovens had heard enough. Before Gill could finish or, more precisely, start her anecdote, they were saying their goodbyes.

10

'Happy Birthday,' said Charlie.

'Happy Birthday,' said Nancy.

Stirling slunk further under the duvet. Usually he woke at four in the morning, railed against the world in general and the Derreks in particular, made grand plans as to his future, fell asleep again around about six and was woken by the twins on the dot of seven. Last night, he had woken with the pre-dawn jitters at 2.17 am, got back to sleep at his usual time, and it was now, as he emerged from under the duvet, 7.01 am.

'Give us a birthday kiss,' said B. The twins jumped into the bed. Stirling was forty. And exhausted. He'd have to fit in an afternoon kip somewhere.

There were no presents, which was fine, for there was nothing material that he wanted. The guest list for his surprise birthday party was nearly as meagre – his brother and his wretched family – which was disappointing. He had always imagined that his fortieth would be a grand affair. A dinner for over a hundred held in a substantial restaurant at which he would feel obliged to make a self-deprecating speech lightly alluding to his considerable achievements before passing among his slightly less successful friends who had always been there for him. Not to be.

Since moving to Norfolk, he had contrived to lose all his friends. Either he had not phoned them or they had not phoned him. It was hard to tell, but a series of impasses had been established which neither side appeared to have the energy to breach. Some families had visited during their first summer, thinking they might as well enjoy a cheap family holiday at Stirling's expense, but by behaving erratically he'd soon put a stop to that. Since then there had been a few Christmas cards, but by the time it crossed his mind to send some in return it had been February. So his fortieth would be a family affair, and not even a complete family, for the brothers' mother was holidaying in Nashville. At least he wouldn't have to make a speech, which was just as well since neither Graham nor Mimi had the slightest interest in anything he had to say.

His brother, typically, arrived early. His silver executive people carrier appeared in the drive, with Hunt and Kent leaning out of the back windows bearing what he assumed were imitation airguns and Mimi looking sparkling in the front, just as Stirling had finished cutting the pieces of toast into sixteen pieces in an futile attempt to gull the twins into eating something.

'Unhuh,' said Charlie.

'Trouble,' said Nancy.

The toast untouched, they disappeared. The cousins had no shared interests.

Graham was done up in a Barbour, plus-fours, wellies and flat cap; Mimi in a snazzy checked suit, pashmina and head-scarf. It was one of their medium irritating jests to 'wrap up warm' on their rare visits even on July days when you could happily waltz around in swimwear. The cousins, wearing fatigues, bombed out of the back. Stirling, wearing a disintegrating pair of boxers, hauled on a nearby overcoat and went to greet them.

Bang. Bang. Kent smashed into one kidney, Hunt the other. Stirling wasn't used to horseplay. The twins apologised if they so much as brushed you on their way past, never raised their voices, and looked worried whenever anyone did. It was hard to believe they were all related. Maybe they were less related than they thought. God knows what Mum had got up to in Nashville before she lost her looks.

'Kent, Hunt,' said Stirling, careful, as always, not to mix the 'k' with the 'h' or the 'u' with the 'e'.

'Uncle Jimmy, where are the twins?' asked Kent.

'Hiding.'

'Yahoo,' said Hunt and the duo ran off to storm The Priory.

'Sweethearts,' said Mimi.

'Happy birthday, bro. You look like a flasher.'

'Slow start. B's shopping and I got behind myself.'

Graham and Mimi surveyed the grounds to see if there were any improvements they could comment upon. There weren't.

'Drink anyone?' said Stirling, and then remembered it wasn't eleven yet. 'I mean, coffee or tea? Ribena?'

'Coffee would be great,' said Graham.

'Have you any infusions?' asked Mimi.

'I'll look.'

They didn't, but the fussy drinker settled for out-of-date Earl Grey and they sat at the milk-and-honey-stained table as Stirling cleaned up around them.

'How's things?' asked Graham.

'So, so,' said Stirling.

'Have to say I couldn't make head nor tail of your piece last weekend.'

'I got a bit lost.'

'It was long, though,' said Mimi.

There was a fairly serious crash upstairs. Stirling dropped his J-cloth and went to investigate. The door to the twins' bedroom was hanging off its hinges. Kent and Hunt, both armed, were either side of the twins' bed; Charlie and Nancy, unarmed, were underneath it.

'Prepare to meet your maker,' screamed Kent.

'Achtung surrender,' said Hunt with a menace, and a knowledge of German, unbecoming in a four-year-old.

'Go away,' said Charlie softly, by a whisker the braver of the pair.

'Children, children,' said Stirling. 'Who wants to watch a video?'

By separating the young an uneasy peace was brokered which extended to the adults who were too consumed with childcare to embark on fault-finding missions. At midday, as was his wont, Stirling suggested 'a walk' and they trudged to the local pub. The children had goujons and chips, the adults decided to eat later. The afternoon passed without mishap. Graham played football with Hunt and Kent, Stirling played an imaginary game with Charlie and Nancy, Mimi and B avoided each other.

Later, Graham and Mimi dressed for dinner because that's what they did. Stirling and B followed suit so they could have twenty minutes alone together. In honour of the depressingly auspicious occasion the Stirlings chose to debut their dining-room. A poorly lit, grim affair with no furniture except four uncomfortable chairs bought with a low bid at Diss auction.

The food was exceptional. The half-case of wine, provided by Graham, a couple of *crus* above anything Stirling had ever tasted. It could only have been improved upon if Graham had poured larger glasses as he introduced each bottle.

Just because they were in Norfolk, it didn't mean the Londoners were going to refrain from talking about their careers. 'The wonderful thing about the current market,' said Graham, sipping at his wine, 'not at all bad, is that it gives the advantage to the more intelligent players. Any old fool can make money in a bull market, it's merely a question of picking up the phone and generating volume, but now you have to think a bit.'

'What's your bonus going to be?' asked Stirling to spite himself.

'I doubt it will be seven figures. Upper middle upper six figures, something in that ball-park.'

'More wine, anyone?' asked Stirling, pouring some into his glass as he did so. He had opened all six bottles, ostensibly to allow them to breathe, but in reality to avoid having to go into the kitchen every twenty minutes for reinforcements.

'There's no real need for you to work, then?' asked B.

'Not financially, of course not,' said Mimi. 'But I find it very fulfilling running my own business.'

'Sorry to be so rude, but what is it you do?' asked Stirling.

'Mimi is Europe's number one party planner,' said Graham.

'It's been a struggle,' said Mimi, exchanging her wine for water. 'The headaches I've had with nannies, you wouldn't believe. Do you have a nanny, B?'

'No.'

'But if you work hard enough you get there in the end and you do feel you're making a difference. Only last week we had

154

a really zingy crowd: Sir Tim Rice, David Seaman, B. A. Robertson . . .'

'Pretty zingy,' said Stirling.

'And it takes not a little subtlety to keep that diverse a range of clients coming back for more.'

'You can't just give them a party bag and tell them to fuck off,' said Stirling.

'Absolutely not.'

'More wine anyone?' asked Stirling.

They had exhausted their guests' careers.

'Don't you ever get bored looking after the children?' asked Mimi, turning down the dessert.

Why did everyone automatically assume that his wife and he were bored? Was it their body language? Something they did or didn't say? Did they appear to lack ambition? Was it that?

'Of course,' said B, 'there are times when it seems as if my life begins and ends with the kids.' She paused. 'Which, I suppose, it does.'

'Have you thought about going back to work?'

Good question, thought Stirling. A question which, whatever their financial predicament might be, he had never been quite doughty enough to ask.

'Doing what?' said B. 'There isn't much of a demand for delightful getting to know you soirées in South Norfolk. Or canapés, for that matter.'

They had exhausted the hosts' careers. There was only one subject left to discuss, and short of offering to do the washing-up, Stirling was stuck. Best to get it over with.

'How's Kent and Hunt's [not easy when pissed] school?'

'Wonderful. It's open all year round, which gives us

maximum flexibility. And they love it. In the holidays it can be quite an effort to convince them to stay at home.'

'Surprise, surprise,' said B.

'It's not often that kids love their school,' said Stirling, covering up. 'They certainly seem very happy, very . . . boisterous.'

'They're real boys,' said Mimi.

Steady, thought Stirling.

'I don't want to criticise . . .' continued Mimi.

Fuck, thought Stirling.

'. . . but I couldn't help noticing that the twins seem – how can I put this, without hurting anyone's feelings? – a bit too close. Have you ever thought about separating them?'

His wife accepted criticism on a limited number of issues. Childcare wasn't one of them.

'I'll do the washing-up,' said Stirling.

'I'll help,' said Graham.

By the time the brothers had struggled through the cleaning up their wives had disappeared to bed. One way of settling their differences.

Stirling put a log on the fire, a 1998 beech.

Graham opened a bottle of port, a 1934 Taylor's VIP.

'The year Dad was born,' said Graham. 'I thought it would be appropriate.'

'I suppose so,' said Stirling, offering his glass. 'I still miss him.'

'We all do. But you have to move on.'

'Where to?'

'You've a lovely wife, lovely children, a lovely house.'

'Yes, but . . .'

'What more could you want?'

'A job which was mildly interesting or challenging. Money.'

'Money's no great shakes.'

'Easy for you to say . . . I don't know what I want but I know I want something. I don't want to die having spent my life watching football. There must be something more to it all than that.'

'Maybe not.'

'You can talk with your four houses, glamorous friends, power job. You could do anything.'

'Yes.'

'But I, I only seem to do nothing. I have to do something but I can't for the life of me work out what. More port?'

'I think I'll turn in. Thanks for the dinner, Jimmy. And if you need any help with money you only have to ask.'

'I know. What's B. A. Robertson up to these days?'

'Who?'

The younger brother went to his lavishly connected wife in bed. The elder brother took his birthday present up to the attic and put on the *Grande Messe des Morts* by Berlioz. He opened a new file on the laptop, saved it as Things To Do, thought for a while, and started to type.

1. Accounts for 2001/2002.
2. Accounts for 2000/2001.
3. Resolve dispute with revenue over accounts for 1999/ 2000.
4. Return children's library books. (Not having replied to their letters he had recently received an e-mail, of all things, from Norfolk Public Libraries. The Stirlings were forty-seven books overdue. Working in tandem with the twins he had found four of them. Library books were his responsibility.)

5. Respond to letters from Dad's friends. (Unforgivable.)
6. Unpack. (Two years in and there were still brown boxes clogging up the third spare room.)
7. Respond to letters from readers. (Fuck 'em.)
8. Check twins' premium bonds. (Probably the only extra source of income available to him.)
9. Apply for driving licence. (If he didn't do it within the next twenty months, which on current form looked at least possible, he would have to retake his driving test, with all that entailed.)
10. Expenses: 1997–present day. (Ask not how much you owe the Paper but how much the Paper owes you. In the past, he had filled the back pockets of his jeans with receipts, washed the trousers, and presented the accounts department with a papier mâché sphere attached to a ball-park figure. But, in a sign of the times, the pesky new managing editor refused to countenance such arbitrary accounting practices.)
11. Fix car radio.

It was enough admin to give him a hobby for the rest of the year. If only he could get started. Instead, he restarted the *Grande Messe des Morts*. Dawn was breaking. A couple of pheasants hove into view. In the corner of his office lay two dozen scarily white envelopes – bank statements. He poured the rest of the vintage port into his half-pint glass. There was something sacramental about drinking a deep red liquid from the year of his father's birth. Would his Dad have opened the bank statements? No. How many times had his Dad gone bankrupt? Too many times.

He could do this methodically, opening each statement as

it was sent and compiling a detailed dossier of his chaotic finances, but he doubted there was enough port remaining for such a considered approach. Or he could take an instant hit and open the most recent statement. Man or mouse?

If required by law to guesstimate the size of his overdraft Stirling would have hoped to get within a year's salary of the actual figure. When he had last looked it had been £150,000 against a property worth £360,000. In the last two years he had earned, say, a hundred grand, so make that sixty after tax and, new one on him, national insurance. They had spent, assuming the worst, as it was prudent to do in such circumstances, four grand a month, which times 24 equalled getting on for a hundred grand. A forty-grand deficit which, added to the earlier figure, still made for less than two hundred grand. Reckless but sustainable.

He was somewhat surprised, therefore, on opening the white envelope, to read the following:

An update on your overall financial position:
What you own:
Your home (based on the last valuation)   £360,000.00
What you owe:
Your overdraft as at 28/06/01   -£327,689.43

The difference between what you own and what you owe
£32,310.57

Off the pace by an eighth of a million, outgoings were treble incomings, they were spending ten grand a month. And what had they to show for it? Nothing. No new cars, no new white goods, no new clothes. All he ever bought was fags and booze.

The figures didn't add up. Unless B was having an affair, make that a string of affairs. He scanned the joint account for evidence: Budgens £87.80; Budgens £76.17; Goffs Petroleum £897.65; Budgens £65.01; Budgens £99.88.

He had been brought to the verge of bankruptcy by a mixture of petroleum and Budgens. What did they use petroleum for? What could be so expensive in Budgens? What was going on? All it needed was a Gulf War or a Budgens price hike and they'd be homeless. Either he would have to ask B to stick to some form of budget or he would have to ask Graham for a loan. He might have to do both. He dropped in on the twins on his way to bed. 'When are our guests going to leave?' Charlie said in his sleep, snuggling closer to Nancy.

Stirling rose at noon, four hours too late to tap Graham for some money.

'The bitch didn't even have the grace to leave a note,' said B.

'My dreams came true,' said Charlie.

'You missed church,' said Nancy.

'How was liturgy?'

'God doesn't like rich people,' said Charlie.

'But he likes poor people,' said Nancy.

'That's good to know,' said Stirling, pouring himself some cold coffee. 'Darling, I was reading some bank statements last night.'

'What?'

'Yeah, I know. Something to do with being forty probably. Anyway, I think we might be overspending.'

'The only overspending going on in this house is on cigarettes and alcohol.'

'It can't be just that.'

'We can cut out the fags, only drink on Saturdays and live on potatoes and lentils. I've done it before, it doesn't bother me.'

'Don't overreact, it's nothing major. Nothing I can't work out.' He lit a cigarette. 'Why do we need petroleum?'

'To heat the house.'

'Of course.' He coughed disgustingly, thought about putting out his cigarette, thought again, and battled on.

His mobile rang. On a Sunday?

'Hi, sport,' said Derrek no longer Junior.

'It's Sunday,' said Stirling.

'Apologies and all that but I thought you should be one of the first to know. Peter and Gareth confirmed on Thursday that on matters sportive I'm the head honcho.'

'Congratulations.'

'Obviously it won't be easy to fill the Big Fella's shoes.'

'Obviously.'

'But I've some ideas of my own to bring to the table.'

'Such as?'

'Top priority is I want all my boys to watch more live sport.'

'More live sport?'

'Yeah, say it's Tuesday night and you have nothing urgent to do then why not get yourself off to a game?'

'But no one wants to read a match report of last Tuesday's game on a Sunday.'

'I'm not talking match reports, I'm talking research. I want my team to be out there, unearthing stories and watching football. You know Rob Parsons took in 178 live games last season?'

'But that's over four a week.'

'Very do-able the way the fixture schedule currently stacks up.'

'But . . .'

'Now, at your age, Jimmy, I don't expect you to rack up those kinds of figures. So I've allocated you a target of a ton.'

'A ton?'

'That's a hundred.'

'I know what it is.'

'A nice 'n' easy hundred games should have you in perfect fettle for the World Cup.'

'What World Cup?'

'Jimmy, hell-o, JapKorea 2002, only the greatest show on earth.'

'That World Cup.'

'No cheating, either. I expect to see programmes from all the matches you visit.'

'Reclaimable on expenses.'

'They're only a couple of quid, Jimmy.'

'Multiplied by a hundred.'

'We'll see. Moving on, I want the new regime to start with a bang, so it's all hands to the pump next week and let's see if we can produce a fuck-off Prem preview to fuck off all the Prem previews ever produced.'

'Sounds fun.'

'And, as a matter of some urgency, we need to find a new Phil Davies.'

'Another one.'

'Yeah, the tosspot's agent rang me to say his client's been offered better terms and conditions elsewhere. Non-negotiable.'

'Not a complete surprise.'

'I dunno, Jimmy. You give people their break, provide them with a pedestal and they turn round and shit on your doorstep. It's a bad business.'

'That it is.'

'Can't chat all day. Remind me to buy you a curry next time you're up in the smoke. Ciao.'

Ciao, yourself. The World Cup. The World fucking Cup.

'How's work?' asked B.

'Don't ask,' said Stirling.

Stirling wasn't up to date when it came to sports kit, but he had done his best: a Fred Perry shirt, baggy off-white shorts, Dunlop Green Flash gym shoes. He stood outside the Bungay Sports & Leisure centre, volleying flies with his catgut-strung Grays squash racket, waiting to play against Bella. Or should that be 'with' Bella? A car horn hooted. If he'd been driving the red car he would automatically have assumed he was doing something wrong. But he was on the pavement, making quite a fool of himself swatting flies. The horn hooted again. There was only one other car in the car park. A green sporty executive number with a woman in the front making 'What to do?' gestures. Bella. She must have locked herself in. He wandered over.

She opened the door for him. Wrong again.

'Hi, Bella.'

'What are you wearing?'

'Squash kit.'

'Why?'

It was like talking to Derrek Junior. 'In order to play . . .'

'Oh, Jimmy, you didn't really think we were going to play squash? How old are you?'

'Forty. Three days ago.'

'How long have you been married?'

'Ten, eleven years.'

'You've never done this before, have you?'

'Sat in a car, in squash kit, discussing the length of my marriage. No.'

'Very funny, Jimmy.' She started reversing the car. 'Come on, we'd better go somewhere more suitable.'

The car park was deserted. But what did he know?

'Can I smoke?'

'Of course.'

Did he really think they were going to play squash? It was a good question. And one he had considered at length. In realistic moments he had decided that playing squash was exactly, and the only, thing they were going to do. At more fanciful times he had imagined that a sweaty game of squash with plenty of huffing and puffing and occasional, and increasingly not so accidental, body contact might be a prelude to some pretty sensational sex. But even at his most carried away he had never envisioned squash playing no part whatsoever in the proceedings. That's why he'd spent the whole of Monday looking for his racket. He should probably say something.

'Big car.'

'It's just a run-around but it does the job.' She attacked a blind corner at a confident 60 mph. Stirling always hesitated before using the word ironic, but no other word would describe him being found dead wearing squash kit. And quite a few other words spoken about the fact that his body was found in the middle of nowhere next to someone else's wife who was dressed in a jumper dress, stockings, he presumed, and ankle-length stiletto boots. Normally he didn't go for small voluptuous women. Normally he didn't go for any women. But Bella was very much on the sexy side of raddled. And, Christ, her tits were big. Which again normally he didn't go for but . . .

'Nearly there.'

'Where?'

'For me to know and you to find out.'

He lit another cigarette.

'Relax, Jimmy, you're making me nervous.'

'I am relaxed. I just like smoking.'

They pulled into the overspill car park behind a pub.

'We should be OK here,' said Bella. She wasn't wrong. It was Stirling's pub. No one ever came here, despite the magnificent extravagance of the overspill car park.

'Do you wanna dog?' asked Bella.

'You sound like my wife.'

'Your wife?'

'B's always banging on at me to buy the twins a dog.'

'Jimmy, I'm not talking about fucking animals, I am talking about making out in car parks. An activity known as dogging.'

'Right. Sorry. Yes. I tell you what, can I buy you a drink?'

'I'm just a girl who can't say no.'

Stirling's barmaid was on duty. The least he could do was offer an explanation for his extraordinary clothes.

'Just been playing squash.'

'That's interesting,' said the barmaid. She looked past his shoulder at Bella. 'Who with?'

'On my own, getting in a bit of practice. I'll have a pint of . . .'

'Adnams,' said the barmaid.

'Yes and . . . Bella?'

'Spritzer, please, sweetheart.'

Sweetheart, thought Stirling, dumbfounded.

Spritzer, thought the barmaid, confounded.

'Or, as it is probably known locally, a white wine and soda,' said Bella.

'In the same glass,' added Stirling.

Forgoing his usual seat with the view of the cash-point machine, he escorted Bella to the back.

'I've never actually been inside a pub. It's really quite horrible.'

'The beer's fine. Never a queue at the bar.'

'But what about the decor?'

'Not the kind of thing I notice.'

'Well, take a look now.'

He did as he was told.

'And?'

'Do you do a lot of dogging?'

'What an impertinent question.'

'Forgive me, all this dogging talk has thrown me. It's all a bit new to me.'

She stared into his eyes. Stirling finished his pint.

'Why don't we settle for a guilt-free fuck?'

'A guilt-free fuck. Yes. Another drink?'

He checked for signs that the barmaid – he must ask her her name one day, this was ridiculous – had overheard Bella's offer. She hadn't appeared to. But how could you tell? Maybe it happened all the time. Maybe the Norfolk fast set met here whenever Stirling wasn't sitting on his own in the corner. To be on the safe side he offered to buy her a drink. She accepted a spritzer.

Back at the table Bella was pouting.

'If you don't fancy me, just say.'

'No, not at all. You're quite the sexiest woman I've met in Norfolk . . . and Suffolk . . .'

'Keep going.'

'Apart from my wife.'

'She doesn't need to know.'

'No.'

She leaned over and kissed him on the lips. Stirling kissed her back, keeping one eye on the barmaid's back and another on the front door. They disengaged, he reached for his cigarettes.

'You're not ready, are you?'

'No.'

'Text me when you are.' And knocking back her spritzer in one, she turned and sashayed out of the door.

'What an arse,' thought Stirling.

'I don't mean to be nosy but,' said Cedric, 'are you a regular at The Hare and Greyhound? If you know what I mean?'

'More an occasional.'

'And, stop me if I'm boring you, but how come you're in Never Pullham and your car's in Bungay when I'm the only cabbie on duty tonight?'

'Simple. I played squash with my friend. I do have friends. And then he gave me a lift to the pub so we could enjoy a few post-match drinks and it would have been a waste of petrol if we had both driven and then . . .'

'He forgot all about you.'

'No. His bleeper went off and he had to answer an emergency call. Heart-attack near Thetford.'

'Doctor, is he?'

'No, he's a fucking vet.'

'Language.'

'Yes, he's a doctor.'

'I'm looking for a new doctor. The one I've got at the moment keeps giving me these pills which make me ever so drowsy. You couldn't give me his name, could you?'

'I just call him Doc.'

'Good friend, is he?'

'How was the squash?' asked B.

'Fine.'

'Did you win?'

'Yeah, of course, but it wasn't a bad game.'

'And how was the Queen of Bungay?'

'Ohh, you know, Queen of Bungayish.'

'Go for a drink afterwards?'

'Just a quick one.'

'I think she might fancy you.'

'Don't be ridiculous. I mean, look at me. What would you like for supper?'

'I've eaten, thanks.'

He made himself some cheese on toast and joined B in front of *Midsomer Murders*. It really was time they stopped watching so much television. B was asleep before the second murder. Stirling stuck it out. Christ, he felt horny. Carefully waking his wife, he led her upstairs.

On average B felt like sex once a month. It was the flipside of her period, as it were, when she became so randy she'd sleep with anyone. Against all rules of probability it had been Stirling's misfortune to be away on that particular night for longer than he cared to remember. But all losing streaks eventually come to an end. After some perfunctory foreplay and a predictably wrong call on the condom they were soon into their stride, with Stirling mumbling away at some fantasy about B being fucked by someone else. Perhaps these things went in cycles. Seven months fucking each other followed by seven years imagining you were fucking someone else, followed by seven years imagining your partner was fucking someone else followed by . . . they both came promptly. Neither had any semblance of patience and both preferred to complete matters before boredom kicked in. Their joint record dated from a lazy afternoon watching women's tennis at Roland Garros when they had rushed to the bedroom with the score at 15–30 and returned to find it was deuce in the same game.

Four in the morning again. There was no point in Stirling lying there pretending he was about to drop back to sleep. He put on a dressing-gown, went up to the attic and checked his e-mails. Seconds later, he put 'dogging' into google.co.uk. There were over 16,000 matches, specifically:

'Dogging UK: The UK's No 1 Dogging Site. For lovers of outdoor fun and frolics in and around cars, an activity known as Dogging. R U Ready 2 DOG?'

Stirling pressed Enter.

'Dogging is the fastest-growing craze in the UK. All over the country, couples who like to watch or be watched are dogging in car parks and wooded areas, and on nudist beaches. R U Ready 2 DOG?'

Stirling pressed Enter. His screen filled with thumbnail pictures of scarcely dressed women disporting themselves in the back of cars. In one of them a man with his tracksuit bottoms round his ankles was being given hand relief while another quite elderly man waited his turn or watched or wondered what the hell the world was coming to. None of the three participants were conventionally good-looking.

'To find dogging sites in your area select a county from the list below.' Stirling selected Norfolk. 'Norwich, Lowestoft, Holkham, Great Yarmouth and Never Pullham.' Stirling selected Never Pullham. 'The Hare and Greyhound, on the outskirts of Never Pullham. 100 yards past the Hardware shop if you're driving from Beccles. The overspill car park is a great place for dogging. No problems with police or landlord, both of whom are regular visitors. Closed on Mondays.'

He was aware you should expect the unexpected but who would have thought that the people of Never Pulham, such a conventional lot, were preoccupied with fucking each other into next week, cheered on by their neighbours, in the overspill car park of The Hare and Greyhound. Should he trade up, get some leather seats? He should certainly buy a new car radio. All those evenings staring out at the cash-point machine when he should have been turned the other way.

He added the page to his list of favourites. It went straight to the top, there being no other entries.

11

Stirling sat in the lounge bar of the Travel Lodge slap bang in the centre of Inverness. The footballer he had been intending to interview was now three hours and eighteen minutes late, so he went to the bar, put another pint on room service and started to think about what he might ask him. He would have to open with a few obligatory questions about the phone company, as that was one of the conditions on which Derrek had accepted the interview on his behalf. Then he might as well follow up with the World Cup, as if anyone cared. Perhaps, what it was like to play under the Mighty Sven – boring Swedish twat. Or grill him on his career highlight, which would inevitably be receiving an OBE from the Queen or some such yawning nonsense.

Before he was halfway through his fifth pint, and just as he was wiping some ash off what he now realised was an exceptionally moth-eaten jumper, the entourage appeared. In the middle, Frankie Sober, England regular and multi-medal winner – although not with England, obviously, dressed in a suit and more dapper than usual. On his right, his agent, dressed smart casual, a man whose name Stirling could never remember, which rarely mattered because he always ignored Stirling if there was anyone else in the room. On his left, a whippy blonde, presumably from the phone company, dressed like a tart.

'Jimmy,' said the agent.

'Big fella.'

'Meet Frankie and Roxanne.'

He shook their hands. 'Drink, anyone?'

'I'll get them,' said the agent. 'Mineral waters, everyone?'

Stirling looked at his glass. 'A pint, thanks. Import.'

'We were expecting Rob Parsons,' said the blonde.

'He's ill.'

'Shame, such an exciting talent.'

'Yeah, well, shit happens. Anyone mind if I smoke?'

'I'd rather you didn't,' said the blonde.

Fucking PRs. 'Fine. So, Frankie, let's get the phone business out of the way first. Just how good is your new mobile?'

'It's the best . . .'

'Aren't you going to use a dictaphone?' asked the blonde.

What was wrong with the woman? 'I wasn't planning to. It's not exactly Watergate, just a cosy chat about mobiles and football. I should be able to record it all with my short . . . in my notebook. If Frankie speaks slowly.'

'Do you mind if I use one?' said the PR.

'If I can smoke.'

The PR looked confused.

'Joke. Go ahead. Be my guest. Great. Frankie, tell me a bit about your phone.'

'It's . . . the . . . best.'

'You can go a bit quicker than that, for Christ's sake.'

'Sorry?' said Frankie.

'Sorry!' said the PR.

'Sorry,' said Stirling. 'Long wait.'

'We're early,' said the blonde.

Perhaps they were.

'Everything cushty,' said the returning agent, bearing mineral water and a much-needed pint.

Cushty – God in heaven. Stirling ploughed on.

'No problems with reception. I don't know about you but I find that where I live, which is Norfolk, would you believe, I often have real difficulty getting a signal and sometimes have to go out to the field – we own a field or paddock or whatever – just to get my messages. Which is a real pain, I can tell you.'

The agent said 'Yup'. The blonde stared at the dictaphone. Stirling finished his pint and manoeuvred the next one into position. He had to stop talking about himself in interviews. No one was interested.

Frankie, the pros' pro, was not deflected from the job he was paid handsomely to do. 'No probs with reception. Even on the recent trip to Albania.'

'Even in Albania,' echoed Stirling, making a note. 'What about that text-messaging stuff?'

'Yeah, it's got all the mod cons. Predictatext and fasttext and . . .'

'Teletext,' said Stirling, chuckling.

'Not yet,' said the blonde, taking him seriously. 'But next year's model will enable you to tap into your home computer or any other information source from wherever you are in the world, won't it, babes?'

Had the PR no shame?

'Yeah, I can't wait,' enthused Frankie.

Stirling had arrived at the outer reaches of his expertise when it came to mobile phones, but there would be 2,000

words to write. He fell back on his old standby – *Shoot* magazine interviews from the Seventies. Favourite mobile? Favourite
fascia? Favourite ring-tone? Most memorable text message?
Longest call? Which footballer's mobile do you most admire?
Most irritating ring-tone in the modern game?

All these and more questions were, despite frequent over-
talking from the PR, politely answered by Frankie Sober while
Stirling jollied things along with a few choice anecdotes and
stories. The blonde's dictaphone tape ran out with a click. The
wall-eyed agent was stirred by the alarm on his mobile going
off.

'One more question, Jimmy, and that's your lot.'

'But . . . big fella.'

'People to see. Faces to meet.'

Shit. He had forgotten to ask anything about football. Derrek
would crucify him. Quick. His interviewee was preparing to
leave the building. Quick, quick, quick.

'Frankie, last question, erm, who, who, who in the world
would you most like to text?'

'The Pope,' said Frankie.

'Lovely.'

Stirling shuffled up to the bar, ordered the most expensive
bottle of red, scanned the menu for something other than
goujons and returned to his seat to jot down anything Frankie
had said which he had failed to note. This, experience had
taught him, was best done when the footballer's aperçus
remained fresh in the mind.

The lounge bar in the Travel Lodge in Southmouth was a
comforting replica of the one in Inverness. Stirling was pleased
to see Gerry Pike sitting in what he considered to be his seat.

'Sorry I'm late, Gerry. There was a mix-up at Aberdeen, the train from Edinburgh derailed, nothing happening at Leeds, usual problems approaching Peterborough, Northern Line banjaxed, and, to cap it all, a reduced service to Winchester followed by confusion over connections to the south coast. Can I get you a drink?'

'Mineral water. But we'll have to be quick, I'm meeting my lawyers in twenty minutes.'

The lawyers. Pike's pickle, as Derrek called it. A hugely popular football manager, Gerry had alarmed a few in the game by standing as a BNP candidate in a local council election and then compromised himself on the eve of the vote by being charged with conspiracy to import illegal immigrants. His chairman was standing by him. Everyone knew what that meant.

'Cheers, Jimmy. I can't talk about the case because it's pre *judice* but, off the record, like . . .'

Jimmy closed his notebook, put his pen down, drank his pint.

'There's been one helluva mix-up. All I was trying to do in my own sweet way was to demonstrate how easy it was to get those bloody nig-nogs . . .'

'Weren't they Kosovans, Gerry?'

'Precisely, Jim. And I can tell you they are entering the country for fun at the moment. No one bats an eye. And at fifty quid a head with a hundred odd crammed in a coach there's some serious money to be made. Not quite football money but getting there. And I was trying to highlight this, bring the issue into the general domain, get some campaign off the ground, and it's me who ends up down the nick. I ask you.'

'British justice.'

'Don't go there, Jim. I tell you, I blame the Lib Dems.'

'The Lib Dems?'

'Pinko homosexualists, the lot of them. And it can't exactly be entirely coincidental that my mug appears on the front page of the *Echo* on the same evening that the punters are coming home to vote. Without that unwelcome publicity we would have run 'em darn close.'

'As it was you got how many votes?'

'Seven.'

'Seven hundred?'

'Seven. The turn-out was low but, yes, it was unforgivable.'

'Well . . .'

'Nasty business, politics. You try to put something back into society which, as you know, Jim, is not something many in the game can be arsed to do – it's all me, me, me with the current mob – and then they turn round and hit you with a trumped-up conspiracy number. Are they taking the piss, are they?'

'When's the trial date?'

'That's what we're trying to delay, isn't it? Take the sting out of proceedings. Give it some low profile. Anyhow, football, that's what we're here for, after all.'

'Big season for you, Gerry?'

'Yeah, well, to be frank, every season's a big one when you reach my age, Jim.'

'Number one priority – avoiding the drop?'

'No, Jim, we may be a small club compared to your Man Us and Arsenals but there's no point being in the Prem if you can't harbour European ambitions.'

'UEFA Cup?'

'Yeah, that's about the mark. The Worthington Cup looks very winnable this year.'

'Any youngsters exciting you?'

'We've got an exciting crop of youngsters, as always down the Field, and it would be nice to think some of them might break through and establish themselves as Premiership regulars in the coming season, certainly.'

'Names?'

'Not off the top of my head, Jimmy. And it would be verging on the individious to start singling people out. Wouldn't it?'

'Absolutely.'

'That enough?'

'More than enough, Gerry.'

'Great. I'd appreciate it if you didn't mention the trial. What with the low profile and everything?'

'Not a problem.'

'Good man.'

You never lose it, thought Stirling. Time for a drink.

'Yes, Derrek. Yes, Derrek. I know, Derrek. They'll be with you within the half-hour.'

'You said that two hours ago.'

'Forty minutes, then.'

'Your dick's on the line here, sonny. Forty minutes or I'm eating it for breakfast.'

'Fine.'

Stirling could actually see Derrek put the phone down. He was ten yards away sitting in his small office: a fat man in a little bubble. He finished off his expenses form – a post-forty resolution – and then gave his attention to his computer. He had two files open on the screen, one titled Frankie Sober, the other Gerry Pike, and he had a notebook open either side of the keyboard. In one he had written 'Albania', 'Walnut' and

'Pope'. In the other, 'every season's a big one when you get to my age, Jim' and 'fascist twat'. Not an abundance of material to work upon, but sufficient. He got to work, typing in first one file then the other like an underprepared examinee trying to dash off two extempore essays before the invigilator said pens down. By the time he reached for the *Oxford Book of Quotations* he was flying.

The Butt was empty.

'Where's Terry?' Stirling asked David.

'Hospital.'

'Who hit him?'

'No one. His liver collapsed. Just over there, actually.' David pointed to the broken banquette. 'It was quite dramatic. One minute he was listening to Ian, the next he was writhing on the floor in agony.'

'Ian can do that to you.'

'He's OK, apparently, but he won't be able to drink for a while.'

'How long?'

'Three months.'

'Christ, that'll put a dent in your takings.'

'What with you in East Anglia, Terry in intensive care, and no young drinkers coming through, it's a grim time to be a publican.'

Stirling's mobile rang, reminding him to switch it off. He took a seat far away from where Terry had come to grief. Three quick pints, sleep on the train, and he'd be home for supper.

'Phone, Jimmy?'

'Who is it?'

'The living Derrek.'

'Tell him I'm not here.'

'Jimmy. Where else could you possibly be?'

He took the call.

'I knew I'd find you in the pub.'

'No shit, Inspector Barnaby.'

'Who?'

'Inspector Barnaby. *Midsomer Murders*. John Nettles.'

'Your pieces, Jimmy.'

Here we go. The important thing was to stand up to the bastards.

'They're crap.'

'They're genius.'

'Crap.'

'Genius.'

'Crap.'

'Genius.'

'Crap.'

'This argument is reductive.'

'I don't care what it is, the fact of the matter is that these two pieces are the worst I've seen in my editorship.'

'It's only been a week.'

'Where are the quotes?'

'I used them sparingly. No point overloading a piece with quotes. That would be typing not writing.'

'Who are these Kosovans Pikey's meant to have picked up on the cheap? There's no mention of them on the club web-site.'

'Lose them, Del, I must have been misinformed.'

'And are you taking the piss or what? Both these pieces start exactly the same way with some nonsense about fucking Travel Lodges and quotes from a bloke called Tacitus who you don't even give a first name to even though we've all told you a million fucking times that Christian names are used on first mention and never again.'

'Cornelius.'

'Cornelius?'

'Cornelius Tacitus.'

'Can you spell that for me?'

'C.O.R.N.E.L.I.U.S. The point is, Derrek, that I made the introductions similar in an attempt in my own sweet way to subtly underline that whether you are an England star or a crim, when it comes to football everything's the same. Everything changes except for football. Perhaps it doesn't work.'

'Too right it doesn't work. Usually I'd demand complete rewrites but everyone's screaming at me for the pages so this time I'm going to have to let them through. But the truth of the matter is, Jimmy, you've let me down, you've let yourself down and you've let the paper's Premiership pull-out down.'

'Sorry.'

'That's not good enough, sonny. You're benched vis-à-vis interviews, your games per season target is upped to 120, and if your match report doesn't really sing tomorrow you can consider yourself verbally warned. Thanking you.'

Match report? What match report? There were no matches. That was why they'd worked their balls off producing a Premiership preview: because the matches didn't start until next Saturday. Idiot.

B was away flying with Hansie, Nancy was on his laptop, and Stirling was watching Charlie on the PlayStation, bonding with his only son.

'Dadda, you know at school during main break . . .'

'You don't have to worry about school, darling, it's the middle of the summer holidays.'

'I know, but when we go back to school and it's main break I think I'm going to feel a bit lonely.'

'But Nancy's always there.'

'Yes, I know, but the thing is I want to play imaginary games with more people and there's no one else at school who will play imaginary games.'

'Esme?'

'She thinks she's a teenager, now.'

'Well, she is ten.'

'I don't want to be a teenager, Dadda.'

'Who does?'

'Were you a teenager?'

'A long time ago.'

'What did you do?'

'I don't know, really. School. Uncle Graham was quite a bit younger so we didn't play much. I went to a lot of sport with Papa . . .' He hesitated, as he always did when talking about his father with his son.

'The phone's ringing. I'll get it . . . Charlie speaking . . . Yes . . . I'll just get him . . . It's for you, Dadda.'

'Hi.'

'Jimmy, Kath here. We need eight hundred words on the whistle as a runner plus teams.'

'What are you talking about, Kath?'

'Norwich v Stockport. We arranged it on Thursday, don't you remember?'

'Yes, yes, of course.'

'Is it a problem?'

He looked at the clock. Quarter to two. Plenty of time. 'No. Thanks, Kath.'

Where was his computer, his mobile, a pen? What was he going to do with the children? Children weren't welcome in press boxes other than the little boys who week in week out regularly packed them.

'Charlie, where's Nancy?'

'On the computer.'

'Come on. Get a jumper or something, we're going to the football.'

'I hate football, Dad.'

'I know, but sometimes we have to do things we don't like.' He hurried upstairs. 'Nancy, off the computer, we're going to the football.'

'I hate football, Dad.'

'I know, I know, I know, but I have to go to work and I can't leave you here on your own.'

Downstairs Charlie could be heard crying. Nancy started crying. He couldn't bear his children crying. He picked up a resistant Nancy and bundled her downstairs. Charlie, with scrunched face, said through his tears, 'But Dadda, you promised.'

'What did I promise?'

'That you'd play an imagination game with us.'

'You did, Dadda,' said Nancy, no longer crying now that she sensed an out.

'And grown-ups should never break . . .'

'Promises.'

'How about spending an afternoon with Esme?'

'She's away,' said Nancy.

'OK, then, how about . . .'

'There is no one else, Dadda,' said Charlie.

'Then you'll just have to come with me.'

They both started crying again.

'I'm going into the field for five minutes. When I'm back I want you both ready.'

'I'm coming with you,' said Nancy, who needed a parent within twenty yards of her at all times.

'And I'm coming with you,' said Charlie, who needed to be within twenty yards of Nancy at all times.

'This is ridiculous,' said Stirling, stomping out on to his property. 'If you come to the football I'll take you to Pizza Express afterwards.'

'No.'

'No.'

'A film. *Bug's Life* or something.'

'No.'

'No.'

'So what are we going to do?'

'Play an imagination game,' said Charlie.

'OK, we'll play an imagination game.'

'I love you, Dadda,' said his son, grabbing one thigh.

'I love you, Dadda,' said his daughter, grabbing the other.

'And, first of all, we'll play my imagination game. Into the red car, both of you.' They merrily did as they were told. Stirling sat in the driver's seat and switched his mobile on. 'Right, when I say "Go" I want you both to start crying as loud as you would if you were forced to watch a football match with You Know Who sitting on your left and the entire Malfoy family on your right.' He lit a fag, dialled Derrek's number, pressed call, and said 'Go'. The racket was unbeliev-able. Fuck, they were good.

'Del, can you hear me?'

'What?'

'It's Jimmy here?'

'What's that noise, for fuck's sake?'

'You're not going to believe this, Del, but I've just totalled the car.'

'You've what?'

'I've totalled the car,' he screamed.

'I heard you the first time. That noise. How many children have you maimed?'

'None. That's Charlie and Nancy. They're in shock. Anyway, I won't be able to cover the game.'

'Why the fuck not? Just get in a fucking cab.'

'But what about the kids?'

'Let their mother look after them.'

'She's not here.'

'Take them with you, then.'

'But . . .'

'End of story.'

The line went dead.

'Right, kids, this time less of the screaming. I need a whimper and keening from you, Charlie, as if you were locked in separate cells in Azkaban. And from you, Nancy, complete silence.'

He hit redial.

'Sport.'

'Derrek, the situation is deteriorating. Charlie looks as if he might be developing whiplash and Nancy's gone very pale and horribly quiet. Hang on a sec. I'm not sure she's breathing, Del.'

'Get the cabbie to drop them off at Casualty on your way to the ground, then.'

'But . . .'

'Norwich does have a hospital, doesn't it?'

'Yes.'

'And I have a paper to run.'

'Can we talk now?' asked Nancy.

'Yes.'

'This is a brilliant game, Dadda,' said Charlie.

'We haven't won yet. The big bad boss isn't going to fall for the kids in peril line. Not when he needs to fill a space with Norwich v Stockport. Which means I'd better take a different tack.' He looked at his adoring children in the back. 'When I put a finger in the air I want you both to make police car siren sounds.'

'Del, good and bad news. The good news is that the kids are fine. Nancy is breathing again and Charlie's whiplash may not be as bad as first feared.'

'Get to the point, Jimmy.'

'The bad news is that a big green car skidded trying to avoid me straight into a white car which in turn jack-knifed into a blue car with the knock-on effect that there was an astonishing pile-up involving cars of many colours. We're talking a major traffic incident, here, Derrek. The A143 could be closed for months.'

'The A143 can go fuck itself. Stop wasting my time and get in a cab.'

'Whatever you say. It might be construed as leaving the scene of an accident but Norwich v Stockport waits for no man.' He raised his finger.

'Nee-nar, nee-nar, nee-nar.'

'Nee-nar, nee-nar, nee-nar.'

'Talk about crap luck. Can you hear that, Del?'

'What?'

'Police. Everywhere. Un-hunh. People are pointing the finger at me. I'm going to have to go, Del. I'll get back to you.' He closed out the call. 'Right, back to the house, kids, and under no circumstances is anyone to answer the phone.'

He put the kids to bed, three and a half pages of *Watership Down* more than putting them to sleep. Where the hell was B? He'd better reconnect the phone. It rang immediately. Amazing.

'Darling.'

'Less of the darling, Jimmy. Have you got tomorrow's *News of the World*?'

'Thanks for the how are you. I'm in Norfolk, Derrek, recovering from a very stressful day. I'll be lucky if I get tomorrow's *News of the World* tomorrow.'

'There's a World Exclusive we need to follow up. Did Frankie Sober say anything about Nell McAndrew?'

'Who's Nell McAndrew?'

'Fucking hell, Jimmy, she's only been *FHM*'s Rear of the Year three times on the trot.'

'Describe her.'

'36–26–34.'

'Terrific. Is she blonde?'

'Yes.'

'Whippy?'

'What do you mean, whippy?'

'It's difficult to explain. How tall is she?'

'How the hell am I meant to know that?'

'You know her bust size.'

'Hang on . . . Anyone know how tall Nell McAndrew is? Five eight, cheers. Five eight, Jimmy.'

'I can't be certain but they may have been together in Inverness when I interviewed Frankie. There was this tallish blondish woman sitting next to him and I definitely remember her calling him "babes".'

'You were sitting opposite Nell McAndrew and you didn't know it?'

'I assumed she was the fucking PR from the phone company, didn't I?'

'You slay me, Jimmy. How you get away with calling yourself a journalist I'll never know.'

'If there's nothing else, I'd better get back to *Midsomer Murders*.'

'Hell-o, Jimmy. You're the only man who's seen them together. Even the Screws are relying on sources close to the pair. This is huge, Jim, I'll have a fight on my hands to keep it in sport. You didn't get a picture, did you?'

'I haven't got a camera.'

'No worries. We can scan one in from *FHM*. Twenty pars, Jim, as soon as you can bang it over.'

'What on?'

'Very funny.'

Buggered if he was going to dignify the story by opening up his laptop, he rang copy.

'Name: Jimmy Stirling. Department: Sport, unbelievably. Subject: Frankie and Nell. Headline: Perfect Match. Copy starts "Following months of dogging, sorry, dogged research, the expenditure of much old-fashioned shoe leather, and the playing of a clever hunch we can now exclusively and globally reveal that Frankie Sober and the 36–26–34 Nell McAndrew are a . . . what's the word for two celebrities going out together?

. . . item, great, thanks. New paragraph. Unassisted, I tracked them down last week to an exclusive five-star hotel and retreat buried in the nethermost Highlands of Scotland. So deep is their love, they didn't even bother to deny it. New paragraph. Instead, the three-times winner of the Premiership and the three-times winner of the prestigious *FHM* Rear of the Year trophy opened their hearts to your correspondent. This time, one couldn't help feeling, it's for real. New paragraph. So, what is the new girlfriend of England's first-choice penalty-taker really like? New paragraph. First, she is fanatically opposed to smoking. Which can only be an advantage in the modern game with its emphases on speed and fitness. New paragraph. Second, the 5 foot 8 inch bombshell was in no way cowed by the great man's presence or, indeed, mine. As we chatted on a diverse range of subjects open bracket see the Big Interview on page question mark of the Premiership pull-out close bracket McAndrew was not slow to proffer an opinion. If anything, she talked too much. In short, Sober's got his work cut out. New paragraph. Third, it would be a mistake to leap to the conclusion that because McAndrew has been fêted in *FHM*, a magazine which, I imagine, derives the majority of its readership from young males incarcerated in one institution or another, she is a dumb bimbo. Far from it. Her knowledge of, to take a subject out of thin air, mobile phones is, quite simply, extraordinary. New paragraph. It is, of course, far too early to tell what implications this shock development will have for England's chances of qualifying for next year's World Cup in Japan and South Korea. New paragraph. Let us instead glory in young love. Summer is here.' He looked out of the window. 'The tulips are in full bloom. And Frankie Sober has found someone to call him open quote babes close quote. End of copy.'

It was short, but it would do. As long as you were nice about people they never complained. He poured himself a substantial drink and went back to *Midsomer Murders*. Quite a lot had happened while he'd been gone, not least the unexplained, as yet, murder of Stirling's two chief suspects. He struggled to get back on top of the plot. The phone rang.

'Darling.'

'Babes.'

It wasn't B, it was the living Del.

'Magnificent effort, Jimmy. You may be a cunt but you're my cunt. Top job.'

Pondering this, and other matters, Stirling went to bed alone, dropping in on Charlie and Nancy on the way. As ever they were in the same bed: cheek to cheek, holding hands, happy, asleep. He sat on the edge of the bed for a while and achieved some sort of calm. For them, if not for himself, he would have to pull things round.

12

Stirling hid in the corner of the multi-media room at Highbury, worrying. It had been a catastrophic week.

At work, he was being sued by two people for his ill-judged front-page exclusive and big interview. Nell McAndrew was claiming that she had never been to Scotland let alone Inverness; further claiming that she had never met Frankie Sober let alone Jimmy Stirling; and further further claiming that she would never call anyone 'babes'. The PR, meanwhile, was contending through her lawyers that she was neither stroppy nor stupid nor particularly ambitious. Worse she had sent copies of her tape of the interview to the editor, deputy editor and sports editor. Peter had questioned his interviewing technique, asking if it was really necessary to talk quite so much about oneself. Gareth had asked if he'd been drunk. Derrek had told him that any old fuckwit knew that Nell McAndrew didn't have an Australian accent. The upshot of all of which had been a verbal warning and a written invitation from the company psychiatrist.

At home, B had said nothing about her latest flying lesson from Hansie. But, then again, Stirling hadn't exactly kept her up to date with his career prospects. Worst of all, in seventeen minutes another football season was about to begin. He stared at the complimentary vol-au-vents. Was he bored enough to eat one?

'Hello, dear boy, long time no see.' An elderly breathless slip of a man was crouched next to Stirling hanging on to the desk for balance and holding a plastic bag in which something clanked.

'Mr Pink. Christ, I haven't seen you since the Football Writers' dinner.'

'Not many people have, dear thing. One minute I was in fine voice at the Royal Lancaster, the next I found myself billeted in a curious residence in Rottingdean. It's taken three months to engineer an escape.'

'Good to have you back.'

'From bedlam to ship of fools. I'm not sure which is the more congenial.'

'Grim, isn't it? Boredom doesn't come into it. A form of Chinese Water Torture – Death by Football.'

'Precisely. Neither heaven nor hell but an everlasting purgatory. Fortunately, there is another option if you care to follow me.'

The Tarantubbies sniggered as the pair shambled past them and out of the media centre. Within five minutes, despite frequent stops for Pink to catch his breath, they were outside the stadium. Within ten they were seated at the bar of Scuffles, yet another of Pink's clubs. It had a Norfolkian charm – that is to say it was empty. It also had a barman and a TV screen showing Sky Sports Soccer Saturday.

'All we have to do is sit here,' Pink explained, 'and watch the tube. They give you everything these days: team news, time of goals and manner in which they were scored, entertaining incidents, managers' interviews, the whole caboodle. It is then a moment's work to ring the office and relay everything to our desk-bound inferiors.'

'So simple, so easy. You don't even need to leave home,' said Stirling.

'Strictly not, but it's nice to get out once in a while and they serve a cheerful enough red here. Fredrico?'

Hats off to Murdoch. This was the way to cover football, sitting in an armchair with a bottle of claret to hand and taking a note whenever Rodney Marsh appeared on the screen. The man was a buffoon but at least he took a passing interest in what he was watching. Every so often a relevant statistic scrolled across the screen, some of which Stirling registered. By the end he was well placed to file a report that was both informative and accurate, exactly the kind of response you would expect from a serious journalist attempting to put a double libel action behind him. Pink, his work done, snoozed. Stirling couldn't help but feel some affection for the old fucker despite him being doubly responsible for his present predicament. As a sports-crazed adolescent Stirling had read everything Pink had written. His high-flown style, flamboyant phrasing and not bad jokes had, more than anything, convinced people that football writing might have some merit. Now his imitators were legion. Halfwits clunking out overblown prose, forever ascribing great import to the trivial, and on the infinitesimally few occasions when football intruded on real life determinedly taking the wrong line. Without Pink's influence, Stirling would never have become a football writer. Without Pink's influence, it might have been a bearable job to do. He briefly thought about waking Pink up to explain the disastrous impact he had unwittingly had on Stirling's life. But he'd probably only start singing Gilbert & Sullivan.

Terry didn't look too clever. Nor, to be fair, did anyone else in the intensive care (renal) unit at St Mary's. In particular, the thing in the far corner who appeared to have an entirely yellow head.

'How are you bearing up?'

'Better than you'd think. The strip-lighting's pretty unforgiving in this ward. I look less ill in the smoking room. Or so I'm told.'

'You look healthier than that, erm, is it a bloke, over in the corner.'

'I'm not sure. It was wheeled in while I was out having a smoke so I didn't catch what it was wearing and since then it hasn't budged or even twitched. Fucking frightening shade of yellow, whatever it is.'

'It seems rude to stare,' said Stirling, staring.

'How are you?'

'Fucked.'

'Not the living Derrek's golden boy.'

'Not exactly. He's already verbally warned me, there's some libel nonsense going on, I can't stop talking about myself in interviews, I find it difficult to remember anything after seven o'clock at night, I may be drinking too much.'

'That bad. How are B and the kids?'

'Twins fine. B probably having an affair.'

'Shit, who with?'

'Bella's husband.'

'Norfolk swings. Are you . . .'

'No. We tried to play squash. It didn't work out.'

'Have you talked to her?'

'She said to text her if I wanted to take things further.'

'That doesn't sound great, given your lack of skill as a texter.'

'Probably for the best.'

'Where are you living?'

'At home with B, of course. We're getting on fine, still talking, just not about what she gets up to when she goes flying with Hansie.'

'He's South African?'

'Irritatingly.'

'Probably good in bed, then.'

'Inevitably.'

His friend had nearly died listening to Ian, and Stirling was talking about himself. He had to get a grip.

'Has Ian come to visit?'

'Regularly. He still feels terribly guilty.'

'It was hardly his fault. I know he's dull, but not so dull he can collapse a liver.'

'It fucking was his fault.'

'Come on, Terry . . .'

'It was Ian's idea to start drinking Viagra-pops, a midlife crisis decision if ever there was one. And there's no doubt that it upset my drink rhythms, the doctors have nearly said as much. All that sweet fruity stuff sloshing around in a bellyful of bitter, little wonder my liver called it a day.'

'I'm sure he didn't do it on purpose.'

'I'm not so sure.' Terry really didn't look at all well. Nor had Pink, come to think of it. Stirling tried to remember when he had last looked in the mirror.

'It's odd being sober. I've more time to read but I enjoy it less. People who used to make me laugh after a drink or two now seem to be writing the most convoluted and repetitive stuff. Plod, plod, plod, I have to take everything a sentence at a time. Three hours a day I've been hammering away at last Sunday's paper and I still haven't finished it.'

'Not many do.'

'The thing is I seem to have lost the ability to laugh. I've been mirthless for two weeks, four days, and seventeen minutes.'

'No fun. You'll start drinking again when all this is cleared up, won't you?'

'May not be able to.'

'Christ, I didn't realise it was that bad.'

There wasn't much more Stirling could say.

The babysitter and Stirling took each other equally by surprise. The babysitter had been expecting a glamorous dolled-up woman in knee-high boots. She received a dishevelled, possibly drunk, man wearing shorts, a Clash City Rocker T-shirt and flip-flops. Stirling had been expecting a sleepy wife. He was greeted by a screaming teenager. It took him a while to convince her he was the co-owner of the house, eventually waking the twins, under her supervision, and asking them if he was their father. A fact they, gratifyingly, confirmed.

Boringly, he had spent all his cash on the way home so he had to borrow from the twins' piggy banks and make up the shortfall with an IOU before the babysitter would consent to leave the premises.

'Where's Mum?' he asked.

'Out,' said Charlie.

'Who with?'

'Friends,' said Nancy.

'Did she mention a name?'

'No. Just friends,' said Charlie.

'No names at all?'

'No.'

'Can we go back to sleep now, Dadda?' asked Charlie.

'Please,' added Nancy.

'Of course. I'll be in the kitchen, TV room, blue loo, bed. Night, darlings.'

There must be some evidence somewhere. B wouldn't go out without leaving a contact number. Would she? No. Writ large on the blackboard was a number he equivocally recognised. He made his way through the family address book. No matches. He took the rubber band off his contacts/address book, arrayed the pages on the kitchen table, checked both sides of each page. No matches. It was a most depressing read. Who were all these people? He opened another half-empty bottle. And stared at the numbers on the board. All those sevens meant it had to be a mobile number. Genius. He rested his forehead on the kitchen table, and fell asleep.

They sat speed-reading the Sunday newspapers.

'Sleep is the new sex,' said Stirling.

'Failure is the new success,' said B.

'Adultery is the new Pilates.'

'Brandy is the new whisky.'

'Have you got the Style section?'

She lobbed it over.

The noticeboard had been wiped clean.

Where was his passport? Where was his frigging passport? He was sure he had put it in a safe place; but he'd checked every place he might, imaginably and unimaginably, have considered safe – three, four, five, six times. He had gone through every jacket pocket remorselessly. He had ransacked the kitchen, nearly scalding himself when he took a torch to the inside of the Aga. He had trashed the twins' bedroom and upturned every perfectly ordered toy basket in their playroom. He had peered and poked into every crevice of the red car, collapsed into the driver's seat, smashed his head against the steering wheel, set off the horn and screamed to himself to get his act together. It was too late. He had phoned Kath. She had phoned him back and said there was a final plane to Munich in two and half hours' time. He had told her neither to worry nor tell Derrek.

He co-opted B and the twins on to the search team. As a family they went through the two dozen sweating weeping bin-bags at the back of the building – putting the rubbish out was one of Stirling's responsibilities. They emptied them one by one on to the lawn, which when he had more time he would turn into a croquet venue, creating a mountain of mulch and squelch. Stirling offered to sift through it alone. It was his passport, after all. He stripped naked, donned Marigolds and dived in. Meat grease, discarded pâté, long-gone cream, remnants of porridge, a nearly full family tin of tapioca, and right in the middle a side of salmon which had decayed into thousands of tiny wriggly pale pink worms. They leeched onto his arms, his stomach, his chin and cheeks, his thighs, his dick. He battled on. Attempting to clear his vision with the back of a Marigold he merely succeeded in rubbing squished worms into his right iris and then his left. He emerged screaming and blinking into the daylight. Ahead of him, Hansie was doubled up with laughter over the bonnet of his people carrier.

'Have you got the time?' Stirling asked.

It took an age for the South African to reply.

'One . . . thirty . . .'

Ten minutes, fifteen max. He threw up horribly. Think, think, think. Peeling off the Marigolds he used the non-wormy insides to detach the strands and flecks of vomit hanging from his mouth. Where, where, where? He had checked his Carling freebie overnight bag, hadn't he? Hadn't he? He walked slowly up to the bedroom, unzipped the bag, turned it over. One change of clothes, a toothbrush, a Bic biro, four books. He shook the bag. Nothing. Searched the bag. Nothing. Strip-searched the bag. In the hidden pocket nestled his passport. At last. Seven minutes. Did he have time for a shower? No. But a quick pit-wash might be hygienic. He rubbed soap into his armpits and groin, doused himself with a couple of glasses of water, repacked his overnight bag and walked briskly to his car.

'Bye, everyone,' he said to no one. 'See you Sunday night.'

The car started first time. Stansted here we come. The South African's people carrier was blocking his exit. He unwound the window. 'Hansie, you cunt.' No one responded. 'Move your fucking car, yarpie.' Nothing. 'Do I have to do every-thing?' he said to the world as he moved from one car to the other. The keys were in the ignition. He started the engine. It was a manual. Sod it, he wasn't planning to drive it very far. Just out of the gate and out of his way. He stalled. Restarted the engine. Stalled. Fuckfuckfuck. Restarted the engine. Mangled the top-of-the-range people carrier into reverse, pressed down on the accelerator, braked sharply, accelerated gingerly, glanced at his rear-view window mirror, realised he wasn't going to make it, yanked at the steering wheel, went for the brake, hit the accelerator, crunched the right side of the carrier into the left gatepost, stalled, restarted, accelerated, moved his right hand down instead of up, ker-powed the other side of the carrier into the other gatepost, stalled, restarted, reversed, hit a post, stalled, found first gear, accelerated, rehit the other post.

'What in God's name are you doing to my motor?' wailed an apoplectic South African.

'Sorry,' said Stirling, emerging from Richard's car. He ran his hands through his hair, dislodging a few stubborn worms, and considered the damage. The people carrier, caught between a gatepost and a gatepost, was emphatically wedged. No one would be leaving the Priory in a hurry.

'I don't believe you, Jimmy. Why didn't you ask me to move it?'

'I did. Didn't you hear me?'

'We were playing with Charlie and Nancy on the PlayStation.'

'As I said, I'm sorry. Very sorry. But these things happen.'

'Not if you're careful, they don't. Who's going to pay for this mess, Jim?'

'Aren't you insured?'

'Yes, but I wasn't driving.'

'Good point.'

He offered the big South African a cigarette, knowing that he didn't smoke.

'Couldn't you pretend to have been driving, simply for insurance purposes?'

'No one would believe I might drive that amateurishly.'

'No, erm, well, I suppose you'd better borrow my car while I arrange for yours to be fixed.'

He literally turned his nose up at Stirling's car. 'Thank you very little, Jimmy.'

'Dadda, phone,' said Charlie, appearing on the patio with Stirling's mobile.

'Who is it?'

'Some rude man.'

'Hello, Derrek.'

'Hi, Jim. My arse, we're getting excited here in the office. And we're not even there. I can't imagine what the buzz must be like in Munich. It can only be fantastic.'

'Fantastic's the right word, Derrek, I'm just walking out of the arrivals lounge at Munich airport,' he paced the patio, 'and ahead of me I can see thousands, literally thousands, of England fans, waving the flag of St George. It's a great night to be an England football fan, Del.'

'Certainly is. I'd better let you go. Rob's doing the main piece, so if you could bang over a thousand words of mood on the whistle that would be magnifico. Come on you Ing-er-land. Ciao.'

Ignoring Richard, B and the twins, he marched across the patio, up the stairs to his office, and locked the door. It had worked at Highbury, could it work in Munich? He channel-hopped furiously in search of mood. Far below, Richard and B began the unavoidable job of refilling the bin-bags. The twins bounced merrily on the trampoline. At some time in the future he must spend more time with his family.

Thank heaven for British Eurosport. Outbid by higher-profile broadcasters when it came to live rights, they were relying on a commentator in a booth in Paris and a roving reporter on the streets of Munich. No other journalist covering the game would be watching British Eurosport, which meant Stirling had, to all intents and purposes, channel-hopped onto an exclusive. Dutifully, he tapped into the computer the vapid observations of Tony from Maidstone, Phil from Wokingham, and token woman Marsha from Carlisle. In the background, a phalanx of men in baseball caps were standing outside an Irish Theme bar singing:

'No surrender,
No surrender,
To the IRA.'

They encored with:

'The Krauts are on their way to Auschwitz,
Hitler's gonna gas 'em again.'

For the first time in years Stirling started to care about the outcome of a football match. He whacked Haydn's *Kaiser-Hymne* on the CD player. He stood alongside the TV as the German players, manfully and straight-backed, sang the third verse of 'Deutschland über Alles'. When Germany opened the scoring after six minutes he scooted from his chair, prostrated himself in front of his tiny screen and yelled, 'Jancker, you beauty.' How good was this? 'David Seaman, ha, ha, ha. Come on, Germany, take the piss.' 'Let's see some width.' 'Vision.' 'Simple ball.' 'Keep it tight.' 'Trolley back.' 'Kahn. What. Bollocks.' (Germany 1, England 1.) 'OK, lads, steady down.' 'Peddle it.' 'Ferry wide.' 'Park, park, park.' 'Yes. No. You wanker, Deisler.' 'The fucking luck of the English.' 'Immerse yourselves, boys.' 'Trolley, trolley, trolley.' 'Intelligence.' 'Pace ball.' 'Goa . . . how did he save that? Seaman of all people.' 'Construct and prevent. Construct and prevent.' 'Refereee.' 'Careful, wall, careful, wall. Bollocks.' (HT: Germany 1, England 2.)

No matter. There was plenty of time. The Germans always made up a deficit, that was so clichéd it must be true. He took another bottle from the mini-bar, pushed the cork in and spurted some Riesling into his glass.

'Contain and impose. Contain and impose.' 'Mark him, mark, Christ.' (Germany 1, England 3.) 'Keep it stubborn.' 'Lathe him, lathe him, lathe the fucker. Pathetic.' (Germany 1, England 4.) 'Invade, invade, invade . . . Heskey?' (Germany 1, England 5.) 'Fuck this for a game of soldiers.'

On the plus side, the inevitability of the conclusion allowed him an extra fifteen minutes to compile his mood piece. It would have been dishonest for him not to call it as he saw it. To the backdrop of Brahms's *German Requiem*, he rattled off a Teutonic take on what many in his trade would unquestioningly describe as 'the greatest night of their lives'.

Work completed, he opened another bottle and considered his deepening financial crisis. Richard's car would cost whatever it cost to mend a car, which, whatever it was, would be more than he could afford. There was no option but to gamble. He typed his brother's e-mail address in and put 'Re You only have to ask' in the subject-box.

Really appreciate Mimi and you making the effort to attend my fortieth. I think I can safely say we all had a fantastic time. And aren't we lucky that our wives and children get along so well?

Anyway. Following on from your considered advice I have decided to play the stock market and was wondering if you could use your expertise to do the investing for me. If we move fast I reckon I can afford to gamble £25,000 and I'd like to put the whole bundle on football clubs' shares going down (Man United, Leeds, Chelsea, Millwall, whoever). To access my bank account you will need to know my six-digit pass-code (123456) and my six-digit password (ABCDEF). The bank's name is The Bank.

If there are any difficulties don't hesitate to get in touch.
Thanking you in advance,

Jimmy

He sent the e-mail flying across the ether and out of his
mind. There would be a record of it in his Sent box, but that
was a place Stirling preferred not to visit. You couldn't live
your whole life in the past.

13

Spanker, a man whom Stirling wouldn't have allowed within a country mile of a primary school playground, approached him as he waited for the twins.

'Rum goings-on in New York.'

'Where?'

'New York, America. Haven't you heard? Some idiot Yankee pilot has driven a 747 into the World Trade Centre.'

'On purpose?'

'No, not on purpose. I don't think it's the kind of thing even a socialist would do on purpose, do you?'

'I suppose not.'

'How's your wife?'

'Fine.'

'Good. She's very much an addition to the community.'

'She does her bit.'

'And always with a smile on her face. Game as a pebble.'

A twin grabbed either leg.

'Dadda, can we go to the sweetie shop?'

'Not today, there's a breaking news story back home.'

They made it just in time to be informed the world might be about to end.

'Wow,' said Charlie.

'What video is this?' asked Nancy.

'It's something I have to watch for work. Why don't you go on the PlayStation? I'll be along in a minute.'

There was a rogue plane heading for Washington, another for Los Angeles, another half a dozen God knew where. He moved from CNN to Fox to Sky News to the BBC. All of them were clueless. Did he know anyone in New York? The phone rang.

'Theatre of Dreams OK for you on Saturday, Jimmy?'

'Derrek, have you seen the news?'

'Most of it. Wolves have pulled out on a move for Gary Kelly after he failed a medical, Mansfield are on the brink of going into administration, Nicky Butt's hamstring is healing faster than expected . . . anything else you want?'

'Derrek, the news. Fifty thousand people have been killed in New York. The world may be about to end.'

'Are you sure?'

'Yes, I'm sure.'

'You're not having me on? Never shit a bullshitter, Jim.'

'Trust me.'

'Hang on a minute . . . Kath, be a love and come in here and switch the magic box over to Sky News, would you? . . . No, I don't know which channel it is, use your imagination . . . you just had it, back two, stop, forward one, bingo, cheers, pet . . . Wow, you're not wrong, Jim. That's one hell of a bonfire they've got on their hands.'

'One way of looking at it.'

'Who's responsible, Jim? The IRA?'

'Probably not.'

'You're right, not really their style. A bit big-time for them . . . Wallop. Did you see that, Jim?'

'Yes.'

'One minute it was there, the next rubble. Phenomenal.'

'It's terrifying, Derrek.'

'For the people involved, obviously, but I imagine we're quite safe on this side of the pond.'

'Perhaps.'

'Moving swiftly on, conference gave a thumbs-up to your piece on the massacre of the Huns. They seemed to think it was very funny. Personally, I thought it was a bit lightweight given the enormity of the occasion, but what do I know? You were in Munich, weren't you?'

'Of course. Why?'

'Just wondering. So, what game have you lined up for tonight, then? I see Colchester are at home.'

'No one's going to be playing football, Derrek.'

'Why ever not?'

'Look at your TV screen.'

'Tragic, I grant you. But the game must go on.'

It was only appropriate that on the Saturday after the world changed for ever Stirling should be stuck in a Virgin Weekend First train compartment with Brown, White and Blue on his way to watch Manchester United play Coventry at Old Trafford. Football seemed destined to remain for ever a constant in his miserable life. He hadn't slept for days. The personal fears that had ensured he hadn't missed a dawn chorus all summer had been overwhelmed by a general dread of everything. Whereas once he had looked forward to the odd thing now he only looked forward to things being over. It was all he could do to make it up to his office to watch Sky News during the day and provide himself with enough terrifying images to keep him awake through the night.

When he did fitfully sleep his dreams followed the same format used by the station to provide live and exclusive coverage on The War on Terror. They were studded with Breaking News Alerts. Every time a character appeared an Aston would flash up on the bottom of the screen of his dream announcing in bold capital letters what the person was about to say. Every scene in every dream was subjected to remorseless analysis by pundits and experts. Kay Birley, Anna Botting and Bob Friend were ever-presents. An endlessly repetitive argument with his new boss was interrupted by 'BREAKING NEWS ALERT: LIVING DERREK GIVEN "AS MUCH AS IT TAKES" PAY-RISE.'

'In among all the mayhem caused by old Bin Liner,' said Brown, chewing on a generously filled spicy chicken tortilla, 'at the end of the day they are American. That strikes me as a fact that's being overlooked here.'

'Hang on,' said Stirling, three hours from Manchester and already longing for a cigarette. 'We don't know how many hundreds of British people are buried there.'

'I think you're missing the essential point, Jimmy,' said White, beating out time with his freebie Carling biro, an irritating tic he had contracted while hosting his TV show. 'However many hundreds of Brits tragically perished you can bet your bottom dollar there will be thousands more Americans.'

'So . . .'

'It's their problem,' said Brown. 'Basically.'

'No it's not. Anyway, I think it's obscene that we're all going to watch a trivial game of football.'

'Define obscene,' said Blue, canoodling the latte, probably

skinny, whatever that meant, he had bought himself at King's Cross.

'Offensive to the senses,' said Stirling.

'Very well,' said Blue, taking the merest sip of latte, 'is it obscene that *EastEnders* continues to be broadcast on the BBC?'

'No.'

'Is it obscene that *The Mousetrap* continues to be staged in London's West End?'

'No.'

'Forgive me, then, but how can it be obscene for twenty-two professional footballers to ply their trade on a sunny Saturday afternoon?'

'Because people should be thinking of other things than fucking football. Because it's inappropriate for sixty thousand people to be shouting "The referee's a wanker" at such a time. Because barely a game goes by without a minute's silence for some nob or other but when hundreds of ordinary people die football carries on regardless. Because, clinchingly, they cancelled the next weekend's football when some bint died in a car-crash in Paris.'

'Who are you calling a bint?' asked Brown, ploughing into an Aberdeen Angus cheeseburger.

'Lady Di.'

'No way was she a bint,' said Brown.

'More of a princess,' said White.

'Would have been Queen, mate, if I'd had anything to do with it.'

'Or if she hadn't died.'

'Or been assassinated.'

'Wonderful woman.'

'Huge loss.'

'Superb charity worker.'

'Trim figure.'

'Why stop at this weekend's games, Jimmy?' Blue asked. 'Why not next week's and the week after that? The whole season, perhaps, and, while you're at it, you could put the World Cup on ice? Would that constitute the paying of enough respect?'

'It's an attractive idea.'

'Do you hate football, Jimmy?'

'Don't be naive. What would I be doing here if I hated the beautiful game?'

'What else would you be doing?'

Stirling feigned sleep and played mental snooker. The left side of his brain broke and scored nine. Brown potting with a 'football is bigger than this' and Blue with an 'out of a clear blue sky', before going in off big style as White outlined his bonkers theory that 'the climate of fear' could be a 'welcome shot in the arm' for the national game as it would mean more people staying in which would mean more people watching Sky which would mean more subscriptions which would mean a bigger TV deal which . . . End of break.

The right side of his brain was fortunate indeed to come to the table with the balls so favourably placed. White was responding to a text message, Blue was reading his own copy and Brown was monologising on recent events in Munich: 'Swede dreams are made of this' . . . 'Hunbelievable' . . . 'Hands up time, I'll be the first to admit I didn't think the igloo dweller was the right man for the job in a country which only invented the game and counts among its residents a certain T. Venables Esq. But cometh the hour cometh the ice-man wearing a suit as sharp and well-judged as young Stevie Gerrard's switch-passing . . . As dignified as he is short-sighted

. . . A prize winner from the land of Nobel . . . English passion linking up with Swedish precision to give the towel-baggers a good old-fashioned hiding.' Crikey, thought Stirling, how many was that?

'Nice,' said Blue. 'Although I do wish they wouldn't frig around with my semicolons. Do you suffer from that, Jimmy?'

'I'm asleep.'

'Fuck me,' said White, 'but that PR ain't half like concrete. Once laid almost impossible to shift.'

'I'll take her off your hands, Chalky boy. What's goose for the gander is . . .'

It was going to be a high-scoring frame.

Stirling remained standing long after everyone else had finished paying their respects. Triumphant, resplendent, alone.

'Jimmy, will you fucking sit down?' said White.

'I'll fucking chin you, sonny, if you don't move. Now,' said Green.

'Excuse me, sir, if you could please retake your seat,' said a steward.

Having made his point, Stirling acceded to the wishes of the majority. The living Derrek had specifically ordered him not to mention the war. It was typical of his pea-brained approach to the world. If it wasn't football it wasn't relevant. And aside from the far from surprising news story that Osama bin Laden was an Arsenal fan, the trashing of the Twin Towers hadn't generated a single football angle. Under Derrek's rules it was, therefore, an unmentionable.

A plane flew over Old Trafford. Stirling dived for cover, reappearing only when the danger had passed. He dusted himself down and as an aide-memoire typed 'Manchester United v

Coventry' at the top of the screen. What would Orwell have done? Told Derrek to go swivel, probably. There were times in a journalist's career when service to the truth had to outweigh any petty personal ambition.

At half-time, he bustled down the row and back into the press room for a much-needed fag. He hadn't checked Ceefax for at least two hours.

'Can I borrow the remote for a second?' he asked Green.

'Once I've seen all the scores.'

By the time the teleprinter had churned its way through four English divisions, some non-league rubbish and the four Scottish divisions the second half was about to begin. Stirling accepted the remote from Green and tapped in '101'. No change whatsoever, nothing had happened at all. Which in its own way was quite worrying.

As the final whistle blew he hit word count. Seven hundred and fifty. On the button. He tacked on a final bracket:

(N.B. Note to subs: Goalscorers, time of goals, entertainment rating, referee assessment, player marks out of ten, officials marks out of five, turning point, man of the match, raise your games, substitutions, time of substitutions, unused substitutes, attendance, weather report, team formations and managers' quotes – all to follow later.)

If he could be bothered. He whacked the copy over to the office. It was possible that they wouldn't print it, he supposed, given their track record when confronted by someone telling it as it was. But that was their problem.

* * *

211

'Dadda, phone?' said Charlie.

'Unggh, what time is it?'

'Cartoon time.'

Charlie handed the phone over and hurried back to *House of Mouse*.

'Hello.'

'Not only are you a cunt you're a wanker which makes you a double cunt.'

'Derrek, good morning.'

'Not for you it isn't. Have you read the paper, yet?'

'No.'

'Ring me when you have. No excuse in the world will save you this time.'

Not so much as a ciao. Stirling struggled out of bed, brushed his teeth, lit a cigarette and went downstairs to watch *House of Mouse* and wait for the papers to arrive. How to explain such anger? It must have been his match report, but if they didn't like it, and they were entitled to their opinion, why not say something at the time? To refrain from doing so was sloppy management.

Stirling listened to the paper boy stuffing the Sundays through the small slit of a postbox. Five attempts, not bad. He wandered over and for the first time for a long time, picked up his own newspaper. 'IT'S WAR' stated the masthead in 96-point type. 'READ OUR 128-PAGE SUPPLEMENT.' And underneath:

WHERE WERE YOU WHEN THE SECOND TOWER COLLAPSED? 50 CELEBRITIES, INCLUDING JUSTIN TIMBERLAKE, MARIELLA FROSTRUP, MARTIN BASHIR AND OTHERS, EXCLUSIVELY REVEAL THEIR WHEREABOUTS.

Nice use of 'others', thought Stirling. The sports section had been buried away between personal and impersonal finance, where it had been allocated a generous one and a half pages. On the top of one was 'The Game Must Go On', with a picture byline of Rob Parsons. At the top of the other was 'United Go Top' above a slightly smaller picture of Stirling. He skim-read his work:

Don't mention the war. Only someone with their head buried so far in the sand that they can't help talking through their arse . . . Nothing remains the same following the tragic events of 7/11 . . . Yesterday afternoon Sir Alex Ferguson rested David Beckham and the younger Neville . . . Coventry, to all intents and purposes, remained unchanged. The referee was Jeff Ashley from Harpenden . . . Where is Vice-President Cheney? Will we, in this lifetime, ever see him, or his like, again? . . . Man Utd went in at the break two goals to the good . . . With the benefit of hindsight what were the 'tragic events' other than the greatest giantkilling feat of all time? . . . Who would have had the cojones to predict that Al Qaida, a bunch of, admittedly hard-working, students managed by a fair-weather Arsenal fan, would pull off such a spectacular shock against the game's only true superpower in their own backyard . . . Manchester United won the game, which was frankly unwatchable, by a margin of three goals to nil.

Staggeringly, the sub-editors hadn't changed a single word. A novel and welcome approach which, rather amateurishly, extended to the N.B. and his final bracket. Not good.

He rang Derrek.

'Double cunt yourself.'

'Don't you double-cunt me.'

'Leaving that bracket in makes me, and the paper, look unprofessional.'

'The bracket is the least of our problems. It's the intentional bad writing above it that means my job is on the line. Peter and Gareth have already launched an internal inquiry to discover how your match report slipped through the system. The war supplement meant it was chaos on Saturday, workies everywhere, but I won't be using that as an excuse. The buck stops at the top. In the meantime, you're suspended pending those psychiatric reports. Goodbye.'

Did that mean he was sacked? And what did Fat Boy mean by 'intentional bad writing'? All writing was intentional. And it wasn't bad, merely different.

He made B a coffee and took the paper up to her for a second opinion, waiting outside while she read it. Normally he would have been on the listen out for laughs. But it hadn't been that kind of piece. It was more thoughtful and penetrating than casually amusing.

'You can come in, now.'

'Well . . .'

'It's fine.'

'How fine?'

'It's very funny. I loved the final bracket.'

'Funny?'

'And it perfectly makes your point that football which is irrelevant at the best of times is doubly so at the worst of times.'

'Absolutely. Thanks, darling. Back to work.'

'Work. It's Sunday.'

'There's a little something I need to clear up.'

* * *

The first e-mail he sent was:

> To Peter.
> Cc'd to Gareth.
> Re: Suspension pending psychiatric reports
>
> I thought it might be an opportune time to express in writing my appreciation of the tremendous job the two of you have been doing in turning the paper round. Those of us who remember the bad days – in-fighting in the canteen and bare-knuckle fighting in The Butt – cannot help but be particularly grateful for your efforts. I am convinced the next ABCs will reflect the excellence of your endeavours.
>
> That said, I think we are all in agreement that to build on this success it is important that the paper remains a broad church capable of encompassing the views of second-rate television artists alongside arguably more thoughtful contributors. Which is not to say that the former should not be exhaustingly flagged on the masthead in order to attract 'younger readers', merely to point out that once 'the youth' have been drawn in we would be failing in our duty if we did not try to educate them. There are those on the paper – as I am sure you are aware – who take a less relaxed approach to this development but I am not among them. It is the year 2001, after all.
>
> All of which brings us to this Sunday's edition (which is a terrific read, by the way) and my coverage of the Manchester United v Coventry fixture. On first reading, I would now admit, this may have thrown some of our more literal readers. They may have expected to read some trite and banal witterings (see usual rubbish from Parsons) mind-numbingly detailing

who scored what and where. Such people may have been initially disappointed. On further readings, however, the evident subtleties of my position cannot but have dawned on them. And while it might be unusual to use 750 words on Man U v Cov as a guise for some trenchant political analysis it does not follow that such a practice is prima facie wrong. Now, perhaps more than ever, our readers need to be kept on their toes and given a good belly-laugh. The final bracket worked rather well, don't you think?

Hoping all this can be cleared up without resort to a psychiatrist.

Yours,

Jimmy

PS If you are thinking of injecting some humour into the paper give us a call.

Because it was destined for an authority figure he reread the contents – a lesson he had learned during his drunken e-mail days – and hit Send.

Now for some fun:

To: Derrek William
Re: Who's a double cunt now?

Dear Mr William

Further to this morning's telephone conversation I would be grateful if you could provide me with details of the following:

a) The name and address of the paper's lawyers.

b) The name and address of your personal lawyers.

c) Any information that you and/or a) and/or b) might consider to be relevant in order to swiftly resolve any legal action which may or may not be pending.

Specifically, I would ask you to draw your lawyers' attention to the question of what the courts might consider to be 'intentional bad writing'. Off the top of my head, I can think of no precedent which governs the issue. Therefore it seems depressingly inevitable that we will have to travel all the way to the House of Lords for a definitive and binding ruling on the subject. So be it.

To avoid unnecessary cunctation I hereby summarise the thrust of my case:

1.1 a) All writing is intentional so the use of the term, in this instance, is almost certainly tautologous.

1.2 If a) then b): it follows we can focus on the second condition of the supposed offence: 'bad'. Can this be subject to an objective interpretation? I don't think so. Whether writing is bad or not can only be determined subjectively. One man's crap is another's genius (see our telephone discussion of August 17 – transcript to follow).

1.3 It is my contention that the Man U/Cov match report was not 'bad' and if the court deem it to be 'bad' I further contend that it was no worse than other contributions to the paper (see, passim, the endless floccinaucinihilipilification trotted out by Parsons).

2.1 If not a) then the court must consider the trappy question of intention.

2.2 In R v Moloney ([1985] 2 WLR 648) – a case, incidentally, which involved a son shooting his father during an argument over their respective abilities with a shotgun – Lord Bridge said that intention may be inferred from the common-sense meaning of the term (that the accused has the express purpose of committing some crime, and acts to do so). However, if the results are the natural consequences of the accused's actions, this supports a belief that intention was present. It was also made clear that, in general, the existence of intention could be left for a jury to decide.

2.3 Which is far from helpful.

2.4 But seems to suggest that you must prove on the balance of probabilities that either a) I expressly filed a crock of shite as a match report or b) I approached the assignment with such a cavalier attitude that it was inevitable the ensuing match report would be flawed.

2.5 Neither of which strikes me as a doddle.

Yours faithfully,

J. Stirling

14

The company psychiatrist appeared to be a perfectly affable bloke. Stirling had been expecting, and hoping, to be mentally examined by a woman. Based on absolutely no evidence he had had a hunch that an attractive woman in her mid-forties might be more sympathetic to his illusory problems. He had imagined it might be easier to open up while lying on a couch if he were in the presence of a female doctor. It was not to be. There wasn't even a couch, which Stirling reckoned had to be a good sign. Instead it was him and 'Dr Mawes, but do call me Rodge' sitting in twin Parker Knolls and going head-to-head. Disconcertingly, Dr Mawes had a clippings file containing everything Stirling had written for the paper. Various articles had been earmarked with yellow Post-it notes with a heavy preponderance of yellow peeping out from the bottom of the folder. Rodge opened up the book as if he were Michael Aspel on *This Is Your Life*, a programme which it was increasingly unlikely Stirling would be invited to appear upon, even as a friend. If he didn't kick on a bit he'd be fortunate to make *Midweek*.

'During most of the Nineties you seemed to take pleasure in going to football matches,' said Dr Mawes, pleasantly enough.

'Perhaps,' said Stirling, guardedly. He had to think of his legal action. It was possible that client confidentiality would cover their tête-à-tête but given the psychiatrist worked in-house for a national newspaper it would be insane for him to rely upon it.

'Latterly, I detect that your pieces are becoming increasingly angry in tone.'

'Ummm, I'd prefer forthright.'

'More forthright then. Has anything happened in the last few years to make you more . . . forthright?'

'No.'

'Anything at work?'

'No.'

'Or home? I notice from the company records that you've moved to South Norfolk. That must be quite a shock.'

'Not really. It's a lovely part of the world full of . . . sky and . . .'

'And?'

'More sky.'

'How are your wife and children?'

'Fine, thanks. Yours?'

Dr Mawes flicked through his file, without laughing.

'Can I smoke?'

'If you have to.'

He had to.

The doctor closed the file.

'Tell me about the late Derrek William.'

'Fat bloke, Arsenal fan.'

'It was he who offered you the job of football correspondent?'

'Possibly.'

'And gave you a very prominent profile in his pages?'

'Ish.'

'His death must have affected you.'

'Not in the slightest.'

Dr Mawes sat there like a lemon. Stirling could never cope with silences. They made him twitchy in the extreme. Particularly when the person who should be doing the talking kept looking at him like that, expecting him to speak, giving him the gimlet-eye, judging him before he had said a word in his defence, taunting him.

'Your father died quite recently?'

'A year and eight months ago, yes.'

'After a long illness?'

'After a short fall.'

More silence. The pressure to tell Dr Mawes about his Dad bubbled up inside him. He wanted to explain how he still missed him, how his life which had been light now seemed wearisome, how death intruded upon his most mundane imaginings, how exhausted he was, how scared he felt for his children, how dwarfed he felt by the finality of unfinished business, how he wasn't really angry, merely lost. He resisted it. He had better things to do with his time than listen to the psychiatrist's platitudes. And three cigarettes later what Dr Mawes referred to as their inaugural session was at an end.

Stirling made his shabby way from psychiatrist's chair to Butt of Lewis. Sufficiently self-aware to realise he was talking to himself he pulled out his mobile to provide a cover for his ceaseless babbling. Mutter, mutter, mutter, bastards. Why had they put him through that? What right did they have? Who did they think they were? Bastards, mutter, mutter, mutter. Give the best years of your life to an institution and they try to commit you. Charming.

The regulars were arranged around their new table.

'Moon man,' said Terry.

'He's back and he's barking,' said Ian.

'Good afternoon,' said Malcolm.

'Who wants a drink?' asked Stirling, rhetorically.

He bought a pint of Import, a half of gin and tonic and a pint of lime and soda with a heavy splash of angostura bitters. Deliberating over what to drink he, on a whim, decided, very temporarily, to join Terry on the wagon. The action, surely, of a sane man.

'Nice piece on Sunday, Jimmy,' said Terry.

'I thought so.'

'That final bracket was mesmerising,' said Ian.

'It was OK.'

'I don't usually linger over sport,' said Malcolm, 'but it took me by surprise turning up next to my You and Your Pension column. And in fifty years I've never read anything like it. Most refreshing.'

'Remind me again who scored for United?' said Terry.

'Very funny. So what's been going on? Any news?'

'Only you,' replied Ian. 'Your suspension pending psychiatric reports is the lead on the noticeboard.'

'Parsons has contacted all users with a couple of spoof e-mails which he is claiming you sent,' said Terry.

'Has he now?'

'They're pretty well done, actually,' said Ian. 'You wouldn't have him down as a natural parodist but he's captured your somewhat erratic style.'

'You can almost believe they were written by the moon man. They're not genuine, are they, Jimmy?'

'Of course not. I haven't sent an e-mail for months.' He changed the subject. 'How are you, Ian?'

Before the diversion could hit its stride Terry shouted, 'Duck, Jimmy.'

Stirling gashed his temple on the corner of the teak table.

'It's the mentalist,' Parsons said with maniacal glee.

'Get off the floor, Jimmy, I need a word. In private,' said Derrek, pointing to the other corner of the pub.

Stirling did as he was told, crouching on a stool and doing his best not to look mad.

Derrek potato-wedged himself into the only chair and beckoned over Parsons, who sat flush on the busted spring and didn't flinch. It was a kangaroo court.

'Numero uno: If you ever threaten me with legal action again I'll sue your arse until it bleeds,' said Derrek.

'What are you talking about?'

'Numero duo: I've got one word to say to you, Jimmy – Germany.'

'Big. Next?'

'Arsenal?'

'Wankers.'

'I'll ignore that. Over to you, Rob.'

'Acting on a tip-off from the boss and with the help of a personal friend who is a stewardess with Ryanair I managed to hack into their passenger lists for every flight from Stansted to Munich on September 1st.'

'Haven't you anything better to do with your life?'

'I assure you it was time profitably spent. There is no mention of a J. Stirling having flown on that day.'

'And?'

'If you add this evidence to the fact that not a single member of the working press is prepared to go on record saying he saw you in Munich.'

'And?'

'It's clear as twat,' butted in Derrek, thick cop to Parsons' slick cop, 'that you never went to fucking Munich.'

'I have in my hands a piece of paper . . .'

'No, you don't,' said Derrek.

'There's been a misunderstanding.' He paused. 'Can I trust you to keep a secret?'

'Depends what it is,' said Derrek. Parsons didn't comment.

Stirling tipped forward on his stool and said softly, 'You two have fucked around a lot?'

'Yes,' said Parsons.

'Derrek?'

'Yes,' said Derrek.

'Good. The truth is I didn't fly out to Munich on September 1st.'

'Nailed out of his own mouth.' Rob attempted to high-five Derrek but the fat man's nearest hand was buried deep in a KP nuts packet.

'I flew out on August 31st.'

'Why?'

'It's a long story. Don't tell a soul but twenty or so years ago I was on the verge of joining MI5. The Cold War may not have been freezing but nor was it showing any signs of thawing. Anyway. I passed the written exams and park bench interview and was fast-tracked over to Berlin. Where, to save money, I was billeted with a foxy young thing called Hanna Schygulla. What can I say about Hanna?'

He lit a cigarette.

'For an unforgettable weekend we forgot about spying and indulged in, how can I put this, more intimate mutual espionage.'

'Details, please,' slobbered Derrek.

'Suffice to say neither of us mentioned the communist threat. Anyway. To cut a long story short I heard nothing from the lovely Hanna for twenty-one years.'

'You must have been shite in bed,' interrupted Parsons.

'It's possible. And then on my fortieth birthday, imagine my excitement, I received an e-mail from Hanna which I can still remember word for word: "I saw your picture byline in a newspaper while I was at the dentist's. It would be fun, I think, to hook up once again if you are coming to Munich for this massive match for everyone involved. Danke, Hanna."'

'Danke, Hanna?' asked Derrek.

'It's German for thank you, Hanna. Anyway, I was intrigued and determined to make a weekend of it.'

'What a pile of bollocks,' said Parsons.

'Not at all . . .'

'So you flew out on Friday, hooked up with Hanna, and . . .' The Fat Man was onside.

'Not so clever. She's married to a prominent industrialist, has seven children and lives in a schloss on the outskirts of Munich. To be honest, she's gone home a bit.'

'No jiggy jiggy,' sweated Derrek.

'Not with her. But the nanny . . .'

'It's a rehash of *The Sound of Music,*' said Parsons.

'Once again life imitates art. The nanny, Derrek, looked like a young Katarina Witt. Perky breasts, pert buttocks, she came to me on a Friday night wearing a flesh-coloured leotard and . . .'

'You made a pig of yourself,' ejaculated Derrek.

'That's one way of putting it. But the reason I'm telling you all this is that I watched the game not from the press box but in an executive box with Hanna and her husband. How else could I have so eloquently written about the German experience on that greatest of all nights?'

'He's got a point, Rob. Jimmy, this nanny?'

'Another time, Derrek, I've a train to catch.'

He bypassed his friends on the way out. Malcolm was snoozing, Ian was talking and Terry was feeling his liver.

The blackboard let it be known that he would be eating alone: C + N staying over with Esme. C U L8R X B.' It read like a text message. Since when had his wife been interested in text? From where had the twins picked up the courage to attempt a sleep-over? There was nothing in the fridge except for a two-chilli-rated microwaveable curry. He poured himself a bowl of Cheerios and a glass of red, and opened that week's *Anglia Ad Trader*: 'SONY TRINITRON portable colour TV, has slight fault, but does work, £5, ono, no timewasters please, Lowestoft 01502 972 493.' Extraordinary. The longer he lived in Norfolk, the odder it became.

There were still three and a half hours to *Newsnight*. What to do? It was too warm for a fire and too late to sunbathe. He checked his wife's knicker drawer. Nothing new. He lay on the marital bed and imagined her wearing nothing but a cerise Lycra thong and being taken from behind by a faceless man while she kissed and licked the compliant Katarina Witt looka-like nanny with no name. Before he could become excited, he became depressed. Forty years old and he could think of no other way to amuse himself. Pitiful. He went to the pub.

There was a new barmaid at The Hare and Greyhound. Another missed opportunity. He had only himself to blame. For two years he had sat in this very seat hesitating over whether he should make some kind of move on the whippiest pint-server in the Pullhams, whether he might, for openers, find out her name. Now he was feeling as horny as all get-out, the barmaid had flown. To be replaced by a woman who looked as if she might be related to the living Derrek. Another busted fantasy.

An executive green sports car moved slowly on by. It looked familiar. Could it be Bella's? Bella – it was becoming quite an evening for the remembrance of missed opportunities. If he had shown a little more vim he might be fucking her now. Gently chewing her arse before turning her over . . . what did she look like? He concentrated hard. No image came. What about her husband? For the life of him he couldn't picture the fucker. The recently departed barmaid? Complete blank. His visual memory had exhausted itself. Perhaps that was what happened when you reached forty, your image bank reached its capacity. You had seen all the faces you might ever remember. Sitting in the corner of The Hare and Greyhound he despairingly attempted to recall the physiognomy of anyone he had met in Norfolk. The task proved beyond him. Shaking his head all the while he ordered in another pint.

'Quiet tonight,' he said pointlessly.

'All the action's out the back, innit,' said the new barmaid.

The overspill car park. Should he go on foot or by car? It was probably better to walk than risk someone recognising the red car. It wasn't that far and the last thing he needed was people gossiping that he was some kind of pervert. If he stayed in the shadows and didn't draw attention to himself he should be fine. He walked slowly round the pub, circumnavigated the main car park using the hedge as cover, darted into the overspill car park and was very nearly run over by a Land-Rover.

'Out of my way, little chappie,' shouted a man Stirling failed to recognise.

He scuttled behind a convenient newspaper recycling unit. Peeking out he could see three cars parked near each other, a twenty-yard gap to an articulated lorry, parked alongside a cab, which, yes it was, was Cedric's, the dirty little fucker blowing truckers when he should be at work, and over in the far corner a vehicle parked at right angles to the rest which might or might not be a green sports car. In the foreground, with his back to him, stood a man who was wearing a Barbour, rugby shorts and gumboots. If he went anticlockwise he should be able to avoid both the Countryside Alliance member and, at all costs, Cedric, before, with maximum stealth, taking Bella's car by surprise. Slow, slow, ever so slowly, he crawled round the perimeter of the car park. Steady as you go, ohhh shit.

The beam from a torchlight revealed that he had, as he suspected, unwittingly crawled into some fresh dog faeces.

'Long time no see, stranger.'

The man holding the torch was Spanker.

'I've lost . . . my car keys.'

'Course you have, leftie.'

Stirling ran like hell for a not-so-convenient bottle-bank on the far side of the car park. He waited for his breath to come back, wiped his right hand as best he could on the side of the container, and took stock. His cover was blown, but as the man who had done the investigating now had his rugby shorts round his ankles and there was no sign of life in Cedric's cab he had been granted a window of opportunity. He lit a cigarette and, as casual as you like, appeared from behind the bottle-bank. It was Bella's car. The filthy, dirty, delightful bitch.

What now? What was the etiquette on this one? What was

U and non U in the world of dogging? What the hell? Through the gloaming he could discern that there were at least two people in the sports car. Only one of whom could possibly be Bella. He hurried on, and on arriving at the driver's window, was greeted by a vista which, despite recent memory lapses, he was unlikely to forget. The seats had been pushed back to maximise the space available. Richard, inevitably, was stark bollock-naked, with his hands tied to the steering wheel and his feet poking out of the back far-side window. Bella, arse facing the car stereo system, black satin knickers hanging from one ankle, was astride him pumping away like a good 'un, and curled up in the back seat was Cedric, who was, no other word for it, masturbating. It was like a bad porn film. Peering through the passenger window and holding the camera was his wife.

'What took you so long?' said Bella.

'We need to talk,' said B.

He put four new logs on the fire. This was an argument it was inconceivable that he might lose. Although it had to be admitted that B wasn't looking particularly guilty or defeatist on her sofa.

'So . . .' said Stirling, opening the debate with all the force of a natural columnist.

'So what?'

'So what exactly were you doing with a camera in the over-spill car park?'

'At least I was invited. What exactly were you doing stinking to high heaven and peering through the window?'

'Research.'

'Since when have you been interested in research?'

'That's beside the point. The point surely must be that it is not often a husband comes across his wife filming the neighbours making out in their sports car while the local cabbie takes a more than passing interest.'

'We are in Norfolk.'

'Even in Norfolk.'

'You left me with no choice.'

'I can't believe what I'm hearing. I left you with no choice. Name one occasion when I ordered you to get yourself down to The Hare and Greyhound to film a ghastly South African and the Queen of Bungay having sex.'

'You did in so many words.'

'What words exactly?'

'Do you remember imploring me to be a slut?'

'No.'

'Demanding that I find someone else to shag so you could watch?'

'No.'

'Lying on my sofa wearing my thong and saying there was a chance you might be gay?'

'No.'

'Suggesting that we should advertise for a bisexual male au pair with a good sense of humour?'

'No.' The debate was slipping away from him and the moral high ground seemed very distant. 'I think I'll go to bed.' He got up to leave.

'Jimmy, you can't keep running away from everything.'

'Why not? I'm tired.'

'Can you remember anything about the last six months?'

'Is that how long this has been going on?'

'Longer.'

'Christ, how many films have you made?'

'I'm not talking about me, I'm talking about you. Can you remember anything from the last year?'

His bloody memory was being called into question again. Wearily, he retook his seat.

'Bits and pieces.'

'Such as?'

'This and that.'

'You have to talk to me, Jimmy.'

He thought for a while. 'Was it fun?'

'Not a word that springs to mind for being yelled at by a South African to get in tighter on his genitalia while his stroppy wife keeps pushing her new Brazilian wax into the frame.'

'And all the while there's a scrawny cabbie indulging himself in the back.'

'Fuck knows what happened there. Richard was banging on at me about his motivation when Bella suddenly leant over, flashed the lights, opened the door, and in jumped Cedric. What could I say?'

'Surely you were the director?'

'More hired hand. Richard insisted on giving direction to what passed for the talent.'

'While lying in a prone position handcuffed to the steering wheel, quite the little auteur.'

'And as Richard was barking at me to go wide for the money shot, Cedric was approaching some kind of rackety closure and the Queen of Bungay was very obviously faking it, thank goodness you stuck your head through the window. I've never been so relieved to see you.'

'I'm always there for you in the crunch, darling.'

'Hardly. What were you doing in the car park?'

'I'm not entirely sure.'

'You said you had to go to London for a Champions Curry with Derrek and Rob.'

'Did I?'

'And that you might be some time because there were a few insignificant work-related problems that needed ironing out.'

'Something of an understatement, but broadly true.'

'What problems, Jimmy?'

'I didn't go for a curry, I went to see a psychiatrist.'

'I know you're not keen on curry but . . .'

'Editor's orders.'

'Why?'

'It's not been the best of months. There was a misunderstanding in Inverness which led to a micro-celebrity whose name I can never remember and a stroppy PR suing me for libel. Then I missed a few games one way and another. Then I finally made it to a game but a fat lot of good it did me because, after all that effort, they suspended me pending psychiatric reports.'

'Why didn't you tell me?'

'I was just about to in the car park.'

'The car park?'

'Well, yes, but it wasn't really the time or place.'

'How did you know I was in the car park?'

'A hunch. There's not much going on around here, as you know.'

'Jimmy, have you ever been there before?'

'Have you?'

'No.'

'I have. That game of squash with Bella, I never beat her

at all. It was her cover story for kidnapping me and keeping
me against my will in that car park.'

'What did you do?'

'I escaped and went for a drink in the pub.'

'That I can believe.'

'Thank you.'

'What are you going to do now?'

The unanswerable question.

'What are we going to do now?'

'Potatoes and lentils?'

'Sounds fine to me.'

15

The text message was stark: 'UR FIRED U ****ER.' Whatever you said about the living Derrek he was a newspaperman down to the tips of his podgy fingers. No one else would use asterisks to disguise a swear word. There was a loud banging at the front door. The doorbell had never worked and there had never been enough users to justify all the expense and hassle of fixing it. A man in leathers was standing outside. Had he been in the overspill car park?

'Coffee?' asked Stirling.

'No thanks, mate, I want to get back to London by nightfall. This is for you.' The biker handed over an envelope with Stirling's name and address written in perfect type. All letters contained bad news and the more care taken over the typography the worse the news. 'What I need from you is your signature and your laptop and your mobile phone.' After which, thought Stirling, there wouldn't be much left. He handed over his mobile immediately, marginally chagrined that it should be repossessed before he had sent a comprehensible text message. He discovered the laptop in the twins' bedroom and unplugged it from the wall and the phone socket, which, at last, provided an explanation for the exponential rise in their phone bills. This, too, he handed over, blissfully unaware that it contained

a history of his visits to dogging sites and a complete record
of his forthright e-mails. Finally, with something approaching
a flourish, he signed one part of his life away.

'Sorry to have to do this to you,' said the biker.

'I think I probably brought it upon myself.' He closed the
door. What the hell – he opened the letter. It was to the point.

Dear Mr Stirling,

Further to your clearly false expenses claim (attached here-
with) we have no option but to terminate your contract
immediately.

Yours faithfully,

The Deputy Head of the People Department

Needless to say, the Deputy Head hadn't had the grace to
sign it herself, leaving such an important letter to be p.p'd by
some illiterate. What expenses claim? He never filed expenses.
He flipped the page to the attachment. 'Entertaining Frankie
Sober: Drinks £98.80'; various Munich taxis; a humdinger of
an invoice, in his own handwriting, from the Hungary Bavarian
for 360 Euros. How typical of the Deputy Head of the People
Department that given a range of grounds on which to sack
him she should have opted for something as mundane as Stirling
having arguably fiddled his expenses. How petty, how prosaic,
how weak. Ah well, at least he wouldn't have to see the
wretched psychiatrist again.

He grabbed a roll of supastrong xtralarge black bin-bags
(Budgens special offer: £1.29) and hurried up to his office. He

chose Vivaldi's *Gloria*, turned up the volume, and got to work. First to be bagged was the tower of newspapers, very few of which contained anything written by Stirling. Next in, over fifty 'Niceday' notebooks filled with vague jottings of what footballers might or might not have said. Then the mountain of ghosted autobiographies which PRs had sent him in the hope that he might review them if not read them: *The Butt Stops Here – My Autobiography* by Nicky Butt; *Sober Is As Sober Does – My Autobiography* by Frankie Sober with Rob Parsons; *Yet More of the Best After-Dinner Football Anecdotes* by Rodney Marsh. In they all went. Ten bags down, two to go. He tipped in three cardboard boxes containing programmes, unopened issues of *Sky* magazine and other memorabilia. Only one pile gave him pause. Stacked in the far corner were neatly filed clippings from a time when he had cared, six box files containing everything he'd had published in the 1990s, pasted and dated. At the front of file one was his first-ever match report. Blackpool 2, Huddersfield 1, 1972. He had written it for Dad when he was, Christ, eleven. Dad had always encouraged him to be a football reporter. 'Yesterday afternoon at a sunny Bloomfield Road, Blackpool ran out deserved winners thanks to a 78th-minute strike from the always dangerous Alan Suddick.' His style hadn't changed a whit in thirty years. There was no point in reading on. He removed the first clipping, found a safe place for it, and tossed the rest into a final bag. His heart pumping from the exercise, he carried the bags, one at a time, from the attic to a corner of the paddock, his bonfire spot of choice.

A pale sunlight covered the field. The sky was clear. Miles and miles of flat East Anglian land stretched before him. The fire lit first time. Unprecedented. A flatulence of football went up in smoke. All that idiocy, inanity and vacuity, all that nonsense posturing and high seriousness and unrelenting stupidity, blah, blah, blah, blah, blah, so much blather signifying nothing. He piled on dried branches, the odd forgotten sleeper, and chunks of leylandii. The flames leapt thirty, forty feet in the air. And as he stood in the corner of a Norfolk field watching the epic conflagration he felt content – no, not content, he doubted he would ever feel content, but released and giddy and relieved. As if a boil that might be mistaken for a second nose had, not before time, burst. He would never have to watch a game of football again.

He stood for a long time alternately inhaling the bonfire and a succession of cigarettes and then went back to his now rather sparse office. His Dad's ashes were in a small container in the freezer section of the mini-bar. He took them out of the fridge, and, minutes later, was sprinkling them on the bonfire. Just because one of us is gone, he thought, it doesn't mean the conversation is over.

As a fair trade for not being given an excess of aggravation for losing his job and leaving the family with no visible or invisible (if you discounted the twins' premium bonds) means of support, Stirling agreed to essay a change in lifestyle. First, and most dramatically, he gave up drinking. It was far easier than he'd imagined, although it did leave him with plenty of time on his hands, which combined with a total inability to sleep meant that both the days and nights were exhaustingly long. Why, oh why, had he burnt all those ghosted autobiographies?

Short of hobbies, he readily consented to B's suggestion that he join the Diss chapter of Alcoholics Anonymous. With a bit of luck he might have bumped into a professional footballer there and, on the sly, been able to write up his drinking experiences into one of those Confessions of a Footballer books which were all the rage at the moment. Instead he found himself surrounded by cabbies, and while this was uplifting – for no one likes to see a drunk cabbie, least of all in the build-up to Christmas – he was less than thrilled to find himself sitting next to Cedric. As per usual in a group situation Stirling proved to be too shy to ask any questions. Instead he listened politely, nearly dropping off at one point, as various cabbies droned on about their repetitive lives. There was a long silence which Stirling eventually realised constituted an invitation to him to speak. 'My name is Jimmy,' he had started conventionally enough, 'and I'm a failed football writer.' He was not, had not been, nor ever would be, an alcoholic. He was simply a heavy drinker. There was a world of difference. On his way out, Cedric asked for a lift home. Remembering what the cabbie liked to get up to in other people's cars, Stirling knocked him back and drove unswervingly to the off-licence to stock up.

In search of hope, he started taking the twins to church on Sunday. He was disappointed to discover that the service was no longer in Latin. How could you have faith with so much understanding and so little doubt? He was infuriated by the discovery that Father Vernon was, to all intents and purposes, a happy-clappy Catholic. He had been relying upon being damned to eternity, instead he was confronted by wishy-washy sentiments on all manner of issues that didn't directly concern him. He thrilled to the sight of Bella taking communion. Coatless, despite the fact that they never turned the central heating on at St Olaf's, she bent forward to reveal the contours of that great arse before moving back down the aisle with maximum supplicance and blanking Stirling as she walked on by.

Once, he went on a walk. On his own. To nowhere in particular. The rest of the time he stayed at home and played with the children, whom he slowly learned to call Charlie and Nancy rather than the twins, which obviously was both disparaging and a hindrance to helping them establish independent identities. They found acres of common ground in fear. Stirling's terror of animals slowly receded as Charlie and Nancy taught him how to confront chickens, rabbits, sheep and, almost, dogs. The three of them went pet-crazy, purchasing a dozen chickens that were neither free nor particularly adept at ranging, a rabbit that sat depressed in his hutch and doubled up as an achingly slow lawnmower, and, a stroke of luck, picking up a couple of sheep, gratis, from the quiet man who was geographically their neighbour.

The mortality rates proved to be medieval. The chickens were undone by Stirling's lack of a gift for DIY when a fox, or whatever, darted through a glaring gap in their coop. The rabbit, meanwhile, having shown a marked disinclination to earn its keep by trimming the proposed croquet lawn, keeled over live in front of the children on a bitterly cold December morning. As for the sheep, for many days Charlie and Nancy and Stirling, seeing them lying prone in the middle of the paddock, deluded themselves that they must be sleeping. A prod with a stick on day five from Charlie confirmed this was not the case. Having never happened across a dead sheep, and uncertain as to what might be required in terms of both protocol and paperwork, Stirling called in professional help. The vet's rapid post-mortem concluded that they had probably poisoned themselves by eating some stray sticks of unintentionally grown rhubarb, or Norfolk anthrax, as it was now known in local veterinary circles. When it came to motive, the vet was clueless. Despite repeated questioning he hadn't the foggiest notion whether the sheep had been struck down accidentally by some quirk of fate or had voluntarily indulged themselves in some bizarre ovine suicide pact. They kept an eye out for a dawn raid from the RSPCA.

Stirling worked hard at teaching his children to overcome their fear of any human other than each other. They were not so much latch-key as latch-thigh kids. Wherever he went Nancy went and wherever Nancy went Charlie went, the three of them wandering aimlessly around, sometimes talking but more often silent. He took them to school earlier and earlier in the hope that they would mingle with their classmates, but to no avail. Esme had finally found another friend closer to her own age and Charlie and Nancy hadn't bothered to seek a replacement. They specifically requested that no one be invited to their birthday party.

Stirling was not surprised. Ever since they had been born they had been as inseparable as the Dioscuri, and Stirling had long held the premonition that on a day of their own choosing they might simply disappear together to roam the world. Checking into Youth Hostels, chatting only to each other, blissfully happy. That day appeared some way off at the moment, given they could barely travel unaccompanied from TV room to kitchen, but it was only prudent to make the most of them while they were still around.

He used his spare time profitably to get back on top of the kiddie movie and literary scene. Together they made many visits to the UCI cinema complex at the heart of Norwich's exciting riverside development and swiftly polished off Harry Potter, Narnia and Lemony Snicket before returning to *Watership Down*. When they weren't reading they played imagination games, Stirling happily undertaking an Alec Guinness multiplicity of roles, from head teacher to cleaner, in Charlie's real-time epic 'My School Day'. Over time he weaned Charlie off his obsessive love for Anne Robinson and eased Nancy's very real worries over the unknown. Stirling had thought that, as he had done with his father, Charlie and Nancy would take an interest in their father's hobbies. But they point-blank refused to watch Sky News.

The more time he spent with them the more he began to understand, if not entirely comprehend, their little ways. Their habit of leaving little notes for each other whenever circumstances demanded they spend some time apart. 'Bouchie Boy. Have to go to Brownies. Enjoy the Simpsons. Missing you. XXXX Love Nancy.' 'Bouchie Girl. Gone to watch cartoons. Enjoy your lie-in. XXXX Love Charlie.'

When one of them was ill, the other inevitably followed, B and he waiting by the phone for the call from St Olaf's that they should come and collect the go-it-alone twin. Sometimes Charlie or Nancy would be verifiably ailing, but more often they were simply exhausted by love-sickness long before it was time for packed lunches and the hellishly daunting prospect of an hour in the school playground without anyone to play with.

The only time they exercised whatever free will they possessed and chose to be alone was when Charlie was performing in a St Olaf's Nativity, Mystery or Resurrection play. On such occasions Nancy would cry off with stage-fright to enable her to sit in the audience and clap wildly at her brother's every gesture as he waved to her reassuringly throughout his performance. Stirling found such antics endearing but doubted that the serried banks of fathers with camcorders were entirely thrilled to be adding such public displays of affection to their video collections. Religious re-enactments aside they stuck together, never happier than when cocooned in the back of the car, safe from intrusion, travelling somewhere, anywhere. Perhaps it reminded them of their happy post-natal month side-by-side in the incubator.

Charlie specialised in numeracy, Nancy in literacy. Charlie learned to tell the time and work the video machine, Nancy read comics and books and sets of instructions to him. Charlie was obsessive, Nancy supportive. For three hours a day every day Charlie would feed his PlayStation habit, doing his brains in against the computer. Nancy would watch patiently, delighting in his rare victories and consoling him when, as almost always, his frustration clouded his sense and he gave an almighty kicking to the control box, having forgotten to save his game.

Stirling was pretty certain that the established pattern would continue for the rest of his, and their, days. Charlie would be an actor, Nancy would be his agent. Charlie would be a hairdresser, Nancy would work front of house. Neither would do anything in particular – living off benefit and chatting away to each other unencumbered by partners or ambition. All three of these possible careers could be pursued in Norfolk. Most of the nearby villages attempted Christmas pantomimes of varying quality. There were five hairdressing salons in Nether Pullham, over a dozen in the Pullhams: it was virtually a home of hairdressing. And if the twins wanted to live off benefit they had come to the right place. His own career might be on hold, or, arguably, over, but his children were sitting pretty.

This abundance of childcare not only passed the time but also allowed B to have her first break in seven and a half years. Neither of them mentioned the sordid events in the Hare and Greyhound overspill car park. There was a tacit understanding that the incident reflected poorly on both of them and any further examination could only be damaging.

The short sharp shock, however, did wonders for their sex-life. Surprisingly, a front-page headline in the paper he used to work for – OFFICIAL: YOUR GRAN HAD MORE SEX THAN U – proved to be correct. The text underneath the arresting headline drew heavily on a study from Spalding University which claimed that if one partner in the marriage wasn't working (as was often the case in the 1950s) sexual activity increased. And if neither party in the marriage was working (rare in these days of low unemployment) it often trebled.

Emboldened, Stirling took his expertise at imagination games from the playroom to the bedroom. For a month he was Cliff (a tanned tennis coach with a limited vocabulary and a penchant for tight shorts). For a week he was alternately Cliff and Bertie (a down-at-heel landowner who played a fast game of whist and was occasionally considerate). Then, on a traumatic night of domestic drama, B had ditched both Cliff and Bertie and, after a week's rest, started a dalliance with Rick (a Harley-Davidson fanatic who was only twenty-four). It was all very like *The Archers*.

Playing the role of Rick required Stirling to purchase pay-as-you-go mobiles for himself and his Mrs Robinson. The pair of them soon became text-addicts, firing off elaborate exchanges to plan the details of clandestine trysts. Whereas Cliff had had little to say about Stirling aside from one throwaway comment about 'your husband needing to work on his backhand' and Bertie was, if anything, over-solicitous about Stirling losing his job and being cuckolded in such short order, Rick had no such qualms. During marathon sessions he would demand that B give him a mark out of ten and compare and contrast his performance as against that of 'the old fella'. When drunk he would cosy up to his mistress on her sofa and implore her to leave her dead-beat husband and spooky kids and come and start a new life with him in his council flat near Loddon. To her credit, B resisted the temptation.

Sticking to his policy of not opening mail, a stance many others had co-opted as a response to the threat of non-Norfolk anthrax, Stirling enjoyed his improved lifestyle free from interruption. There was no earthly reason to call the bank to alert them that it had been a while since any monies had entered his account. Far better to lie low in the Waveney Valley and wait for them to come to him. There was no real reason to call anyone else.

'Now you're working from home, one of our two wishes has come true,' said Charlie.

'What's the other one?'

'To have a watch which tells us where you and Mumma are all the time,' said Nancy.

'Darlings, darlings, I'm not going anywhere.'

The phone rang, jerking him from his seat.

'Hello,' he said very quietly.

'Jimmy.'

'Kath.'

'You are coming to the Christmas party tomorrow, aren't you?'

'Am I invited?'

'There's a seat for you.'

'I'll be there.'

'Where will you be?' asked Nancy.

'London.'

'When?' asked Charlie.

'Tomorrow.'

'Bad Dadda.'

'It will be the last time.'

'Bad Dadda.'

'I promise.'

That night he dreamt of his father. This happened regularly but, on this occasion, something was different. His Dad was standing with a half-full pint outside the Bowlers Bar at Lord's chatting away to someone who resembled The Buffer. He couldn't hear a word they were saying but they both seemed very jolly. His Dad finished his pint, disappeared back into the bar, and returned, in record time, with two pints. He was smiling. He had never smiled before in one of Stirling's dreams.

Stirling arrived at Gringos, a second division Tex-Mex eatery with a profound bias towards guacamole, half an hour early, a sure sign that country living was beginning to affect him. Kath had gone to the trouble of providing placement. At the table with a sign reading 'The Premiership' the following were expected:

Derrek William Junior: The Gaffer, Big Man, Boss, Skipper, Fella

Like father like son, thought Stirling.

Mr Blue: Chief sports writer (football)

God in heaven, was he still using that ridiculous nickname?

Rob Parsons: Chief football writer (sport)

What was it with these brackets? He felt like an Indian among chiefs.

Frankie Sober: Legend

Wanker.

Frankie Sober (Plus One)

Nell McAndrew?
Kath.

It was a line-up to truly test the secretary's fabled stoicism. Roll on the carnations.

He moved on down the divisions; checking out the Vauxhall Conference, the Doc Martens, The Screwfix, before finding his name on Table 12. Kath had run out of leagues before being able to find a place for Stirling. He was on the subs bench. Literally. Surrounded by a collection of work experience sub-editors (Allan, Paul, Linzi) who hadn't been at the paper long enough for anyone to ask them their surnames.

The menu provided more disappointment. Spicy Cheesy Nachos with Guacamole; Spicy Chicken and/or Spicy Beef Fajitas with Guacamole or Spicy Chicken and/or Spicy Beef Enchiladas with Guacamole or BBQ Ribs with BBQ sauce; Fruit Salad with Cream; complimentary half-bottle of Pinot Grigio (£19.95 excluding service). Half-a-bottle? He would either have to dip into his pocket or hope that Linzi, Paul and Allan were teetotallers. He hadn't drunk any of the foul stuff since the Football Writers' Dinner. Better go easy or he might suffer some godawful Grigio flashback.

Finding a convenient toilet he sent a text message to B, as himself.

'Scared and confused. XXXX.'

The reply was instantaneous. 'Tell them all to fuck off, Tiger. XXXX.'

It was sound advice but he doubted he had the strength of will to carry it through. So many to slag off, so little time. He looked in the mirror. Not at all bad. A bit of colour in the cheeks, not exclusively caused by busted capillaries. Bags under the eyes better than they'd been for some time. Hair something of a mess, but adequate. Superficially speaking, he didn't appear unemployable. Although, he supposed, others would have to be the judge of that.

'Hey, good-looking.'

'Terry, what are you doing here?'

'Thinking of having a piss. You?'

'What are you doing at this party?'

'I gatecrashed.'

'No one has ever gatecrashed the Sports Desk Christmas Party.'

'Yeah, well, I hadn't heard from you for a while . . .'

'How is everyone?'

'Depressed.'

'What's new?'

'They're going to turn The Butt into a theme bar.'

'Fuck.'

'Abstinence is the new absinthe as someone put it in a leader column.'

'And you?'

'Four months, three weeks, five days, thirteen hours . . .'

'Can I have your complimentary Grigio?'

His ex-peers were as ugly as ever. Derrek Junior, in a replica shirt even though it was traditionally a smart casual affair, was considerably fatter. Parsons was wearing shades, a T-shirt with 'Football is a Game of Tomorrows – Sir Geoff Hurst', and chatting to that PR woman who for all Stirling knew was probably still suing him. And Mr Blue . . . Mr Blue appeared to have grown a few inches. At his age. Most odd. Stirling shuffled over to take a closer look at his heels.

'Jimmy.' The Fat Man struggled to put one arm over Stirling's shoulder and gestured to the people gathered in Gringos with the other. 'All this could have been yours, my son.'

'Terrific.'

'I can't, in all honesty, say you're missed, though.'

'We all have to move on.'

'The team's really started to gel in your absence and I wouldn't be at all surprised to see the Robster pick up a gong or two at season's end. Did you read last week's in-depth interview with Lee Dixon?'

'Of course not.'

'Fascinating stuff. And, you have to agree, tempting Mr Blue on board from under the noses of the competition was a sensational piece of transfer business. They all wanted him, we got him. Definitively my best signing.'

'Who else have you signed?'

'Early days, Jim, early days. But 75 K per annum for that kind of quality. You can literally feel it on the page.'

'Seventy-five thousand.'

'Cheap at double the price, I can tell you.'

Having failed in his bid to reach Stirling's shoulder, the living Derek slapped him on the back. 'It's a funny thing, Jim, but there was a time when I looked up to you, when I saw you as some kind of mentor, I think the term is. And look at us now. Me running the show, you . . . you . . . where did it all go wrong, Jim?'

'Can I get you a drink?'

'No point. None of us drink any more. Clean living is the new yoga. But don't let me stop you.'

'I won't.'

'And don't get completely pissed, we've got a little surprise for you later.'

Giving up booze had done nothing to improve the Fat Man's breath, thought Stirling, as Derrek barrelled off to exchange a high five with Parsons. He scanned the room for Terry. No luck. Perhaps he had decided, on closer inspection of the guests, to go and lie down in a darkened room.

'Where did it all go wrong, Jimmy?' said Mr Blue.

'Is it just me or have you grown recently?'

'As a writer, as a human being.'

'Admit it, you're wearing stacks, aren't you?'

'What are you talking about?'

'You're three inches taller than when I last saw you. Either you're wearing concealed heels or you're a medical miracle.'

'Sorry.'

'How old are you, anyhow?'

'Twenty-nine.'

'Twenty-nine. Fuck me.'

'Are you OK, Jimmy?'

'I'm fine, I just need a drink.'

He found Table 12 and unscrewed the cap on his complimentary Grigio. The lunch proved to be better than expected. He swapped his Nachos, Fajitas and, after some negotiation, Fruit Salad with Cream for various Christian names' complimentary Grigios and avoided any conversation beyond the perfunctory. By the time Derrek rose to his feet, Stirling was in an excellent mood.

'Straight from the kick-off,' said Derrek, 'and as a mark of our gratitude for all her unstinting effort over the last year' – to no one's surprise, he produced a mid-size bunch of sprayed carnations from behind his back – 'let's give it up for Kath.' The blushing secretary came forward to accept her reward and a sweaty kiss which was slightly nearer the lips than she had been expecting. 'What a year, hnuh. Arsenal win the double and I get the top job. If things keep going this well England will piss the World Cup in JapKorea. But it wouldn't be sport if you didn't lose some as well as win some. Over the last year we have lost Jimmy Stirling.' The Fat Man paused. Not a few people applauded, as if such carelessness might be a cause for celebration. 'And won, after I don't mind admitting some hard negotiation on my part, the man we on the desk like to call The Bluester.'

The living Derrek clicked his fingers and pointed at the journalist, who rose to his feet. Fuck, thought Stirling, he'd even grown during the time it had taken everyone else to eat lunch. There was much banging of hands on tables and a shout of 'Maestro' from Rob Parsons, who clinked mineral waters with his fellow bracket.

'Moving swiftly on. As you know, in our business points mean prizes and over the last six months I have been secretly awarding everyone in the room a mark out of ten for their weekly efforts.' He produced a wedge of paper from his back pocket. 'I am therefore in a position to hand out this year's trophies. Kath, be a sweetheart.' The still-traumatised secretary produced half-a-dozen cheap, pale gold figurines.

'In the world of film people compete for Oscars.' He pointed at the plastic imitations. 'In my world I would like you all to compete for Derreks.' He held up one of the plastic imitations and, struggling a bit, simultaneously read from his prepared script. 'And the nominees in the category of most football matches watched are Rob Parsons and Dave Fanchetti. And the winner is Rob Parsons with a score of one hundred and eighty.' Derrek gave it the full darts treatment. Parsons shook the Fat Man's hand and accepted the eponymous award.

'Tremendous effort, Rob,' said the Fat Man. 'You can say a few words if the mood takes you.'

So that was the surprise. He must have won a Derrek. Was it possible that he was about to win his first award, ever? It had to be. Which would mean he would have to make a speech. He beat an unsteady path to the toilet to freshen up. But what could he have won a prize for? During the living Derrek's editorship he had only managed to conduct two interviews and watch one game of football. Having said that, he had been at the paper for long enough to be in line for some lifetime achievement thingy. He reappeared into the grimy light of Gringos.

'As some of you may be aware my old man pegged out this year.' Derrek was winding things up. 'And, in his honour, I would like to dedicate the final Derrek of the afternoon to him. So it is that in my Dad's memory I award the Derrek for Cunt of the Year to . . .' He stalled for dramatic effect but there could be only one winner . . . 'Jimmy Stirling.'

One man applauded, Terry having resurfaced, unexpectedly highly, on the Division Two table. 'Go to it, Jimmy.'

Stirling made his way forward to accept his trophy. He unscrewed one of the many untouched half-bottles of Grigio on the Premiership table and poured himself a hefty glass.

'It's been a great year for cunts. But not for perhaps the greatest cunt of all time who failed to see it through. No matter, his son survives him. As the People Department might put it – the vacancy is filled.' Terry laughed. 'No one could be more surprised than me to be so honoured.' He picked up the Derrek with the inscription 'Cunt of the Year' Blu-Tacked on its plinth and punched the air with it. 'Thank you.' There was limited applause, more from relief than respect. But Stirling hadn't finished. He had barely started.

'There could be no more perfect coda to what, barring a malign miracle, is the end of my football writing career. For over a decade I have written about matters football and during that time not a single remotely interesting thing has happened.' He lit a cigarette. 'Worse, far worse, during that time a childish game played by childish people has been transformed from an intermittently entertaining diversion into the defining adult passion of our time. The anaesthetic, the analgesic, the placebo for all the sad and lonely people who inhabit this land. How did it come to this?'

'Come to what?' interrupted Derrek.

'It was a rhetorical question, Fat Boy.'

He cracked open another Grigio.

'Not for the first time Peter Cook may have put it better than I am able to. He did so in a monologue written just before he died which, if I may, I would like to quote in full.' Stirling lapsed into a pretty decent Cook impersonation, being four-fifths drunk proving, in this instance, to be no hindrance.

'Derek supports Arsenal and you can see it in his face – that drugged zombie look that comes from substance abuse, genetic malfunction or even the occasional visit to Highbury. It started off innocently enough. His Dad, Derek (no fucking imagination, these cunts), was an Arsenal fan and to placate his wife, Bo, took the then young Derek Junior to watch an Arsenal–Ipswich match as a punishment for wetting his bed. Fair enough, you might say, but Derek, being a cunt, became addicted to ninety minutes of boredom and began to watch the Gunners on a regular basis. He even interrupted his Saturday masturbation schedule in order to travel secretly to North London from Chadwell Heath. There he watched George

Graham, Frank McLintock and nine other wankers stupefy thousands of otherwise ordinary decent folk.'

Derek was the first to his feet, reacting Pavlovianly to the ex-Arsenal manager's name. 'George Graham, George Graham, George Graham,' he began to chant to the tune of 'Here we go', clapping his hands and stomping his feet. 'George Graham, George Graham, George Graham,' he continued, opening his arms and encouraging his flock to join him. Slowly, from the Premiership down to the Screwfix, they too arose. 'George Graham, George Graham, George Graham,' chanted the room.

Stirling waited patiently for them to finish. 'That was written in 1994. Cookie got out just in time, for there are Dereks everywhere now, grinning oddly and chatting to other Dereks about how nice it is to have the league wrapped up before the clocks go back, even though mathematically they are second. And then getting their napkins out and making little lists about why they are better than Real Madrid. Funny lot – the Dereks. Rather insecure, tend to stick to their subspecies, marrying Derekesses and keeping things Arsenal by spawning yet more Dereks and Derekesses who can continue the family tradition for becoming somewhat over-excited at the acquisition of yet more silverware. The Dereks have proliferated to such an extent that it is not an exaggeration to state we are living among a plague of Dereks.' He smiled at Derek. 'However they spell the name.'

'D-e-r-r-e-k,' said the Fat Man smugly. 'You were always shite with Christian names.'

Stirling poured another Grigio, lit another cigarette. 'The sadness is that, dim as they are, the Dereks are by no means the worst of it. They were born to be Dereks, and we cannot heap too much blame upon them for the accident of that birth, however horrific. Far, far more evil is Rob Parsons.' Stirling gestured with his hand, glass and lit fag at the man who loved PRs. 'A man of so little charm, so little substance, so little humanity, that he finds the depth and meaning so pervasively lacking in his life from the mindless and endless pursuit of a little game played by dull men. How can someone watch 180 games of football a year and not be committed, in the mental health sense of the word? How can someone define their whole existence by events on a football pitch over which they have no control and still be deemed old enough to drink? Not that the fucker does. How can someone reduce his life to one subject and still have nothing of interest to say about it? Beats me, Rob.'

'Ich bin ein football connoisseur,' said Parsons, rising to his feet and punching the air. 'And proud of it.'

'Frightening,' said Stirling. He scanned the table. Water, water everywhere and not a Grigio to drink.

'In Parsons's defence, a phrase I doubted I would ever use, he may be the victim of his beliefs. Football, he has told me over and over again in that monotonous way he has with words, is a religion to him. This is neither original nor true but it works for him. As Parsons sees the world The Arse is God, Arsène the Chosen One and Highbury, I suppose, St Peter's Cathedral without the mitigating works of art. Childish, foolish, insane, all these words come to mind, but what really grates is the crushing materialism of his chosen religion. A creed where winning is everything. A credo which demands the richer get richer and sod the rest. Blessed are the sleek, for they shall inherit the earth. Blessed are the moneymakers, for they shall be called the children of Arse. Parsons's brand of fundamentalism is no more becoming than that practised by Osama Bin Laden.'

'Wanker,' shouted Derrek.

'But at least Parsons believes in something. Which is more than can be said for that prat over there with the supercilious grin and the stacks. Stand up Tristan, Tristam, Tristram, whatever your fucking name is, and give everyone a chance to see how much you've grown in the last half-hour.' Mr Blue stayed seated. 'What a fraud. What a chancer. What a vainglorious cunt. He used to be a half-decent industrial correspondent, you know. But then he and his fancy friends thought what fun, and how lucrative, it would be to turn their hands to soccer as they initially called it. Oxbridge tossers the lot of them. Sages in their own lunchtime salad, all of them so very capable of knocking out thousand-word essays on the flimsiest of pretexts. Clogging the pages with ill-considered references to Marcel Proust during appreciations of Stuart Pearce. Forever seeking substance and nuance in the most quotidian footballing event. Desperately trawling through the week's matches for an angle on the human condition without realising that none exists. Football as metaphor for this; football as allegory for that; eat football, think football, read a little bit of Nietzsche . . .'

'I think you'll find it's Nitzchy.' Mr Blue called out.

'Nietzsche.'

'Nitzchy.'

'Nietzsche.'

'Nitzchy.'

'Fuck off. And out of the mixer comes another tranche of football nonsense. And such serious and ordinary nonsense. All of it founded on the wrong-headed premise that what they are writing about and, by solipsistic extension, what they are writing is in some way important. Children, children, it's only a game. A game that used to be funny before the comedians took an interest. A game that had a few redeeming qualities before the banks started charging interest. A game which now has become a sour corporate joke. A textbook example of how a monopoly provider, cheered on by its friends in the press, can abuse its position. And they call it beautiful. Fuck the lot of you. Bored beyond tears at being surrounded, besieged and assailed by Dereks, dunces and shams, I, with customary grace, retreat to Norfolk. Having been sacked, I resign.' He relifted the trophy. 'Thank you, again, for giving me something to show the grandchildren.'

'Poor shout,' said Derrek Junior.

'Truly poor shout,' echoed Parsons.

'I'm sure it's Nitzchy,' said Mr Blue.

Stirling strode in triumph out of Gringos, stopping only for a snap appraisal from Terry.

'At least you kept your dignity.'

There was far too much adrenalin in his system for Stirling to be able to handle the A train to Diss. What's more, long experience had finally taught him, his saver ticket wouldn't be valid until seven o'clock anyway. He needed to be somewhere where he could take stock. Somewhere which would afford some peace after the clamour of all those idiots. He made his way to Lord's.

St John's Wood station was deserted, it was drizzling, it was dark, it was December. There clearly wouldn't be any cricket going on, he thought rather fatuously as the excitement of his swansong wore off and the Grigio kicked in. He trudged on, too ill to smoke. His hair was dank and the international travelling coat that had been the centrepiece of his inheritance from his father was sweating up.

The Grace Gates were open. There were lights on in the Pavilion. He composed himself, made a rudimentary attempt to spruce up, and thanked God that he had decided to wear a jacket and tie for his farewell party. As long as you had a jacket and tie on, no one would complain however distressed you might look.

'Evening, sir,' said the doorman.

'Evening,' said Stirling. 'Wet out.' Now all he had to do was make it to the Bowlers Bar, order up a lager or something equally refreshing, and then he could settle down to work out what to do with his life.

'Charlie Stirling's boy.' It was The Buffer.

'Jimmy.' It was Malcolm.

'What are you doing here?' said Stirling.

'Bridge night,' said Malcolm.

'Easy money,' said The Buffer. 'Some wine?'

'No, no, no. Why not?'

At least it wasn't white. He joined their table.

'Norfolk, isn't it?' asked The Buffer.

'Yeah.'

'Long way to come on the off-chance of a drink. Are you OK?'

'Not great. I've just been voted Cunt of the Year at the Christmas Party.'

'In fifty years in the business, I've never won that one,' said Malcolm. 'Something for the CV.'

'There is that.'

'I haven't seen you in The Butt lately.'

'I was sacked.'

'Heavens, whatever for?'

'Various reasons. Intentional bad writing, poor admin,

refusal to cooperate with the company psychologist, bad attitude, but, primarily, for, supposedly, fiddling my expenses.'

'They can sack you for that?' asked The Buffer.

'Apparently.'

'Ridiculous.'

'I'm genuinely sorry to hear that, Jimmy. The paper's not the same, you know. Overrun by thrusting young things wearing their trousers too high.'

'Never a good sign,' said The Buffer.

'I rarely read it any more,' said Stirling. 'Who cares about celebrities?'

'Is that what they are?' said Malcolm, efficiently finishing his half of gin and tonic. 'Whatever, things could be about to change. I was so dispirited by the general carry-on I stirred myself to have a word with a few people close to the blessed owner. Our time may come, Jimmy.' Excusing himself politely, he moved, with purpose, to the bar.

The Buffer recharged their glasses. 'It really is good to see you again.'

'Thank you,' said Stirling. It had been a while since anyone had been so effusive. He offered the man a cigarette.

'I've actually been trying to get in touch with you, but the mobile number you gave me didn't ring any bells.'

'Repossessed.'

'I suppose it would be. Anyway, the thing is those chip machines are attracting what I would have to call substantial interest.'

'They can't be.'

'They most certainly are. And you may be in line for a divvy, young man.'

'There's no need for that.'

'Of course there is. One way and another I knew your Dad pretty well. And any friend of his . . .'

'Honestly, it's very kind but . . .'

'He loved you, you know.'

Stirling didn't know what to say.

'I can't promise you anything but, just in case, who do you bank with?'

'Christ, erm, no . . . it's gone. Sorry.'

'Think, Jimmy.'

'I know my passcode.'

The Buffer pulled out a bookie's biro and a cab receipt.

'A, B, C, D, E,' said Stirling.

The Buffer didn't write anything down.

'And my pass number,' continued Stirling, 'is 1, 2, 3, 4, 5, 6.'

The Buffer remained unmoved.

'And the first line of my address is The Priory. And the postcode is, hang on, NO4 NOW.'

The Buffer made a note.

'And the bank is called . . . The Bank. That's it.'

'Come on, Freddie,' shouted Malcolm from the bar. 'Bridge waits for no man. Confusion to our enemies.' He was holding a pint of gin and tonic and a bottle of second-cheapest claret.

'Take care, Jimmy,' said The Buffer, as he heeded the call.

Stirling was exhausted by the shock of seeing all his ex-colleagues again, the emotional power of his speech, having to recall his postcode. He poured himself the rest of the claret, took a glug, put his cigarette out, and, closing his eyes, started to put some serious thought into what he might do next.

16

This editing lark is a doddle, thought Stirling. He had gifted the four offensively large-screen TVs to The Butt, calling up the IT department to do the donkey work, and replaced them himself with a mini CD player on which he could play, on a loop, lesser-known works by Vivaldi. Both as an example of affirmative action and in recognition of the suffering she had endured under the last despotic and nepotistic regime, he promoted Kath to be his deputy. Kath proved more than capable of doing the work so he, sportingly, extended her brief to include his own job. A nifty piece of delegation which enabled him to arrive at the office for the start of the working week around about Friday lunchtime. B was happy, Charlie and Nancy were happy, and Stirling couldn't, realistically, complain. 'Gloria in Excelsis,' he sang along to the music, and a very big Laudate to Malcolm, Terry and Ian.

Their putsch against the last editors had, thanks to divine providence, produced the right result. Cobbling together the various strands it appeared that the Paper's owner, in a rare moment of sentience, had called upon Peter and Gareth to respond in a grown-up manner to 'the tragic events' and produce a more serious newspaper. The duo had responded by filling page upon page with celebrities giving their opinions on the serious issues of the day, the nadir or zenith being reached when Nerinder from *Big Brother 2* was given a weekly column to 'opine' on the state of race relations in the United Kingdom today. After a month of this and other nonsense Malcolm, Terry and Ian had sued for constructive dismissal. They claimed their jobs no longer bore any relation to those they had been employed to do. Lawyers for the Paper stalled, and before matters could be resolved Peter and Gareth were poached by the reigning Newspaper of the Year. Faced by three expensive legal actions and a vacuum at the top of his paper the owner, anxious as ever to have a quiet rest of his life, had finessed the issue by making Malcolm editor, Terry his deputy, and giving Ian a roving brief.

Malcom and Terry, operating from their new table in The Butt, had worked smoothly and swiftly. During a single, albeit extended, drinking bout they had downsized all the high-trousers, any of their sympathisers and the living Derrek. This had left them with a fortune to pay in enforced redundancies and a very limited payroll to fill the paper. Forced to priori-tise, they had slashed the pagination given to sport from twenty to four – twelve less than books and two more than style 'n' fashion. To run the new reduced section it was necessary to find someone cheap who wasn't particularly interested in sport. They had called Stirling.

If you could divide people between sackers and sackees, and it seemed to Stirling it was as reasonable a categorisation as any dreamt up by the social anthropologists, then he geneti-cally and instinctively belonged in the latter category. In a long and undistinguished career he had been sacked often and not once been in a position to sack someone else. He was proud to be one of life's sackees. But with responsibility came hypocrisy, and temptation. He fleetingly considered keeping Parsons and Mr Blue on the staff, but with only four pages to be filled there was no earthly reason to do so and the last way he wanted to spend his working day and a half was listening to them moaning about not getting into the paper. Or worse, talking to him about football.

Parsons he chopped by phone, ringing him just before closing time on Friday night.

'Late change of plan, Rob. I'd like you to go to Halifax, tomorrow.'

'But it's United v Arsenal.'

'That's as maybe. I want my chief football writer open bracket sport close bracket to go to Halifax.'

'But Halifax aren't even playing at home tomorrow.'

'How do you know that?'

'I'm paid to know these things.'

'Not any more, chummy. Consider yourself canned. Ciao.'

'Hang on, Jim. The United game kicks off at midday, which means I could be out of there by two and where is Lincoln?'

'Lincolnshire.'

'If I drove like the clappers I could be there for the second half.'

'Too late, Robbie. The decision's been made. Thanking you.'

It had been fun, but not as satisfying as he had expected, the pleasure to be derived from the undoubted element of surprise being undermined by the speed of execution. He took Mr Blue out for a long lunch, ostensibly to hear his ideas for the section. As if Stirling, of all people, would be interested. On and on his chief sports writer had droned. How he was really keen to contribute to the paper's extensive Champions League coverage, how he had already lined up 'big interviews' with various Premiership players, how desirous he was that his column be expanded from its present 1,500 words to a more suitable 2,500, how much he felt he could and would contribute to the section under Stirling's dynamic new leadership.

Only when Stirling had ordered up his third brandy and an eighth mineral water for Mr Blue did it begin to dawn on the employee that he might have misjudged his boss's plans.

'Fascinating,' Stirling had said, 'but perhaps I might, at this late stage, interrupt you. One, there are no plans to increase the sports section from four pages in the foreseeable future. Two, there will be no Champions League coverage, nor interviews nor football columns. There will, in short, be absolutely nothing for you to do. But you will be paid handsomely not to do it.'

'What about the World Cup?'

'What World Cup?'

'The football World Cup,' Mr Blue said slowly.

'That World Cup.'

'Potentially the biggest global sporting event ever contested.'

'We'll play it by ear.'

'I'll be going?'

'No.'

'What do you mean, no?'

'Don't take it personally. No one will be going.'

'But how can you stage such a huge football occasion without me there to cover it?'

'That's one for FIFA to ponder. We can't afford it.'

The twenty-something was visibly shrinking in front of his very eyes.

'Correct me if I'm wrong, but are you basically saying that you don't want me to write anything?'

'You're not wrong.'

'But that's ridiculous.'

'That's as may be.' Stirling tried to sugar the pill for his crestfallen employee. 'There'll be a ten grand bonus if your byline stays out of the paper until Christmas.'

'But my work . . . my reportage . . . my in-depth interviews . . . my canon. What will I have to put forward for the awards?'

'Very little, if you play your cards right.'

'You're mad, Jimmy.'

'Never saner.'

'You're preventing me from becoming a definitive football writer.'

'Why would anyone want to be definitive about football?'

'It's what I was born to do.'

'Shit happens.'

'Do you really really hate football, do you really hate sport, do you really hate me . . . that much?'

'Another mineral water?'

The twenty-something stood up.

'I'm bigger than this. I don't need to take this shit from an embittered, drunk, failed old man. I've got a future. I'm one of the three best sports writers of my generation. There'll be plenty of offers. Wait till Malcolm hears how you've treated one of the paper's stars.'

'Malcolm knows.'

'Fuck you,' screamed Mr Blue. He threw an untouched mineral water at Stirling at the very moment the new sports editor bent down to pick up a cigarette he had somehow dislodged during the cut and thrust of debate. The agua minerale hit an upcoming waiter in the face. The resting actor scowled, the football writer cowered.

Stirling re-emerged from under the table. 'Not looking so tall now, are we . . .' It struck him that he still didn't know how to properly pronounce his Christian name. 'Bluester.' He turned to the waiter. 'Sorry about that. Another brandy with the bill, if you will. And feel free to double the service charge.'

To cover for the departure of his two, in their own heads, top writers Stirling hired Pink and refrained from firing Frankie Sober. The former had a term written into his contract stipulating that he would be fired instanter if he was so much as rumoured to have been heard singing Gilbert and Sullivan; the latter was instructed to write about anything other than sport. Pink proved to be a welcome addition to the team and Sober unintentionally hilarious. Kath's idea to divide up a page with Pink operating on the left under the byline Drinker and Sober on the right under the byline Thinker was a master-stroke.

Every week Pink would file a delightfully discursive thousand words on whatever might rise to the top of his head, and every week Sober would be packed off to pass comment on Matisse/Picasso, anything that might be on at the National, and once, less successfully, the ballet. Initially, Sober littered his copy with clumsy football references, but over time he learned that it was possible to write a review of an Ibsen play without mention of the sport. He attracted a loyal following, readers particularly praising those articles where he assessed a production from conflicting points of view – The New Sober and The Old Sober. They were less keen on his constant references to Step Four of the Alcoholics Anonymous programme, but Stirling continued to keep them in on the grounds that it would be cruel and possibly counterproductive to remove the big man's crutch so early in his journalistic career.

The other three pages took care of themselves. One was dedicated to results, another to reports, and a third to readers' letters and corrections. Throughout the section, or soupçon as he referred to it, Stirling strove to be eclectic rather than definitive. If there was a guiding principle to his editorship it was that every page should include something that would surprise both the reader and himself.

To this end he invented the sport of Skimming, based on the Ancient Greek practice of throwing pebbles into the sea, and in between the Sailing and Swimming results would always make room for an imaginary update:

Skimming: The Night Nurse Invitational, Prestatyn. Men's Quarter-Finals (three-quarter tide, moderate north-easterly, choppy). P. J. Buongustaio (It) 3 (9) bt H. Todd (US) 4 (4); M. MacNamara (UK) 12 (9) bt T. Huff (Ger) 0 (1); The Earl of Buccleugh (UK) 5 (8) bt D. Daunt (UK) 5 (5); T. Blanc (Fr) 4 (2) ((1))* bt C O'Driscoll (Ire) 3 (5).
*a.e.p.

The reports on actual events were less easy to make readable. It was predominantly football, after all. But Pink and he found that, provided they kept their wits about them, it was entirely feasible for them to cover three matches each off the tellies in The Butt. Although, inevitably, such sharp working conditions led to the occasional fallacy creeping into the paper. This discombobulated Stirling not a jot. Indeed he welcomed the mistakes, as they provided copy for the following week's corrections section and the greater the scale of inexactitude (wrong man scoring winning goal for wrong team during match he wasn't even playing in) the more space was required to make effective amends. Which had the benign side-effect of reducing the number of readers' letters that Stirling would have to write that week. Not that he minded writing his readers' letters, quite the reverse, but even as big a fan of his own writing as Stirling had to concede that the page had more pizzazz when it wasn't entirely given over to one man arguing with himself in as many pseudonymous guises as were needed to fill the space.

Satisfactorily quickly his pages began to cohere. Stirling admired his elite team's response to Cup Final day, an event taken most seriously by their ponderously overstaffed competitors. Finding their groove early, Pink and he were able to cover both the English Cup Final from Cardiff (match report by Pink, further analysis by Stirling) and the Scottish Cup Final from Glasgow (roles reversed) with sufficient speed to enable Stirling to knock off an 'I was there' piece on the 2,000 Guineas at Newmarket. In a bold move he had completed the racing segment not with a list of Today's Racecards but with Today's Results, complete with predicted SPs and Tote returns. 'This afternoon's winners, this morning,' he promised on the masthead.

The columns were trenchant. Pink segued from a detailed description of a rare and recent haircut, via a few trichologist anecdotes he had picked up during forty decades covering football, onto a diverting disquisition on the role of the crimper in the modern game. Sober went marvellously overboard in his unstinting praise of a hitherto unheralded dance and mime troupe from Rwanda.

The results page was endlessly fascinating, with an entire column given over to Stirling's favourite sport as the Skimming season got into full swing. And the letters section was abuzz with genuine readers' responses to Stirling's world exclusive the week before that P. J. Buongustaio was being investigated by WASP (World Association of Skimming Professionals) for failing a drugs test and other, as yet unspecified, misdemeanours. Which all went to show that, provided the writing and presentation were snappy, no one in their right mind was the least bit bothered whether a sporting event had in reality, whatever that might be, taken place. How else to explain the enduring appeal of Roy of the Rovers?

Arriving at the office on Thursday afternoon, Stirling was immensely gratified to see that Ian had scribbled on the front of his section 'Enviable work.' He had come in early in the week to have a discussion with Malcolm about the paper's coverage of the World Cup, an irrelevance Stirling had been banking on falling outside the compass of the great man. He was uncertain quite how his new sports journalism would adapt to the logistical challenges posed by the tournament. Even if they split the workload, with Pink pretending to be in Japan and Stirling in South Korea, it would entail them watching a punishing amount of football, much of it at breakfast time, when neither was at his best.

Serendipitously, Stirling had been rehired during one of the Paper's campaigning phases. Over the last two centuries the Paper had, intermittently, taken a strong line on a variety of issues – pro military action in Crimea, anti the banning of absinthe; pro Chamberlain, anti the creation of the NHS; pro Andropov, anti Gorbachev – but never had the workforce been so united on a single issue. It was all hands to the pump to save The Butt from those who would turn it into a wine bar. Prescient as ever, David the barman had inserted into his lease a clause preventing the brewers or their nominees from being able to repossess the premises if someone was drinking within it. The key element to the campaign, therefore, was to keep the pub permanently occupied. So it was that the editor and his sports editor convened in The Butt, not through choice but necessity.

Stirling pushed past some stroppy developers maintaining a picket line to gain access to The Butt. He was early, but Malcolm was earlier.

'Jimmy, if you could start drinking that pint on the bar it would allow me the chance to finish this one off and take a breather.'

He did as he was told.

'Bad news, I'm afraid. It seems as if you are a victim of your success.'

'Success is the new failure.'

'So the ex-features editor used to say. I'm not quite sure how but we've sold an unconscionable number of adverts which have to run during this World Cup thingymajig.'

'In the sports section.'

'That is one of the conditions. I argued your corner with the bods in marketing, suggesting, for instance, that we run an all-ads supplement for the duration of the infernal tournament, but they are insistent we have some copy to leaven the promotions.'

'Fucking marketing.'

'And usually I would laugh in the face of such commercial considerations but the thing is, what with the campaign and everything, we are not in a position to lay off more staff.'

'It's a question of priorities.'

'Unfortunately.'

Whenever priorities were shuffled, Stirling always finished near the bottom of the deck.

'How bad is it?'

'Thirty-two pages bad.'

'Christ.'

'Hence the need for a meeting.'

'In all honesty, Pink and I are overstretched filling four.'

'I can give you all the work experiences it takes.'

'Terrific.'

'See it as a challenge, Jimmy. There must be something you can conjure up . . .'

'I don't know, Malcolm.'

'More drink, anyone?' It was Terry.

'I'll line up a gin,' said Malcolm.

'And I'll have a pint after Malcolm.'

Terry strolled over carrying a pint of fizzy orange liquid.

'What's that?' asked Stirling.

'Tizer. It's the only soft drink David has left. When the Tizer's gone . . . great section, by the way.'

'Thanks. Any thoughts on the World Cup?'

'A wall-chart?'

'Too much hassle,' said Stirling.

'Unreadable columns by washed-up ex-pros?'

'Too expensive,' said Malcolm.

'Big pictures?'

'I suppose there's always big pictures,' said Stirling.

The answer to his conundrum came to him as he found himself accidentally watching Mr White's *Totally Football*, which had been improbably relocated to Tokyo and, due to a sudden absence of 'breaking news alerts' anywhere in the world, was being screened on Sky News as well as Sky Sports News. Appalled, he watched Brown and Green chewing away at stubborn sushi and regurgitating their tired opinions on The Swede and little Michael and young Stevie.

'There's absolutely no question our boys can go all the way,' said Brown, masticating wildly.

'And if we can squish the Swedes – an ironic game for Sven for obvious reasons – then I fully expect it to be brown pants time for the Argies,' said Green.

If this be news, thought Stirling, something must be done. And, in his temporary role as sports editor, he was in the position to do it. It was up to him to use the thirty-two pages at his disposal every week to bring some balance to the world, to make his paper's coverage so moronic that even the fatuous would be forced to concede their vacuity. He had to drown them in their inanity, hoist them with their own punditry. He had to prove that there could be too much football. And what better way to do it than taking things to their logical conclusion and printing page after page after page of the nonsense? No cricket, no rugby, no golf, no tennis, no racing, no pictures, no skimming, just thirty-two straight pages of football analysis. It was beautiful in its simplicity and symmetry. He rang Malcolm. 'Give me four stenographers and I'll give you a definitive World Cup section.'

Back came the televisions from The Butt and with a minimum of fuss the sports desk was rearranged to enable each of the court typists to have room for their machines and access to their own screen. Each stenographer was allocated a TV station and tasked to make a comprehensive note of everything said by every commentator, analyst, link man and pundit. At the end of every programme a convenient workie would be dispatched with reams of paper to the emergency typing pool where temps would transcribe it all into the computer system.

All Stirling had to do was sit and wait for everything to come to him. By happy coincidence the channels had assembled thirty-one experts to cover the thirty-two nations competing in the tournament, twenty-nine of whom were British and two Irish. It was a moment's work, therefore, to type in big bold print on the front page WORLD CUP 2002: EVERY WORD FROM EVERY GAME – VERBATIM and then lob an expert's name on the top of each succeeding page and cover it with 4,000 words of their incisive analysis. The comments of the verbose were run uninterrupted by the flimflam of advertising. The reticent were spared from blushing by Nike, Adidas or Whoever. The only problem was Gascoigne. Minutes into the start of the Geordie's broadcasting career the stenographer – a veteran of thirty years of court reporting – threw her headphones down in despair. 'Impenetrable,' she said. 'So it is,' confirmed Stirling, having wandered over to listen in. For three decades the steno had listened to the dispossessed and criminally hesitant try to explain away their actions, but Gascoigne had her stumped.

No matter, there was always Pink and Sober, drinker and thinker. Before a ball had been kicked Pink had determined that this was a below-average renewal – a conclusion which had nothing, or very little, to do with the fact that it was the first one since 1954 that no organisation had seen fit to pay him to cover live – and the snatches he saw looking over the stenographers' shoulders failed to alter his opinion. Sober, meanwhile, had not before time been smitten by Nell McAndrew, a *coup de foudre* which had the delightful consequences of the celebrated celebrity dropping her libel action against Stirling and injecting some lead into the columnist's pencil. Thrilled to be attending cultural events in the company of someone less informed than himself, Sober became expansive. The ex-England penalty taker's demolition of the entire oeuvre of Pedro Almodovar rated among Stirling's favourites, not least because Fränkie had gone the extra mile and bothered to spell oeuvre correctly.

The facility of his work, however, only added to Stirling's disappointment when his menu gourmand of a section was hailed as a 'breakthrough' success. The sad souls who hung around the watercooler waiting for someone with whom they could chat about the Arse and Arsène revelled in the clearly over the top, absurdly and ironically expansive coverage. They wrote letters of praise which Stirling didn't publish. They left messages requesting back issues which Stirling erased. They sent e-mails which Stirling moved to trash. Mistakenly, unwillingly, he had tapped a vein. In so totally misunderstanding the market he had perfectly understood it. Sales soared. There was, heart-sinkingly, talk of awards. Presumably for the stenographers.

Stirling sought refuge in Norfolk. B, Charlie and Nancy were even less interested in the World Cup than he. B had taken up gardening, high-stepping it around the estate in Stars 'n' Stripes bikini and black wellies. Charlie and Nancy started taking books into school so that when the England games were shown after morning prayers they could dip out and catch up with their reading at the back of the classroom. When pressed in the playground by six-year-olds carrying the Flag of St George as to who they were supporting, they replied Romania. Who, unbeknown to their classmates, hadn't qualified.

The wave of faux nationalism engulfing the nation rendered

Stirling publess. His new pub, The Fighting Cock, was awash with men and women in replica shirts talking incessant football. Even The Hare and Greyhound had commandeered a portable television for the occasion. What had once been a quiet place appropriate for contemplation was now a hotbed of punditry. Stirling had spent a couple of nights in his old seat with the view of the cash-point machine, but the incessant babble emanating from the experts queuing up at the bar had made it impossible to concentrate. The Dereks had taken over his asylum.

He had popped into the overspill car park on his way home. Nothing. Even the dogging community was obsessed with the World Cup. Would it ever end?

In desperation, Stirling took up golf. He followed up on a twelve-word effort in the *Ad Trader* and purchased for a tenner a set of clubs from an end-of-pier karaoke compere in Great Yarmouth. He discovered there was a two-year waiting list for probationary membership of the Bungay & Beccles Golf Club. He gave up golf.

Back in the office, his innovative sports editorship swiftly hit the wall post-World Cup. Pink was back in Rottingdean, the stenographers had been laid off and Kath had taken a holiday. These factors combined to leave Stirling presiding over a sports section which was both zero sum and zero page. Malcolm noticed. Stirling responded by savagely foreshortening Kath's holiday, re-employing the stenographers on double money and taking himself off to Muirfield for the Open, semi-determined to turn things round.

To his dismay, the football writers, fresh back from JapKorea, had been let loose at a golf tournament. Even more dismayingly the Honourable Society of Edinburgh Golfers had allowed not only women into their clubhouse but also White, Green,

Brown and Blue. The Tarantubbies, as anyone might have warned the Honourable Society, quickly clogged up the club-house bar with their post-World Cup analysis.

'At the end of the day the best team won,' said White. 'But what a day and what a team.'

'Sven, hey, what a cunt,' said Green.

'I don't like to say I told you so but I tell you he played the wrong Neville,' said Brown.

'It was a tournament defined as much by what didn't happen as what did happen; a tournament which . . .' said Blue, now Chief Sportswriter (Chief) at some top people's paper.

'For fuck's sake, we're here to watch golf,' screamed Stirling. 'Can't any of you let it go?' And then his mobile went off and he was forcibly evicted from the clubhouse.

It had been a while since he had watched live sport of his own volition, thought Stirling, as he strolled down the fourth staring at Colin Montgomerie talking to himself. Watching Monty a little too closely perhaps as, walking with the same care and attention he devoted to his driving, he tumbled head-long into a vertiginous, cavernous bunker. THWACK was the sound made by dishevelled journalist hitting perfectly prepared sand from a great height. Clinchingly for any career prospects Stirling might, against the odds, have continued to harbour, Peter Alliss was on hand to provide expert commentary on his fall live on BBC 2.

'Oh dearie, dearie me. (Long sigh.) Someone has taken one too many with their lunch. I mean, really. (Longer sigh.) He is not going to find it at all easy to get out of there in one. What an idiot. It wouldn't surprise me in the least if he turns out to be one of these interweb chappies. I mean they really do let any old riffraff in these days. (Longest sigh.) Really.'

Stirling lay on his back looking up at a clear blue sky. For too long he had struggled against the inevitable. For too long he had been angry. For too long he had continued to do something because he couldn't think of anything else to do. For too long he had lived in the shadow of his father's death. It was time for a new start. He stood up, brushed at the sand which fell like dandruff from his hair and shoulders, and steadily and slowly rose from the bunker.

It was only when the cabbie dropped him at Waveney station that he realised he had no money.

'Sorry. I'll get some from the cash-point.'

'Oh, yeah.'

Stirling left his jacket, and one of his shoes, as surety and hopped over to the hole-in-the-wall. Flustered by losing an argument as to whether his jacket was worth £24.80 plus supposedly optional tip he pressed 'Yes' for the first time in his life in answer to the question 'Would you like to see your balance?'

The figure '-£251,162.73' came up on the screen. No. He looked at the screen, genuinely astonished. Incredible. Quickly he took out his card and repeated the process. '-£251,162.73' came up again. Alleluia. Alle-fucking-luia. He had made a hundred grand since he last looked at a bank statement. Considerably more if he factored in the family outgoings. On the push of a button his financial status had been transformed. He might not technically be rich but he certainly wasn't bankrupt. The Buffer had delivered, The Buffer had come through for him. The Buffer had saved him.

He phoned in his resignation from the train, resigning not on a point of principle nor because he had fallen out with management – he was management, for Christ's sake – but out of boredom. Malcolm respected his motives.

'Thanks for helping out, Jimmy. The paper's fucked, by the way.'

'I thought it might be.'

'Sometimes you can be too good.'

'Perhaps.'

Scrabbling through his bag he unearthed the page of his address book on which he had written The Buffer's number.

'Hello.'

'Hi, is that the Buf – Freddie?'

'Speaking.'

'Jimmy Stirling here.'

'Jimmy, how the devil are you?'

'Much better thanks to you.'

'Me?'

'That cash you sent has allowed me to resign.'

'What cash?'

'The chip machines cash. Minutes ago I accidentally checked my balance and I'm less poor than I could ever imagine.'

'I'd love to take some unearned credit but . . .'

'It wasn't you?'

''Fraid not. The chip machines went belly up.'

'But . . .'

'It looked good. In fact, better than good. The orders were flooding in. Easy Street beckoned. Holidays were booked. And then we happened upon a slight technical hitch.'

'How slight?'

'The finished product was either stone cold.'

'Cold chips.'

'Or tongue-blisteringly hot.'

'Too-hot-to-eat chips.'

'The bastard things were either unarguably teeth-shatteringly inedible or arguably contaminated with radiation. Either way, fat-all use to anyone.'

'Busted chips.'

'Indeed. So, Jimmy boy, you're in funds.'

'Ye-ess.'

'Do you know much about this interweb thingy?'

'No.'

'Shame. I always like to take a punt on industries everyone else has written off. And I was on the point of ringing you to see if you might like to come on board.'

'I'll get back to you, Freddie.'

'There's no rush. Do you play golf?'

'No.'

'Real shame.'

'See you at Lord's, Freddie.'

And then he rang B.

'There's good news and good news.'

'About fucking time.'

'The first is that I've resigned.'

'And that's good.'

'Very good. And the second is . . .'

'You've had a sex change.'

'The second is that we're a hundred thousand less poor than I thought we were.'

'How come?'

'I've no idea. But we'd better spend it before someone realises their mistake.'

'Dadda, can we go to a football match?' asked Charlie.

'No.'

'Dadda, you promised,' said Nancy.

'Did I?'

'Yes,' said Charlie.

'When?'

'Last night,' said Nancy.

'Are you sure?'

'You promised you would take us,' said Charlie.

'And grown-ups never break a promise,' said Nancy.

'If you insist, but why on earth do you want to go to a football match?'

'It's what boys do,' said Charlie.

'Not necessarily.'

'Oh,' said Charlie.

'Why do you suddenly want to go to a football match when last time I threatened to take you we had to pretend to be involved in a pile-up on the A143 in order to avoid seeing the wretched thing?'

'Because . . .' said Nancy, looking at Charlie. 'Bouchie boy?'

'Because . . .' said Charlie, looking at Nancy. 'Bouchie girl?'

'I'm waiting.'

'Because,' said Charlie and Nancy together, 'Harry likes football.'

'And who's Harry?'

Nancy chewed away at the back of her left hand, Charlie at the back of his right hand.

'Who's Harry?'

The confession came out in a rush.

'He's our new friend and he likes playing imaginary games,' said Charlie.

'Which means I don't have to be Ron and Hermione and all the teachers and Dobby any more,' said Nancy.

'And he has a PlayStation,' said Charlie.

'And he's even better than Charlie.'

'Nearly better than me.'

'And he loves football.'

'And he goes to watch Norwich every week.'

'And we told him you used to be a football writer.'

'And he told his Dad.'

'And they both thought it was brilliant, Dadda.'

'And we promised Harry we would try and go to a football match.'

'And . . .'

'Children don't break promises. I'll see if I can blag us some free tickets.'

He opted for Millwall at home. With any luck there would be sufficient hooliganism to scare them off the game for life. As they drove into Norwich he filled them in on the rules of the game.

'One team will be wearing yellow and the other blue and the team in yellow will attempt to kick the ball into the blue team's goal at the same time as the team in blue will attempt to kick the ball into the yellow's goal. Then, after ninety minutes, they tot up any goals which may have been scored and we can all go home.'

'Is that it?' asked Nancy.

'That's it.'

'It's not exactly Quidditch,' said Charlie.

He offered to buy them scarves, replica shirts, bobble hats, foam fingers, a selection of Delia's pies, foam fingers again, a programme, but they politely declined. The three of them sat silently in their seats with a partially obstructed view.

'What's that?' asked Nancy.

'A stanchion.'

'Not that, that.'

'What?'

'The yellow thing running around in the middle.'

'Clive the Canary. Norwich's team mascot.'

'He's great,' said Charlie. 'What position does he play?'

'He doesn't play. This is as far as it goes for Clive the Canary.'

'Oh,' said Charlie.

'Oh,' said Nancy.

The mascot left the field to mild derision from the crowd and wild applause from Charlie and Nancy. His space was taken by twenty-two footballers. The game began.

'It's very noisy,' said Nancy.

'It's very violent,' said Charlie.

Minutes passed.

'Can I swap seats with you, Dadda?' asked Charlie.

'Sit down, for Christ's sake,' said a twat in Row Z.

The twins went into a huddle. Nancy nudged Charlie. 'Would it be very rude if we left now?'

'Not at all.'

With joy in his heart and a spring in his step he escorted his children from the stadium.

'For Christ's sake, sit down, will you?'

Stirling gave him the finger. 'Wanker.'

'Bad word, Dadda,' said Nancy.

'If you didn't have your kiddies with you I'd have you, tosser.'

'Bad word,' said Charlie to the man in Row Z.

Leaving rapidly after fifteen minutes of the first half ensured they were in plenty of time to beat the traffic.

'What are we going to tell Harry?' asked Nancy.

'Easy,' said Stirling, and turned on the car radio. 'Listen carefully whenever they go over to Norwich v Millwall and make a note of anything the reporter says.'

Charlie took out the pen and diary he carried everywhere. As they approached the Lowestoft turning the publicly funded service delivered.

'Over to Rob Parsons at Carrow Road.'

'No goals but plenty of excitement here as both sides set out on the long road which may lead to a return to the Premiership.' Rather like you, pally. 'There were thrills right from the start as Jones hit the post for City and, at the other end, Headon was harshly adjudged to have handled in the area. Smithers missed the penalty.' Had they been at the same game? 'Passions were raised when some handbags escalated into afters and Millwall's Simpson was fortunate indeed only to be cautioned. Plenty to look forward to in the second half. Don't go away.'

'Over to Daphne McElwee at Rotherham v Grimsby.'

'What was all that about?' asked Charlie.

'All you need to write is "No goals", "Ref a bad guy", "Norwich robbed."'

'This is the way to watch football, Dadda.'

P.S.

Ideas,
interviews
& features . . .

From Marmalade to *Midsomer Murders*

Louise Tucker talks to Will Buckley

Where did you grow up?

I was born in London and lived there until I was 36. Then I moved to Norfolk.

Have you always wanted to be a writer?

I've always been a reader but never thought I might be a writer. Before summoning the chutzpah to write I had a stab at a number of careers. First, I was a lawyer, but:

a) My barristerial career came to a close after a misunderstanding with the Crown Prosecution Service following some lazy prosecuting in Gray's Essex as a result of which I unthinkingly conceded I was fallible and the authorities responded by banning me from East Anglia.

b) My soliciting career hit the buffers after a misunderstanding with a client (I told him to fuck off), and some sloppy drafting of a recording contract for seventies rock giants Marmalade, led the partners to repossess my telephone. It is next to impossible to solicit in such circumstances.

c) My freelance career working as a sidekick to a man who had once been the Krays' private detective of choice, on behalf of a defendant in the second Guinness trial, was terminated due to lack of funds. Weeks later the trial was halted after the defendant claimed that were it to continue for a day longer he would in all probability kill himself. Which, bar the odd stenographer, was pretty much how everyone else felt.

Second, I was a game show host. Rather

an unnerving occupation. The viewing figures didn't stack up and Channel 4 didn't repeat their mistake. The upshot of the show was an Inland Revenue investigation after they refused to accept that someone could do such a degrading job for so little money.

Third, I was a fringe comedian who lacked the ability to make anyone laugh. Not in itself a problem, but I had naively assumed that some of my fellow comedians might, on occasion, make me laugh. Didn't happen.

Fourth, I was an ideas man. Nothing much got off the ground but one of my partners became, in 1991, the first person in the British Isles to use the verb 'blue-sky' un-ironically. Because of, or despite, this no one would fund our projects.

After the above, journalism began to seem quite an attractive option.

There are a lot of similarities between your life and Jimmy's. Is there much of you in him?
Perhaps and maybe. For a start, I doubt it matters very much. Certainly not to people who don't know you, and it is every author's hope that their novel will be that breakthrough book which reaches a wider audience than is contained in their address book.

It is, however, beyond dispute that I live in Norfolk, am the father of twins and work as a sports journalist. So, unarguably, does Jimmy. The starting point is therefore clearly ▶

> ❛Novels which are intended to be comic tend to be, superficially at least, more autobiographical. ❜

From Marmalade to
Midsomer Murders (continued)

◄ autobiographical. From that moment on, however, everything is up for grabs. There are things that did happen which quickly unravel into things which didn't happen, and then there are those which didn't happen which develop to include things which may have happened. After a while you can no longer be sure what is invention and what is exaggeration.

All that may be certain is that novels which are intended to be comic tend to be, superficially at least, more autobiographical. The fact that people have laughed at something in the past can give you the confidence to take it further. And if you want your readers to laugh at someone, better he/she resemble you than someone else.

> 6 You have to take writing seriously without becoming too serious about it – a tricky balancing act. 9

As a result of the connections between you and him, how did your newspaper colleagues or neighbours respond to some of the characters?
My newspaper colleagues thought it was a clever ruse to render me unsackable on the grounds that a supposedly venerable paper such as the *Observer* would never be so petty as to dismiss someone for expressing a profound disaffection for the subject they were employed to cover.

As for the neighbours, I think they might have preferred it if the book had come with an index. If I had added, say, 'Stirling joins PTA (p. 64); PTA passes smoking ban (p. 65); Stirling leaves PTA (p. 66),' they could have saved themselves some time – not that time management is a high priority in Norfolk. There were rumours that some local groups had chosen it for their book clubs, but at the time of writing no one has leaked the result of their deliberations.

Bereavement is the catalyst for change for Jimmy. Was that your experience?
Almost certainly. My dad died suddenly, and it affected me far more than I suspected. We had managed that sometimes problematic transition from parent/child to good friends, so his sudden absence was all the more overwhelming.

And I was living in Norfolk. And I hadn't passed my driving test. And I spent a lot of time looking at bonfires. And there finally comes a time when you decide that one way of coping might be to try and write something which, were he still alive, he might enjoy. Not that he would be able to, of course, but you do what you can.

Time is often cited as the most necessary thing for a writer and the most difficult to find. How do you balance the requirements of a full-time job, fatherhood and the desire to write?
Probably by doing all three in a half-assed manner.

The writing usually swings when you can dedicate a chunk of time to it. If you spend Monday faffing around not doing much, Tuesday is often better and then Wednesday better still. Sabbaticals are great.

The main difficulty, if you are not making even the majority of your living from your books, is that they can become sidelined. ▶

❛It is counter-productive to keep asking yourself why you are writing, yet foolish never to question your motivation. ❜

From Marmalade to
Midsomer Murders (continued)

◀ From there it can be a short step to seeing the books as a hobby, at which point it might be better for all concerned if you took up golf. You have to take it seriously without becoming too serious about it – a tricky balancing act.

It is counter-productive to keep asking yourself why you are writing, yet foolish never to question your motivation. Perhaps the best answer is that it provides a way in which you can attempt to make sense of your life and, with luck, the longer you struggle away at it the better you become. So you do what you can in the time you can make available.

Deadlines help. Famously, Anthony Burgess, on being assured he had only a year to live, set himself the target of 2,000 words a day, every day, to be completed before the pubs opened. He upped this target marginally in the hope of completing ten novels of 100,000 words each. In the event – 'because of hangovers, marital quarrels, creative deadness induced by the weather, shopping trips, summonses to meet state officials, and sheer torpid gloom' – he managed five and a half novels. But as he writes, 'still, it was very nearly E. M. Forster's whole long life's output'. Quite an achievement, but he was labouring under a fairly severe deadline.

One of the overwhelming problems for Jimmy is that he's bored – with his work, his home and his life. To a certain extent his boredom feels like a modern phenomenon: that sense that there is so much opportunity and yet we still don't quite get it. Do you

> 6Deadlines help. Anthony Burgess, on being assured he had only a year to live, set himself the target of 2,000 words a day, to be completed before the pubs opened. 9

think his boredom is a function of just his job, location or age, or is it part of a wider twenty-first-century malaise?

There is something comical in the amount of choice available to us and yet how fundamentally inconsequential those choices are. Your mobile comes with thirty-something ring tones yet why express preference for one over another when all of them alert you to the boring fact that your phone has rung?

It becomes comi-tragical when people see such non-choices as expressions of their personality. The ring tone, the replica shirt, the brand of trousers … *Auld Lang Syne*, Arsenal, Armani … welcome to the real me. Confronted by such fatuity, it is hard not to be bored.

Jimmy's boredom, however, is exaggerated for comic effect: boredom leading to anger leading to pratfalls. He knows he needs to do something yet is unsure what thing, and in his confusion chooses to do the one thing that if he had been thinking straight he would never have done. He is trapped in East Anglia in that his family want to live there and he wants to live with them. He is trapped in his job in that he does not possess the confidence to be able to find another one. He can't do anything about being forty. All these things conspire against him. He senses that somewhere along the line he made compromises which he can no longer unmake, that he is in a cul-de-sac of his own creating. Little wonder he's pissed off. Some younger reviewers expressed impatience with Jimmy's failure to escape his ▶

> ❝I would suspect quite a few writers are sustained by fantasies. But, fuck it, how bored would we be without them? ❞

LIFE *at a Glance*

BORN

London, 1964

EDUCATED

Eton, Cambridge, the Bar.

CAREER

Varied. Has worked for the *Observer* since 1998.

FAMILY

Lives in South Norfolk with his wife and three children.

From Marmalade to *Midsomer Murders* (continued)

◄ predicament, yet they are at an age when anything seems possible whereas Jimmy is at an age when if he doesn't look sharp he'll end up doing nothing.

The one consolation of reaching such a stage is that boredom can become a panacea for anxiety. It is often better to be bored than anxious. There is something to be said for watching *Midsomer Murders* rather than juggling calls on three different mobiles, all with different ring tones. However, there does come a time when watching *Midsomer Murders* can seem to be 'part of a wider twenty-first-century malaise'.

What are you writing at the moment?
The usual knockabout sports journalism. I would suspect quite a few writers are sustained by fantasy, and while writing the book I gulled myself into believing that it would change my life. When it conspicuously didn't, I berated myself for being so foolish as to have ever believed such a conceit. But, fuck it, how bored would we be without our fantasies?

What's your next book?
The new book is another comic novel. It is a genre that is easily dismissed but it seems to me that making people laugh is both harder and more beneficial than making them cry. Anyone who is diligent can be serious; very few people can be funny. ■

Top Ten Comic Novels

In no particular order, here are a few modern comic novels you may have missed:

Karoo *by Steve Tesich*
In the opening chapter Saul Karoo admits: 'My drinking problem began a little over three months ago.' His problem is that however much, and whatever, he drinks he can no longer get drunk. Yet such is his reputation that everyone expects him to be drunk. This is one of many contradictions that assail Karoo as he doctors other people's scripts for Hollywood film companies that invariably employ someone called Brad.

The Magic Christian *by Terry Southern*
'When not tending New York holdings Guy Grand was generally, as he expressed it, "on the go".' Grand likes to make things hot for people. He uses his wealth to discover just how far people will debase themselves to earn an honest crust. Peter Sellers liked the book so much he made the film.

Is This Allowed? *by William Donaldson*
Every Donaldson book is worth reading but the jokes are arranged best, and most darkly, in this autobiographical novel. This book is extremely funny, and massively underrated. The libel report of his novel autobiography, *From Winchester to This*, was longer than the book.

The Mortdecai Trilogy *by Kyril Bonfiglioli*
Bonfiglioli claimed to be 'abstemious in all things except drink, food, tobacco and talking' and 'loved and respected by all who ▶

Top Ten Comic Novels *(continued)*

◄ knew him slightly'. His main character is a beguiling mix of Bertie Wooster and Flashman who behaves, on occasion, like an aggressively heterosexual Uncle Monty.

Never Mind, Bad News *and* **Some Hope** *by Edward St Aubyn*
Recently republished in America in one volume, this trilogy is sharply honest about the upper classes and, as a consequence, grimly funny. St Aubyn is keener to exit the aristocracy than be invited to their parties and uses his distance to great comic effect. Unlike Gore Vidal he doesn't think much of Princess Margaret.

The Ecstasy of Owen Muir *by Ring Lardner, Jr*
When J. Parnell Thomas asked him, 'Are you or have you ever been a member of the Communist Party?' Lardner replied, 'I could answer the way you want, Mr Chairman, but I'd hate myself in the morning.' While he was in prison he wrote this novel. Later he would co-write *The Cincinnati Kid* with Terry Southern and Altman's *M*A*S*H*.

Country Life
by Will Buckley

The main attraction of living in one of the quieter parts of South Norfolk is that it affords you plenty of time to think. Whether this is beneficial depends on the state you are in.

When we arrived here – Jesus, nearly five years ago – I was possibly rather disaffected. I knew no one, the main source of entertainment was whether we would be flooded, and, being unable to drive, I had to walk two miles to buy a packet of cigarettes. It was like being back at school.

Living in such an environment you can become undone by bleak thoughts. One way to counter such moods is to make light of them. This I attempted to do in various newspaper columns. While living in London I had found columnists banging on about 'My Rural Idyll (Episode 213)' lame and irritating, but irrelevant. Yet more self-serving guff: 'We moved to the countryside and, before you ask, yes we are so much happier than when we lived in Islington. Only the other day at the farmer's market …' Now I was living 24 miles east of Lowestoft I had a chance to disrupt the cosy picture painted by fellow journalists, presumably deeply in hock to local estate agents. Instead of drawing the reader's attention to outsize marrows I dwelt on dead pets (four rabbits, two sheep, a babysitter's dog), despair (the Express Queue at Budgens) and chicanery (the machinations of the PTA). One of the pieces was, considerately, given the headline 'Village of the Damned', which led to a neighbour noting that it couldn't be a coincidence that since my arrival the locality had been subjected to plague and pestilence. ▶

Country Life *(continued)*

◄ Another, in which, tiring of the PTA, I had blithely suggested that the Mendham Guy Fawkes Night Under 5s' Fancy Dress Competition had been fixed led to the threat of legal action. It was proving to be self-damaging guff.

Better, on reflection, to put such observations in a novel, which is the last place anyone would come across them. This was a subsidiary motivation; the primary one was more prosaic – 'What the fuck else is there to do?'

Most journalists have a book inside them. Sadly, so do many non-journalists and, being both more pragmatic and richer, they are quite happy to pay journalists to write that book for them. I might have ghosted Denise Lewis's *My Autobiography* but her people said I was too dishevelled. I might have gone back into the toilet book game but it had been annexed by celebrities. It would have to be a novel.

Once I had started, the lack of distraction proved to be a boon. There was no one to go for a drink with, so I went to the pub regardless, sat in the corner and wrote down what I might write next. No one seemed to mind although one big bloke with long hair did come up to tell me that if he'd been younger he would have taken the piss out of me but he wasn't going to because he was more of a new man now.

The process of writing the book provided something to ponder when the pace of life became intolerably slow. On the rare occasions when we were invited to dinner and the conversation focused in on, as it

> ❛ The main attraction of living in one of the quieter parts of South Norfolk is that it affords you plenty of time to think. Whether this is beneficial depends on the state you are in. ❜

invariably did, what one owner of an estate (land not car) whom I had never met had said to another owner of an estate whom I will never meet, I could switch off and wonder what to do with Chapter 9. On Lottery Day in Budgens I could marvel at the seven items the locals had chosen to place in their baskets and still have time to worry away at a wrinkle in the plot.

Just because nothing ever happened didn't necessarily mean life was boring. Things that the 'opinion formers' in the newspapers kept telling us it was very important to have an opinion upon began to seem not very important at all. This point was illustrated one Sunday in church (there is no cinema) when a woman from CAFOD, trying to drum up funds for the leaving collection, asked the congregation if anyone had heard of David Blaine. The silence that followed was long, profound and life-affirming. Not everything that happens within the M25 need detain us.

If writing a book helped, its publication did not. There was far too much time at my disposal to obsess over Amazon ratings and whole days to be given over to analysing misbegotten forays intended to publicise the book. Did I really manage to lock myself out of the premises half-way through a three-hour seminar on sports writing I was giving in a holistic centre in Cheltenham? And why didn't my two lecturees come and save me?

The only escape from such fretting is to start writing another book. ∎

> ‘If writing a book helped, its publication did not. There was far too much time at my disposal to obsess over Amazon ratings.’

If You Loved This,
You Might Like ...

Tilting at Windmills: How I Tried to Stop Worrying and Love Sport
Andy Miller
Sport-phobic Miller tries to overcome his hatred of all things athletic by becoming a champion crazy golfer.

Fever Pitch
Nick Hornby
The classic memoir of loving football and hating oneself.

The Mystery of Men
Guy Bellamy
Four middle-aged male friends decide to insure their lives: if one of them dies, the others get the money. But nasty events start to happen and the money seems less of a reward.

The Old Devils
Kingsley Amis
Winner of the Booker Prize, Amis's famous comic novel catalogues the attempts of four couples in rural Wales to achieve their one remaining ambition: drinking Wales dry.

Scoop
Evelyn Waugh
One of the funniest books ever written about the life of a journalist.

It's What He Would Have Wanted
Sean Hughes
Angst-ridden comedy in which thirty-something Shea is forced to confront his true family values after his father's death.

Find Out More

PLACES TO VISIT

Norfolk
www.visitnorfolk.co.uk
www.north-norfolk.gov.uk
Jimmy Stirling may moan about it, but
Norfolk is considered by many to be a
beautiful county. Edged on one side by the
coast, on another by the Fens, and
crisscrossed by waterways, it offers some of
the most varied scenery in England. These
websites offer lots of information about
activities and attractions.